Wanderamid's Crystal Ball

I.V. Phillips

Cover Design by LLPix Photography and Design
www.LLPix.com

Copyright © 2012 by I.V. Phillips

I Dedicate

This Book

To My Family, Friends

And

Especially To

My Wonderful Son,

Michael

Those Who

Dream

With

Open Eyes

Through

Their Thoughts

And

Surprised

This

Crystal Ball

Is

For You!

Table of Contents

CHAPTER ONE

FOUR QUARTERS END

Themore students of Whilom Elementary darted out
of their classrooms and rushed through the long and
narrow hallways with walls made of old stone. With
empty backpacks strapped across their shoulders, they
waved their open hands excitedly high over their heads,
shouting happily, as they directed towards the front doors,
anxious to begin their long-awaited summer break. Then
they saw the school principal, Ms. Biddock, was blocking
the exit. She showed no alarm at the swarm of students
running towards her while she folded her long arms firmly
in front her towering body.

The students realized too late, she was not about to
move away from the colossal wooden doors secured by
the enormous brass bolt locks.

The ones nearest to her warned the others far back
behind, "Slow down! She's not…." However, their
warning was too late, bringing them to a complete stop.

"Oww," they moaned after they ran into each other.

The students in front leaned their bodies as far back
as they could, to avoid running into her, and succeeded by
inches. They rubbed their furrowed eyebrows and tilted
back their aching heads, until they noticed the stern

expression imprinted upon her face. She stood confident, as they silently gazed up at her piercing green eyes looking down into theirs, frozen wide-open, and unable to blink.

Without any warning, her voice blared through the school hallways.

"All that you have studied this past school year should not leave your minds! You will all be tested the first week you return!"

The students stood with trembling knees and their chins drooped down to the pounding of their chests, all resulting from her firm lecture. When she slowly unfolded her arms their chins lifted, their mouths closed, and their knees, gradually steadied along with the calming of their throbbing hearts. Then, the students looked past her, to the massive doors behind her, and to their way out.

Finally, she calmly turned her back on them to unbolt the tightly secured locks. They grew more impatient, watching as her long, bony fingers turned them one at a time, nervously giggling quietly at the sight of them, lightly covering their mischievous grins.

With every inch of sunlight bursting through the opening of the doors, warm air touched their faces and they were instantly gratified. Their smiles returned completely. Butterflies in their stomachs grew along with the desire to leave through an exit that would eventually separate them from the long, mind-numbing school year.

The schools fourth quarter finally ended.

Their hands fell from their mouths and they began to express their freedom loudly, "Go fast, go, go!"

The doors had not opened entirely when they began racing through. They gave the door, Ms. Biddock stood by, a swift push, hitting her arm, causing her to lose balance!

"Noooo!" she yelled, as she struggled to control her poise, swaying back and forth, but did not succeed. Her long legs guided her many steps, until uncontrollably, she fell heavily to the floor.

The students ran past her as she sat with her head leaned against the wall of cold stone, watching how neither one of them stopped to help her.

"Keep going, don't stop!" urged a student, nudging the back of another with his knuckles. His eyes wandered in slow motion towards the direction of Ms. Biddock's dull expression, but then sharply focused back to the students already outside.

The teachers in front of their classroom doors stood motionless and in awe after they witnessed her fall. Then, one of them quickly whispered strongly to the others, "Hurry, go get your things—or she'll give us a lecture."

They turned around stiffly, hoping she had not seen them, but she did, then in a panic rushed back inside their empty rooms, grabbing only their belongings. Ms. Biddock sat, glaring at them as they rushed back out, looking the opposite direction from where she watched them heading towards the school's rear exit.

One student stayed behind, unnoticed. Ms. Biddock's lecture did not trouble her; it was her final year at Whilom Elementary. She watched as the teachers left, wondering only for a second why they did not help her.

"Ms. Biddock." She slowly walked up to where she sat helplessly on the floor.

Ms. Biddock turned with the same dull expression, motionless on her face, staring right through her as she stood by the edge of her feet.

"My name is Rena," she announced in a soft voice and then held out her hand. "Let me help you up."

Ms. Biddock leaned forward, as if to take hold of her hand, only to slap it away. "Run off with the rest of them!" Her long, bony finger trembled as she aimed towards the doors the other students ran through moments before.

"Huh?" Rena gasped and then placed her stinging red hand over her mouth. She began to walk quickly, steadily in reverse, hoping for those doors to touch her back.

Ms. Biddock slowly turned her head away, removing Rena's presence from her view. Gradually, she lifted herself off the floor as Rena finally reached the colossal doors, not hesitating once as she kept going, just as Ms. Biddock so furiously demanded.

Although Ms. Biddock stood solely on her feet, it was no different from when she sat helplessly on the floor. Her heart sank to the pit of her stomach as unwanted feelings surfaced from the past humiliations she suffered as a child in school. During those times, her anger grew more, hardening her heart, the anger she never imagined she could ever have.

*   *   *

Before that ever happened, she had a happy childhood with her mother, whose loving words kept Ms. Biddock from evolving into one of pure evil.

"No one else has such unique eyes, Emera," her mother said and meant every word, unconditionally.

When it came time for Emera to begin school, she began to worry deeply about how the other children would treat her, due to her unique appearance. Just as she feared, her worries became real. Emera immediately became an outcast, not only for being taller than the other children were, but also because of her piercing, green eyes.

"Hey! Look at her eyes!" a student scoffed, bringing attention to others, who then joined in his mockery.

Their laughter continued all throughout her school years, which seemed forever to Emera. On the way to her classes, they would push her, hard enough that she would fall to the floor. They jeered and pointed, "Let her use those long arms to get up."

No one would help her—not one, even the teachers who watched the taunting of Emera, turned away as though nothing happened.

The steady bullying progressively turned her into someone bitter, mean and heartless to all, all except those she truly loved—and who truly loved her.

One night as Emera slept, her mother sat at her roll top desk in the living room, carved with the word "Believe", and began writing inspiring words on colorful paper squares. She sneakily placed them where Emera was sure to see them, to keep what spirit she had from withering away. As a child and then growing teenager, Emera read them many times over, until one day they formed special powers within her. Unfortunately, the amount of encouraging words balanced with the taunting ones, any thoughts good or bad that entered her mind... happened.

Towards the end of school, all the students and teachers became increasingly suspicious with unexplained occurrences, such as; being slapped across the face, pushed and pinched by an unseen force, only during Emera's presence. They thought it was a warning, from her, and so their mockery quickly stopped. Nevertheless, their silence was too late. Emera's revenge had only begun and the worst were, as they feared, yet to come.

When school ended, the students who made Emera's school years suffering ones, planned to leave their town secretly. They packed all they could carry and waited for night to fall. Earlier, they strongly advised their families to leave ahead of them with the rest of the town's people, who heard rumors of unexplained happenings, fearing for their town. They were to keep going, never to look back; assured they would be together again.

Did they leave as planned—secretly? Did they see their families again?

*   *   *

Ms. Biddock walked sullenly to her office. As she reached the entrance, she found the door left completely open, her three felines roaming the old floorboards, seemingly waiting for her. A smile gradually formed on her face, as they paced towards her, then she raised her hand at a stop.

"Stay still, only for a second."

Her arms lifted and stretched out wide, as she began twirling in place with eyes closed lightly, smiling, and swiftly transforming her boring office into one of rareness.

"There now, that's much better. Don't you think?" She patted their heads and then walked to her desk to sit in her queen-like chair, covered in green velvet, placing her long tired arms gently on the thick padded armrests.

They purred loudly, rubbing against her legs.

"We're going to do a little homework right now." She leaned over against the desk and slid the black carrying bag, which contained her grimoire, towards her and pulled it out, placing it in front of her. When she opened it, it magically grew to an enormous size! The felines stood poised, curiously watching as its edges expanded wider than the desk.

"Now lets' see. We must find a spell to get me out of this boring town," she murmured. "If I even see another student today I will cast him or her away. Hmm, let us see. Ahh, here's something we haven't tried. There has to be a way to get back without the crystal ball, there just has to be!"

She placed her index finger on the page she chose and glided under each word.

"I think this spell could help. Now the three of you behave and don't make any sudden moves. Go on—over there," she shooed them and they walked calmly to the corner while she continued to read.

Meanwhile, outside on the school steps, Rena stood watching everyone's cheerful face as they hurdled onto their bikes and rode off carefree under the beaming sun, while others walked on. Suddenly, she had an overwhelming urge to look back.

CHAPTER TWO

INNER POWER REVEALED

Rena turned around and faced the colossal doors once again; staring at the crevices that had gone unnoticed all those years walking towards them. Her eyes gazed downwards slowly and then realized one door remained unclosed.

'She probably didn't leave yet,' she thought, knowing that if Ms. Biddock had left, the door would not have been open. Although she was frightened by her moments before, she understood why Ms. Biddock reacted the way she did. It must have been hard to watch the ones she thought were her friends, walking away from her.

"Hmm," she murmured, scratching her chin, thinking if she closed them, she would only regret it after. "Maybe Ms. Biddock will apologize to me."

With each minute that passed, her curiosity grew, until finally she had made up her mind.

"Hello? Hello?" she peeked, bug-eyed, cautiously between the partly open doors. "Can anyone hear me?"

A quantity of sunlight shined through the old classroom windows with rays beaming through the unclosed doors into the empty and narrow hallways. Slowly, she walked inside and then stopped when she reached the corner leading to Ms. Biddock's office. The entrance door was open and the light on, hinting she was still there. Rena continued quietly and as she did, heard a faint voice mumbling, believed to be that of Ms. Biddock's.

"Maybe the teachers came back," she whispered under her breath.

"I've used many words to describe what I seek! I've searched for other passages till there was blood on my feet!"

Rena stopped instantly, "Or—maybe they didn't." She kept still, and the loud, bellowing cry startled her once more.

"I ask again, help in my finding, the place where these memories and I were once binding!"

The hallways once lit from the suns warm rays, appeared dark before her eyes, not moving once as she watched a storm develop inside the school and all around her. Thunderous sounds suddenly pierced her ears and twisting winds came about, causing all the classroom doors to slam abruptly. She covered her ears with trembling hands; her eyes squinting as she cringed with pain. It was at that moment she had decided—it was time to leave, however, just as she was about to turn back, she was overwhelmed with a similar interest that had lured her before.

With eyes half-closed, she struggled to continue through forceful winds, using only the light that glared passed through the frosted glass atop the office entrance, to guide her way. Her arms stretched out in front of her, reaching for the door, determined to take hold of the doorknob, and succeeded.

With trembling hands and all her weight—all ninety pounds, she pushed hard as she could, however, the winds on the other side were just as strong, pushing the door against her and then finally closing. Yet, she tried again, squeezing in between the opening, immediately attracted to the ceiling, turned open sky, with monstrous swirling clouds, followed by thunder and lightning. With one hand, she kept hold of the door, while the other kept her tangled hair in the wind away from her face. It was then when she saw a woman staring directly at her with green glowing eyes!

"Ms.… Biddock?" she asked, unsure if it was even her, and at the same time wondered if all was really happening, until the winds against her face made her realize, it actually was.

Ms. Biddock turned her head slowly, with her arms firmly held out under the treacherous sky, cleaving to a gold, carved wand, with lightning soaring out from its tip.

Rena was able to recognize only one letter carved into the wand, the letter M; afterwards, she was attracted to the desk, covered completely by an old, green leather bound book, bright lights beaming out from its oversized pages.

"Didn't I tell you to leave?" Ms. Biddock yelled, as her black layered gown flapped uncontrollably along with her loose hair floating wildly away from her face.

"I was only—" Rena tried to explain.

"ONLY!" she furiously interrupted as her seemingly weightless body levitated gracefully over the floorboards, her black felines with eyes similar to hers guarded her space.

Rena watched as they sat in line with their hypnotic stare that prevented her from moving. Then, they hissed, and all their control instantly ended.

She hurriedly apologized. "I'm sorry. I didn't mean to upset you." She backed out of the office quickly. The door slammed sharply, inches from her face.

With her empty backpack still strapped securely over her shoulders, she ran against uncontrolled winds the best she could. In the dimmed hallway, she slid her hand against the wall of stone, guiding her way back to the exit she wished she had never gone through.

Ms. Biddock called out to her in a deep, echoing voice. "Come back, Rena! Come back!" Her arm extended slowly out in front of her towering body, reaching with the tips of her long, bony fingers, barely touching Rena's hair flowing in the wind.

"Stop following me!" Rena cried out as she turned her head. "I'm leaving!"

However, Ms. Biddock already realized, she was the one to help her return home and make sure she would.

Rena kept ignoring her calls and focused only to escape the nightmare she carelessly entered.

As she neared the exit, she thought, 'I will make it.'

A new smile emerged along with hope as her hands reached out and touched the brass handle!

"Yes, I will make it," she whispered excitedly and then felt the straps of her backpack tugged. In an instant, her smile disappeared.

"No! No!" she yelled, as Ms. Biddock dragged her, preventing her from leaving with only her heels and buttocks touching the floor. She twisted her body side to side, kicking her legs as hard as she could, trying to break free from the principal's seemingly tight clutch.

"Let… go of me," she struggled. "Somebody, help me!"

Nevertheless, due to the surrounding storm, her shrilling cries were not loud enough for anyone to hear. The students who anxiously left the building before her were already frolicking around outside, clueless to what was happening inside the school.

"I won't tell anybody… uh… what I saw, I promise," she tried to assure her. Then quickly after, she stopped resisting, tilted her head back, and saw Ms. Biddock circled by thunderbolts, flashing around her, coldly ignoring her plea.

Rena slowly looked back hopelessly towards the doors, she tried desperately to reach, before abruptly abducted, become further away. She had to think of something, quick. One at a time, she pulled her arms out from under the thick straps of her backpack, keeping herself steady, so not to attract her attention. It worked, and she was able to free herself, but then the strong winds kept her on her hands and knees, preventing her from standing. After countless struggles, about to give up all hope, she unexpectedly balanced onto her feet.

Ms. Biddock continued, unknowingly, hauling an empty backpack behind her.

Rena reached the massive, colossal doors; again, and took hold of one enormous brass handle, but before she could pull the door just enough to fit through, the winds changed direction and forced it closed. The thought of surrendering terrified her so that it miraculously revealed hidden strength she had all along. She pulled as hard as she could, one more time, and ran through just before it slammed shut behind her. She was free and jumped off the school steps running, never to look back again.

Ms. Biddock turned the corner the same time she heard the heavy slam of a door. She stopped and quickly pulled the backpack she held with a tight grip and it smacked hard against her face. Her eyes rolled and her head bobbed. A few moments after, she came to and realized Rena was truly gone.

"NOOO!" she screamed with tightly closed eyes as her body shook with anger and then swung the backpack with such tremendous force through a closed door and window, followed after by a strong gust of wind, carrying her cry of rage.

Broken glass fell out on the school premises, leaving it and the remaining broken windows with only their chipped, white frames.

The children outside heard when Ms. Biddock screamed along with the sound of cracking glass.

"What was that?" shouted a girl, looking around in alarm when she heard the noise.

"Get out of the street!" a boy warned, as he watched glass fall onto the school lawn.

They were unable to move fast enough; the blast of wind knocked them all down, sending the ball that they played with, flying through a neighbor's closed window. At that same time, Rena ran around the corner and stopped, waiting impatiently until all the glass fell completely. Then, she walked carefully, ducking down quickly to grab hold of her backpack that fell thereafter.

Finally, there was no stopping her from running home and away from Whilom Elementary.

"Hey, what happened in there?" he yelled out to her while the others stood up from their fall to the ground.

Rena kept running without so much as a nod, ignoring anyone or anything near her. The blank expression on her face kept him from asking again. He turned to look at his friends, seemingly in shock by the brief heavy gust of wind that knocked them off their feet.

"That was… Rena," said the girl. "She was in… my sister's class."

"Well, don't tell anyone what happened. I don't think they'd believe us anyway."

They all shook their heads with widened eyes, speechless, and then walked away towards their homes. An old woman stormed out of her cottage in anger, slamming her door against her porch railing. They stopped dead in their tracks and turned their heads sharply to the direction that startled them. She stood motionless, staring with devilish eyes; her hair held up in loose curlers with pins twice their size, wearing an old worn-out robe. Her eyebrows furrowed as she pointed her crooked finger at them and yelled, "Your parents are going to pay for a new window and all of you will put it in!"

They all looked at one another, and then a boy, who worried about getting in trouble, shouted, "We don't know how to put a window in!"

"Well you better learn and learn fast!"

The girl spoke out in their defense, "But, it wasn't us. It was the wind!"

The old woman ignored her excuse and with buried rage just under the surface of her skin, entered back inside, slamming the door behind her, causing the remainder of the glass to fall. Even though she said nothing else, they were sure she would to their parents.

The boy who yelled out to Rena reminded the others, "Don't forget! Don't say anything! Let's just go home and stay there until tomorrow. That old woman can't prove anything."

"But she has our ball!" shouted another boy, afraid they would get in trouble for something they didn't do.

"Yeah!" the others shouted.

"We'll talk about it tomorrow. Only Rena knows what happened in there."

They all nodded their worried heads and once again, went their separate ways, back to their homes, where they stayed out of sight for the remainder of the day and throughout the night.

Ms. Biddock watched everything that happened as she stood by the classroom entrance. She noticed Rena never once stopped to talk to anyone, although, it was no guarantee she never would. She floated back through the constant winds to her office; her hair blew unevenly above her shoulders, up and aside from her face as her green piercing eyes glowed throughout the dark, squally hallway.

When she arrived at the entrance, she used her powers to push the door wide open against the forceful winds inside her office, never touching the knob. Her three black felines were huddled under the desk, seemingly waiting for her, untouched by the treacherous sky above. They walked towards her and she bent down, brushing her hand over their heads.

"My dear little friends," she greeted them lovingly. Their presence comforted her. She proceeded to her desk, to search a different spell in her grimoire, to cast on Rena before she entered her home for the night. It was the only way to make Rena help her return to Wanderamid, where she had unwillingly entered into the town of Whilom, after foolishly placing a curse on two young girls. She cursed them with powers that of a witch, which included all the disadvantages of an evil one, meant only to be a lesson, a lesson that without warning backfired.

She peered deeply through the open ceiling into the treacherous sky and said aloud, "Rena has all the advantages: she has a big heart, she is very brave and has lots of energy. She has shown to be tricky, too This time the spell will be said with a twist, so any backfiring will be certainly missed!"

After, she looked into the grimoire and began turning the pages, one after another, until she finally came upon a spell that ended her search. Anxiously, she picked up her gold, carved wand, raised it directly above her, and recited the words loudly and firmly, *"That which evolves, close to the ground and resembles fire, will award you the dream you frequently desire. The winds in the darkness will cover you, and prayers from another will lead you to—dreams you envision every day, but not precisely in the same way. If assistance is truly in your heart, then I will soon be back to where I'm now not part. Pieces of this puzzle come together, as you roam, the last piece being the one guiding you home!"*

The ceiling swiftly closed with a shrilling, razor sharp sound and the winds quickly perished. All mystical surroundings immediately switched back to original form. She waved her magic wand around herself, instantly covered by falling, radiant particles, becoming once again the principal, with her hair up in a French twist bun and dressed plainly in her school attire.

When she closed her grimoire, it immediately shrunk to a standard sized book, conveniently fitted for her black carrying bag, used for witches' tools. After placing it and her wand inside, she was finally prepared to leave. Before she and her black felines exited the school grounds for the summer, she secured her office and walked to the classroom she was near earlier.

The broken windows and door needed restoring along with clearing debris.

Once again, she reached back in her bag to retrieve her powerful wand and waved it over the broken door and windows.

"Restore those windows and this door, like they were not long before."

She grinned at her felines. "Now everything is back the way it was." As she began to walk away, she remembered, "Oops, I almost forgot!" She turned quickly and waved her wand yet again.

"Transform this room back to its norm, the way it existed preceding the storm."

Ms. Biddock was finally satisfied. She continued towards the colossal doors and secured them. Afterwards, she smiled down at her dear companions.

"Come on," she waved her hand for them to follow her.

They left through the back exit, ending their stay at Whilom Elementary. Eventually, she would return after summer break.

Would she ever return?

Before long, a promising and powerful sign would reveal the beginning of what would soon become—an interesting spell.

CHAPTER THREE

MAGICAL DANDELION

A feeling of relief came over Rena as she ran around the corner onto Whisper Lane, where she lived. She thought then she had completely escaped her ordeal with Ms. Biddock.

The children were having fun on the cobblestone street, unaware of the disturbance that occurred previously in front of the school. Some rode their bikes over ramps while others enjoyed a game of volleyball, without a net.

One of Rena's friends ran up to her, when she finally caught her breath, after a long run.

"Rena, what took you so long to get home?"

For a moment, she thought about what to say and not wanting to lie, told her partly what happened.

"I… forgot my backpack and had to go back inside the school to get it."

"Oh… well… come on. Let's get in the volleyball game."

"No thanks, maybe later."

"Are you all right?" She noticed Rena's pale face.

"Oh, yes, I'm fine," she chuckled nervously. "There was a dog chasing me, that's all."

"A dog?" her friend asked, puzzled and then unexpectedly shouted out to the others, "Hey, Rena saw a dog!"

The children playing volleyball suddenly ended the game and the ones riding their bikes screeched to a stop! There was an instant of silence, with only a fading sound of a bouncing ball. They ran over to Rena and her friend.

"Where did you see a dog?" asked a curious boy. "There hasn't been a dog around here in like three years."

Rena looked at everyone staring, impatiently waiting for her to respond. She had forgotten the dogs in the neighborhood and everywhere else near their town, disappeared with no reason.

"No, no," she answered nervously, wiping the sweat from her forehead. "I meant to say a hog, not a dog."

All of them began laughing and then walked away shaking their heads.

Her friend continued to stand beside her, trying to keep a straight face.

"Rena, there aren't any hogs running around here."

"Well, there was some kind of animal chasing me," Rena whispered nervously.

"OK… well, let me know if you change your mind about the game."

"I'll just sit here for a while before I go inside," she responded.

"All right, I'll talk to you later." She smiled and then walked back to the volleyball game the others had already started again.

Rena sat down gently on the curb in front of her cottage and placed her backpack, covered with a butterfly print, alongside of her. She thought, 'I shouldn't have walked back inside the school and I shouldn't have said, DOG.'

Although she truly wanted to tell her friend what really happened, she was not sure she would have believed her, especially after mentioning a hog. She stayed there to rest and then eventually drifted off into a daydream about traveling anywhere she wanted. If there was ever a time she wanted to be somewhere else, it was then.

She wrapped her arms loosely around her legs and then rested her head on her knees, glancing at the red wide-brick sidewalk in front of her home.

"If it could only happen now," she whispered tiredly.

From the corner of her eye, she saw a sparkling dandelion and was instantly captivated with its' larger than normal puffball with tips, flickering from the bright sun. Her tired eyes soon after revived, drawn by its' mystic appearance. Gradually, she stood and walked towards it, not letting it out of her sight, and then knelt down on the grass to pull it out. She held it in front of her closed eyes, making what she hoped to be, a magical wish. As a rush of air from her breath broke the large puffball, they gently opened, watching as the light wind carried it to the sky. Left with only its long stem, she then threw it towards the red wide brick sidewalk when it vanished before her! For a moment, she searched the same direction aimed, but it was nowhere in sight. After, she stood up, walked back to the curb for her backpack, and then waved to her friend before entering her home for the night.

"Bye!" she shouted.

"You're going inside, Rena?" her friend asked aloud.

"Yes!" she replied, walking up to her porch.

"See you when I get back from vacation!"

Rena turned briefly before entering her cottage.

"Have a good time!"

Her mother heard the front door open.

"How was your last day of school, Rena?" she asked while preparing dinner.

"It was OK." She was not sure whether to tell her about what happened in school, it was too unbelievable, so instead she asked, "Do you believe in magic, Mom?"

"Well, just because you didn't see something doesn't mean it didn't happen," she replied. "So, the answer to that question is, yes I do. Why?"

"No reason," she shrugged her shoulders then walked towards the stairs.

"Would you like to go anywhere special tonight, like to the movies?"

Rena paused with one foot rested on the bottom step.

"I don't know… maybe not tonight."

"All right then, we'll watch a movie here," she replied in good spirits.

"OK," Rena smiled and then proceeded to her bedroom to change into her sleepwear.

After the day she had in school, she thought it would be best to stay inside the rest of the night. When she placed her shoes in her bedroom closet, she discovered a red shoebox on the floor. She was positive about it not being there that morning. Excited to see what was inside, she opened it and found a new pair of pearl white sneakers with lavender colored laces and silver sequins on the sides.

"Cool," she whispered under her breath as she removed them out of the beautiful box and then immediately after, ran down the stairs to her mother. "Thanks, Mom," she said, gratefully. "I'll help pay for them out of my allowance."

Her mother was completely surprised with what she said; gently lifted Rena's chin and then looked into those big, dark eyes she adored. "No honey, they're a gift from me to you. It's time to eat now. Put them over there in the corner."

She made all of Rena's favorites: steak, homemade French-fries, sliced thin, and baked Italian bread. For dessert, she made her special chocolate cake with the sweetest chocolate icing.

"Mom, it looks delicious and smells really good."

They began to fill their plates and then her mother stopped suddenly.

"Let's say grace first."

"Oh, I almost forgot," admitted Rena.

Afterwards, they enjoyed every bite of their meal, not leaving a single crumb.

Their stomachs were completely satisfied.

"That was so good, Mom. I don't think I can move," she said rubbing her stomach.

"Thanks, I thought you'd like it," she replied proudly.

They sat a little while longer and then Rena's mother began to clear the dishes from the table. Rena helped, placing them in the sink filled with warm, sudsy water.

"Mom, have you ever made a wish on a dandelion?"

"Oh, a lot of times, when I was a little girl," she recalled and then gave a big sigh. "But, they never came true. Maybe one day you'll get a chance to make a wish on one."

"But I did. I saw one out front on our lawn and made a wish on it, right before I came in," she replied. "It was so beautiful Mom. I never saw anything look so magical. It had the biggest puffball with tips, sparkling... like they were on fire."

"That's strange," she thought aloud with a bewildered look on her face.

"Why?" Rena asked, puzzled.

"Well, I haven't seen a dandelion on our lawn or any other in years. It must have been a special one, just for you," she smiled and then curiously asked, "What did you wish for?"

"Mom, if I tell you it won't come true," she chuckled.

"You're right," she laughed. "I know that! Well, I hope your wish comes true."

"Mom, will you holler for me when you're ready to put on a movie? I have to lie down for a while. I think I ate too much. I'm really full."

"Go on," she smacked her hip playfully with the hand towel. "I'll come up when I'm finished."

"Thanks again, for the great dinner and new sneakers."

She picked her sneakers up from the floor on the way up to her room, where she finally changed out of her school clothes, then immediately flopped onto her comfortable bed. As soon as her head rested on her over-puffed pillow, her mind wandered off into a deep sleep.

Rena's mother dried the last dish and thought about how Rena described the dandelion, 'Biggest puffball—with sparkling tips like fire'. She kept repeating it over in her mind. "It even sounds magical," she muttered to herself.

Her belief in mystical happenings made her wonder; Rena could have possibly stumbled into one.

After setting the last dish down, she walked to the end of the stairs and hollered, "Rena… Rena, I'm ready! It's movie time!"

When there was no answer, she immediately went up to check on her, only to find she was sleeping. To avoid waking her, she placed a light kiss on her cheek and tiptoed out. As she reached to shut the door, she noticed the window open, snuck back inside, slowly closed it, then quietly backed out, leaving it partly open. Afterwards, she went all the way down to the den where she too drifted into a deep sleep.

The hours passed and it was the middle of what seemed to be, a peaceful night, until the crickets began chirping loudly under the starry, sparkling sky. A gentle zephyr wandered atop Whisper Lane, seeking an answer to someone's prayer. Rena's window opened slowly and it entered, carrying the spirits of children whose prayers were unanswered. The lost souls gathered to assist other children lost, so not to arrive at the same fate they had.

"She is the one, she can do it, she will help her," they whispered softly.

The spirits could not help guide a child in need, without the bravery and heart of someone who had not yet passed. They chose Rena to help a certain one lost and unable to find her way home.

The peaceful zephyr passed over her slumbering body, circling above her delicately with voices anxiously saying repeatedly, *"You must help her find her way home. She doesn't have enough time."*

Sparkling particles gently fell thereafter, disappearing over her and then the spirits drifted out through the window screen they had entered.

Rena tossed and turned throughout the remainder of the night.

All the spirits whispered, repeated in her dreams.

* * *

After what seemed to have been a long and uncomfortable night, the first light had risen, starting a new day in Whilom. Rena gradually opened her eyes and stretched her arms out in front of her as she let out an enormous yawn. She felt exhausted and could not understand why, after all, she went to bed early the night before. Nevertheless, she was curious about the weather. She rubbed her drowsy eyes and anxiously got out of bed to gaze out her open window and felt the morning chill air against her face. The sky was clear, completely empty of any clouds and she thought at that moment, it was going to be a perfect day. She pulled out her favorite green jeans and a yellow, butterfly print shirt from her dresser drawer, before washing up.

Her mother realized Rena was awake when she heard the water running in the bathroom.

"Rena!" she shouted when the sound of running water stopped. "Straighten up your room before you go outside!"

"I will!" she replied happily.

After she did what her mother asked, she rested comfortably on her bed covered with a soft, butterfly print quilt, wondering how she would spend the day. All her friends would be leaving for their summer vacation getaways, so she thought about taking a walk to Fountain Lake Park, where she has gone many times before—alone.

She quickly rose up and then ran down the stairs into the kitchen where her mother sat dressed in clothes worn only when cleaning, sipping on a cup of steaming hot coffee. It was a definite sign; she had taken the day off. She had planned to spend it with Rena, but had not expected her to wake up so early.

"Good morning, sweetie."

"Good morning, Mom," she replied, as she reached for the loaf of bread and then plunked two slices into the toaster.

"I didn't think you'd get up this early, especially on your first day off from school. You'll have to stay near the cottage if you go outside. I have a lot of housework and I might need you to help a little. We can go to the movies after."

Rena's toast popped out of the toaster.

"Sounds good to me," she said, placing her toast onto the plate.

"Good, then it's a plan."

Her mother set her empty cup down in the sink, then fitted her hands inside latex gloves before grabbing the cleaning caddy.

"Oh, by the way," she added, "Did you straighten your room like I asked you?"

Rena stopped buttering her toast and looked up at her innocently, smiling, "Sure did."

"Great, then I'll start cleaning downstairs in the den. Love you, sweetie."

"Love you, too, Mom."

Rena turned on the TV and began eating her breakfast. The weather report scrolled at the bottom of the screen, predicting rain for the afternoon. It was disappointing news for her. How could it rain the first day of her vacation? She stuffed her mouth with the rest of her breakfast and ran down the stairs to tell her mother before she could swallow it all.

She stood in front of her, unable to speak as she kept chewing and then finally, "Ahem!" She cleared her throat. "I'll be right back. I'm just going for a little walk, before it rains."

She turned around quickly and then ran back up the stairs.

"Wait, Rena, don't forget what I told you. You need to be near the cottage."

When Rena reached the top step, she turned briefly to look down at her.

"I know. I won't be long."

Her mother shook her head and smiled. Rena continued the rest of the way up to her bedroom, put on the new sneakers given to her the night before and then ran down to the front door.

"See you later!" she shouted. "Oh, I shut my bedroom window, too!"

She hurried out the door.

Her mother stopped what she was doing and wondered aloud, "She shut the window? I shut it last night. Hmm, maybe I didn't."

Meanwhile, Rena saw her friend's parents getting ready to leave for vacation. "Hi!" She smiled and waved.

"Hi, Rena!" they smiled and waved back briefly, as they were too occupied fitting their overstuffed suitcases inside the small trunk of their car.

Rena laughed discreetly and proceeded to the park, which was a mere two blocks away from her home.

* * *

A little while later, she approached closer to the entrance. The beautiful light green water came into view, glittering from the sun's rays when flowing against the mountainside. She could hear the birds singing high up in the trees spread apart from each other when walking in, kicking through a pile of leaves that had fallen on the ground. As she headed towards the old, crooked dockside, she took a moment, staring at the reflection of the sky in the water and then heard a rustle of leaves behind her. She turned around cautiously and saw three boys walking towards her.

One of them shouted, "Hey, what's going on?"

His smile caused her to blush.

Rena knew the boys from the neighborhood. They attended Imagine Middle School, where she would be attending at the end of summer break.

"Hi," she smiled shyly at him and then partly turned away.

He turned to his friends. "Hey, go on, I'll catch up in a minute." Then, he gave his attention back to her. "Your name's Rena, right?"

She looked at him, confused why he stayed behind.

"Yes," she answered hesitantly.

"I called you when you were running yesterday, by the school, but you didn't answer. Oh, and my name is Jodon."

She smiled again and nodded.

"What were you running from?" he asked.

"Nothing... I was just... late getting home."

He took a couple steps closer.

"I saw you get your backpack. Someone threw it out the window. There was glass everywhere. This morning all the windows on the second floor were fixed, like it never happened."

Rena stood, speechless.

"Hey, Jodon!" his friends called out. "Come on!"

"I have to go. Maybe we can talk later?"

"Sure," she replied, as her thoughts were elsewhere.

"Bye," he smiled and then walked away.

Rena stared back into the water and then afterwards, stepped onto the old dock, walking all the way to its end. She sat and admired the few larger and unique cottages built slanted on the small mountain across the lake, thinking about what Jodon had said, gazing over at the bridge beside the dock that gave the owners private access to the park. It was then she sensed the once light wind, strong against her face, causing the branches to sway back and forth, enough for the birds that were once singing, to fly off and away silently, with only the sound of fluttering wings.

'It looks like it will rain anytime', she thought.

Regardless of the weather, she closed her eyes and concentrated only on the sounds of the lake flowing past her and the leaves falling from the trees behind. At that time, it was the perfect place to be and she could have stayed there forever.

Suddenly, without any hint, there was a rumbling sound of thunder quickly followed by another. Rena opened her eyes and saw the clouds hanging low, covering the treetops across from the lake. She stood with her eyes glued to the sky. Before taking the first step leading back to the beginning of the dock, it began to pour! She was instantly drenched before she began to run towards her final leap off.

A boulder inscribed with huge letters that read 'Fountain Lake Park' was in her path. She tried to avoid running into it, but it was too late, as she stumbled and bumped her forehead hard against it, plummeting into the muddy ground.

There her lifeless body lay unconscious, under the pouring rain.

After what seemed like hours had only been five minutes. She awakened from her heedless fall with a painful, throbbing headache, completely drenched from her head to her new sneakers. As she sat up slowly with her hand pressed tightly against her forehead, she immediately became curious as to what caused her fall. Large raindrops dripped off her long eyelashes, making it difficult for her to see, and then a peculiar sight came into view. She stared, unmoving; countless raindrops beating against her skin, and then crawled slowly towards the odd object, trying hard not to blink. The rain tapped continuously on her back as she hung her head down over it. It was a glass ball, like fortune-tellers.

Her eyes widened with amazement.

"A crystal ball—maybe it's real," she said, astounded.

She immediately picked it up and held it in the palms of her hands, allowing the heavy rain to wash it clean. Instantly, a numinous presence was in front of her, revealing a mystical, cloudy appearance that caused her heart to beat as fast as the rhythm of the rain. Soon after, a clashing thunder burst along with a huge bolt of lightning missing Rena inches from where she was kneeling. It frightened her greatly and her hands flew up in the air, sending the thick glass ball flying, landing onto the muddy ground ahead of her. She crawled towards it, again, and then picked it up before running towards an old neglected storm drain tunnel, the one she and her friends never entered. It was the perfect place to separate from any further piercing lightning bolts.

As she neared the entrance, she slipped onto her stomach with her arms stretched out and her fingertips touching the edge of the tunnel's concrete floor.

"Oh, no!" she gasped and then watched helplessly as the ball slid from her hold and rolled inside the tunnel.

She anxiously went in after it on her hands and knees and was about to grab it, when a bright light shined out that brought her to an immediate stand. It was then she knew, without a doubt, she had discovered something incredible.

As she stood calmly, waiting to see if the bright light would dim, she heard a faint sound of dragging feet further inside the unexplored tunnel, the most disturbing sound she had ever heard. With one hand, she partly covered her eyes and with the other, poked it with her trembling finger before swiftly pulling it back. She felt no heat from the bright light and so without further hesitation, grabbed it! The once faint sound of dragging feet had become clearer; frozen in panic, she was unable to move.

From the corner of her eye, she saw a shadow and unwillingly, stayed still in her body filled with fear. Eventually, she forced herself to walk backwards, but was only able to move an inch at a time, unable to take her eyes away from the direction of the terrifying sound, not even for a second.

A silhouette of an old woman appeared out of the darkness, walking continuously towards her in a long dress and a shawl that hung over her shoulders, trimmed with diamond-like sequins, sparkling in the dimming light as her long hair clung to it. Rena had no idea what to expect and remained extremely cautious.

"Hello," said the old woman.

The sound of her voice baffled Rena. It was not one of an old woman, but more from someone her own age.

"You look like you're afraid of me, don't be, I won't hurt you. What's your name?"

She continued walking towards her.

Rena struggled to speak and then finally, with an apparent break in her voice, she answered, "Re—n-a."

"Hi, Rena," she responded politely and then stopped when she sensed her fear.

"What's… y-your name?" she asked in a trembling voice.

"Avanna—Avanna Marsail," she smiled. Her tired eyes suddenly widened in amazement, when she saw what Rena held so protectively in her arms. "Where did you find the crystal ball?"

"I fell over it—when I ran off the dock."

Rena wiped the dripping water off her face and felt a slight lump on her forehead, sore to the touch, as her eyes scoped the empty, damp tunnel.

"Have you been staying here?"

"I guess you can say I've been… waiting here."

Rena sensed weakness when Avanna spoke and noticed there was no sight of food anywhere. She had begun to realize Avanna was quite harmless, allowing her to be more at ease in her presence.

"Have you had anything to eat?"

"I haven't had an appetite lately, but when I get a little hungry, I wait until dark and walk by the cottages to pick apples and pears off the trees in the yard."

"Why do you stay in here?" she curiously asked.

"I have to, I have no place else to go. I'm lost. I've been praying every night for that crystal ball," she answered, silently overjoyed Rena found it, however, there was doubt she would give it to her.

"Do you want me to help you get home?" Rena asked and then added, "And why do you keep calling this a crystal ball?"

Avanna turned her head to one side and then to the other, searching for a spot to sit. She knew her answer to Rena's question would be a long one, hopefully to convince her to believe and give up the crystal ball she so desperately needed to get back home. When she finally found a spot, ready to answer her question, Rena sat across from her, ready to listen.

The rain outside had since dwindled and gave Rena more time before going home.

"Are you ready?" Avanna asked.

"Yes, I'm… ready," she answered, shivering in her soaking wet clothes.

Avanna noticed and offered her shawl. "Here, take this, it will keep you warm."

"Thanks," Rena responded gratefully. She wrapped it tightly over her shoulders and then eagerly waited for her to begin.

CHAPTER FOUR

AVANNA'S ANECDOTE

Avanna was sitting with the crystal ball at arm's reach, only steps away from leaving Whilom, where she thought she had been bound to forever.

She began telling her version about the crystal ball.

"I didn't think I'd ever see the crystal ball again and I would be stuck in a world I know nothing about, forever. When I came here, I was so tired and fell asleep right over there." She pointed to where Rena was sitting. "I felt the crystal ball pulled from my arms. That's when I woke up and saw three boys standing around me."

"What did you do, and what do you mean being stuck in a world you know nothing about?"

"I'll explain that to you," she replied and then continued, "I yelled for them to give it back, but they laughed at me and called me a 'crazy old woman'. Then they left with it."

She lowered her head, embarrassed, and then slowly looked back up at Rena.

"When they ran out of the tunnel I stood and tried to chase them, but I lost my breath as soon as I stepped outside. That never happened to me before. I thought I would die! All this time the crystal ball was by the dock and I didn't even know it. I could have been halfway home by now."

Her legs had become numb, tingling from sitting on the damp concrete floor. She stood to stretch them, pacing to the entrance and then back again.

"Avanna, are you all right?"

"Yes." She leaned against the wall tiredly and then let out a huge sigh while she thought, 'She won't believe me'.

It seemed useless to continue, until she saw the sincere look on Rena's face. She sat back down, carefully across from her.

"I know it's hard to believe that's a real crystal ball, but it is. I couldn't be here without it. You see, I went into a tunnel in my hometown, Wishing Willow, to get out of a storm. That's where I found it, covered with dust. It had to have been there a long time. When I wiped the dust off, a bright light shined out from it!"

"That's what happened to me." Rena reacted anxiously. "Did it scare you, too?"

"No," she replied. "That didn't scare me at all; it's what happened after. When the storm became stronger, I kept moving back, but then this strange force pulled me all the way. I tried to run back out, but it was too strong! After, there was a loud humming sound that made me sick."

"What did you do then?" Rena asked interested in hearing what happened next.

"Well, I kept my eyes closed the whole time. I was too afraid to open them. I couldn't wait until it was over. When it finally stopped, I felt better, then, I opened my eyes and saw I was in another world, not at all like mine. It was hard to believe. I tried to go back, but there was only an outline of the tunnel, flashing and fading away. I was too afraid to go back."

Avanna suddenly felt sick reliving that awful day, although she realized she had to continue for Rena to understand, the power of the crystal ball.

"Everything will be all right. You don't have to finish," Rena said.

She thought back to the day before. It was somewhat unusual for her, discovering Ms. Biddock's' hidden identity. A part of her wanted to leave while at the same time, she needed to hear the rest of her story, no matter how impossible it seemed.

"No, I want you to hear all of it," Avanna said, excitedly. "Everything I've said is the truth. You have to hear the rest. When I was in that world, I found many tunnels, like this one. I went through them and then back out after I found they weren't the ones leading me home. They're all in different places and not easy to find. You have to search for them. The only way to travel through them is with that crystal ball." She referred to the one Rena held tightly in her hands. "To really understand what I'm talking about, you'd have to see for yourself. This is the sixth tunnel I've gone through. You know, I'm really the same age as you."

Rena sat quietly as she listened to the strangest story ever and then her eyebrows lifted as she asked in disbelief, "If you're my age, why do you have gray hair?" The sore lump on her forehead left her with a lingering headache that created doubt in Avanna's story.

"I'll tell you." She gave a slight sigh as she sensed doubt from her expression, watching as she pressed the palm of her hand against her forehead. "Are you all right?"

"Yes," she nodded with eyes squinting. "I'm fine; I just have a little lump from my fall."

"Maybe you should go home," Avanna suggested. She sensed Rena was not well enough to hear the rest.

Rena quickly dropped her hand.

"No, it's all right. I can stay," she said, curious to find out what supernatural powers the crystal ball supposedly had.

Avanna began to hopefully clear any doubts in Rena's mind.

"Each time I go through a new tunnel, I become a little older. My hair gets grayer, and I get more wrinkles. My body gets tired faster, too. I have no idea what I look like. The closest I ever came to a mirror was by looking in rain puddles. I probably look older than my own mother." She wiped a tear off her pale cheek. "I miss her a lot. I don't know if I'll ever see her again."

Rena was surprised to hear Avanna had become older by going through tunnels. If she had not seen the crystal ball light up the way it did, she probably would have never listened to her. Nevertheless, she did see it, and with her own eyes, remembering her mother's words the night before, 'Just because we didn't see something doesn't mean it didn't happen'.

"You don't look old. You only look tired." She walked over and gently patted her shoulder, "I'm sorry you haven't seen your family for so long."

"Thanks… Rena." She gave a slight grin. "I haven't thought about my mom in a long time. I've been too busy trying to get back home. There were times, though, when I heard her calling for me… or thought I did. It seemed so real."

Rena thought about helping Avanna get back home, although, like Avanna, there was a chance she could enter into the wrong tunnel and be lost for a very long time, possibly forever. There was even a chance she would die of old age while searching for the right one as well! All those possibilities entered Rena's mind, but she was not about to part from the crystal ball, it was her find and she was not ready to give it away.

"Do you have any brothers or sisters?" she asked.

Avanna's mouth fell open, "Oh, no, how could I forget?"

"Avanna, your memory isn't the same. It's not your fault."

"But I forgot about my little brother," she replied embarrassed.

"You'll see your brother and your mother again, don't worry," she assured her.

Avanna's glassy eyes stared down at the tunnel floor. The emptiness she felt inside increased along with the memory of her brother.

"No," she remembered sadly, "He… disappeared two weeks before I did. My mother was very sad when no one could find him. Now that you have the crystal ball, I have a chance to get back home. Maybe Jack's been found!"

Rena kept silent. Avanna could only use the crystal ball if she went with her. It was a huge decision for her to make.

Would she give in and hand it to her or was Avanna too weak to go alone?

The once faded memory of Jack had become clearer, giving Avanna reason not to give up hope. She believed Rena was the answer to her prayers and in time, she too would become the answer to Rena's prayers.

Rena thought about inviting her to lunch.

'A sandwich would give her some energy,' she believed and then asked, "Avanna, would you like to have lunch with me and my mother?"

"Thanks," she replied gratefully, "but I wouldn't feel comfortable. I mean… I'm thirteen years old and I look like I'm an old woman."

Rena turned away with a mild grin and walked towards the exit to check the weather. She knew Avanna was right. Her mother would think that she was a stray old woman, and she was not supposed to be talking to strangers, young or old. Avanna went over to where Rena stood and they stared at the cottages slanted on the mountainside, while the seemingly calm sky turned dark before their eyes.

Rena glanced over at another direction and saw the curtains from one cottage window open with glowing green eyes glaring, locking into hers. Ms. Biddock was the only one she knew with eyes like those.

Rena gasped and stood breathless.

Avanna heard her and turned to see the frightened look on her face.

"Rena? What's wrong?" She tapped her on the shoulder. "Rena, hey, what's wrong?"

She followed the direction Rena's eyes locked to and saw green eyes glowing, staring out from a window.

Ms. Biddock focused on what Rena held in her arms.

"Oh, it's the crystal ball! She has the crystal ball! I don't need her to go to Wanderamid now!" She was excited and relieved, while her black felines calmly paced around. "The spell must be stopped. But, how can I do that?"

Meanwhile, Avanna quickly pulled Rena back into the tunnel and broke the hold those unusual eyes had on her.

"Who is that, Rena? Do you know who that is?" She slapped her cheek lightly, but the expression on her face remained unmoving.

Finally, Rena had begun to slowly come out of a daze and asked, "Did... you... see her?"

"Yes. I saw green eyes glowing through a window, looking straight into yours."

Rena panicked.

"It's the principal of my school. She's a witch! She knows where I am. We'll have to run to my cottage, we can't stay here any longer or she'll come after us. Follow me and hurry!"

She ran out of the tunnel as fast as she could. Avanna tried to follow.

Ms. Biddock could not allow them to leave her sight and quickly bellowed, *"Those in view about to flee, barricade that path with a branch from that tree!"*

She aimed her long arm firmly towards the big tree with the biggest branch on their path. A huge lightning bolt struck the branch and fell directly in front of them, missing them by inches. They had only one option, to return into the tunnel they frantically ran out moments before. Ms. Biddock did not try to harm the girls with her dangerous aim; she only meant to delay their getaway, or she would never get the crystal ball.

The spell she created the night before had already begun. The clouds in the sky became thicker and darkness increased greatly with silent, flickering lights of lightning. It was too late to put a stop to it, and no one could change it, not even Ms. Biddock.

She walked out onto her balcony and held her arms out wide, levitating carefully over the railing. The spell instantly kept her from using any powers against it. Without any warning, her body swiftly dropped straight down onto the slippery, muddy slope of the mountain, traveling instantly at great speed. Stunned by her unexpected fall, she managed to swerve back and forth to avoid colliding with the trees on her path. Even as the mud continuously splattered on her face, her squinting eyes were able to catch a glimpse of the lake as it became closer. She dug deeply into the ground with her long, bony fingers and the tips of her shoes, slowing down before finally coming to a stop, ending her terrifying ride with her stiffened chin hung over the edge, the lake as her view. Her body, completely covered in mud, added to her weight, making it difficult for her to stand.

As she lay on the ground, she wiped the mud from her mouth and spit out what went inside.

"This spell will be stopped!" She became furious and struggled to get on her feet, wobbling while she extended her mud-covered arms and then levitated over the calm lake, once under her chin. Only one foot made it over and she fell. She paddled continuously to bring her head above water, refusing to give in to a spell she created and then began swimming across, towards the opposite side where Rena and Avanna were waiting, for the worst was yet to come.

After the water washed the mud off her face and she was able to keep herself afloat, she noticed the bridge she could have easily walked over. Without any powers, she kept forcing her long, bony arms to paddle, which from afar resembled a pair of oars.

"I thought you said she's a witch," Avanna chuckled as she watched Ms. Biddock swimming in the lake.

"She is a witch! You weren't at the school yesterday. You don't know what she's capable of doing."

"Look!" Avanna pointed towards the lake.

Rena looked with a puzzled expression and thought, 'Yesterday she was floating above ground and today she's swimming in the water? Why isn't she using her powers?' She turned to Avanna and asked, "What is she up to?"

"Well, if she really is a witch, like you say she is, we should be worried—r-right now," she said with a nervous tone in her voice.

Rena turned her head slowly, afraid what her eyes would see. Ms. Biddock had made it across! Drenched to the bone, she walked with eyes glowing, unhurriedly towards them, staring their direction and then suddenly stopped.

They waited alertly for her next move.

"Look! What is she doing now?" She watched as Ms. Biddock began walking again, her every step had become weaker than the one before.

When she could go no further, she raised her arm, pointing at the crystal ball.

"She wants the crystal ball, that's what she wants, but why?" she wondered aloud.

Rena quickly covered it with the shawl.

"No!" Avanna cried out. "Don't let her have it! I'll never get home if you do!"

Her desperate plea startled Rena. She turned to see Avanna's eyes filled with tears, terrified Ms. Biddock would take the only hope Avanna believed could bring her home.

"Rena! Rena!" Ms. Biddock yelled. "Please, bring me the crystal ball!"

"No, go away!" she yelled, wondering at the same time why she was not using her powers to take it.

While it seemed Ms. Biddock lost her powers, she still had the power to frighten them.

The thick clouds suddenly swirled powerfully as they lowered more. Ms. Biddock realized her time was about to run out. She looked to the sky with her unusual eyes and called out in a compelling voice, *"I cancel the curse about to arise, to dissipate in the sky! Reasons are before me, I plead with this call; help me retrieve —my crystal ball!"*

After those commanding words, the crystal ball began to pull away from Rena's arms. Avanna combined what little strength she had with Rena's, to prevent Ms. Biddock from taking it. However, they were powerless against the overwhelming force and hoped for some kind of miracle.

"No! You… can't… have it!" Rena cried out.

They kept pulling as hard as they could. The tunnels damp floor touched their backs, as they kept their heads turned to the side, keeping her in full view.

Ms. Biddock thought her powers had returned full force and she had control of the spell. She pulled harder, eventually bringing Rena and Avanna back on their feet, however, soon after, the spiraling clouds turned into one massive tornado, directing towards her.

"NOOO!" she yelled. "It's mine—It's mine!"

She gazed up at the tornado and its funnel swiftly vacuumed her inside! It spiraled up the mountain slope, through the trees, where she fell back onto her cottage balcony. Any control she thought she possessed, was no more.

Rena and Avanna took a hard fall backwards when the overwhelming force broke.

"Avanna… are you all right?"

"I… guess," she answered, slowly standing back up as strong winds were hitting against the tunnel cement walls. She knew the tornado was close by and peeked out to see. "Rena, Look!"

Rena went to stand by her and cautiously peeked outside. The strong winds instantly dried her wet hair and dampened her soaked clothes. She gripped tightly to the tunnel wall with one hand as she watched the tornado circling Ms. Biddock's cottage on the other side of the lake.

There were no thoughts to escape; the winds would surely carry them away. They both waited for a change in its path.

* * *

The winds blew powerfully all around. Caged in a storm and suddenly, bound. Her home was a prison, she prayed for the calm. 'A witch's nightmare', she sighed, as she held a powerless wand.

CHAPTER FIVE

THE SIGN

Strong gusty winds, accompanied by heavy rain, caused some of the branches, overhanging the tunnel, to snap and fall onto the roof. Rena and Avanna stood trembling with folded arms covering their heads, afraid it would collapse on them. It seemed the tornado had a mind of its own; it continued circling Ms. Biddock's cottage. Eventually, it would have to move sometime and to some other place.

"Rena, we can get out of here with the crystal ball. It's the only way," Avanna said with certainty.

If they stayed, the tornado would destroy the tunnel and Avanna had neither spare time nor strength to search for another. Rena understood her plea to leave, but the thought of that being their only escape, terrified her. An unpleasant feeling came over her when she imagined possibly never being able to return home.

"There has to be another way," she replied desperately.

She longed for the tornado to move away or better yet, disappear. Then, she thought about leaving Fountain Lake Park the way she had arrived.

"We have to take a chance and run to my cottage. I have to make sure my mother's safe. Come with me and I'll help you figure out how you can get back home later, all right?"

She knew it would be difficult for Avanna to leave the only place she felt closer to home. Although they had only known each other for a short amount of time, Avanna believed Rena would help her.

"All right," she replied. "I'll go with you."

Even though she was weary about meeting Rena's mother and Rena knew her mother would not approve of her bringing home strangers, they had to put any doubts aside. She wanted to be near the crystal ball Rena was not ready to give away, before seeing its powers.

As they were about to escape, the tunnel floor began to vibrate, strongly under their feet.

"It's coming!" Avanna shouted.

Both struggled not to fall.

"Rena, we can't take a chance going out there. I'm afraid! We can't go out there and we can't stay in here."

Rena covered her face with trembling hands and then they dropped to her sides.

"I'm afraid, too," she confessed, and then quickly after a roaring gust of wind hit strongly against the tunnel wall, she asked, "Will you hold the crystal ball?"

"Yes. Why?" Avanna asked, confused.

"I'm taking my necklace off. I want my mother to know where I was last. It will show her I'm all right."

Three more trees fell, struck by lightning.

"Watch out!" Avanna shouted.

Both swiftly turned their faces away and when they looked back, they found themselves barricaded inside.

*   *   *

Rena's mother heard strong, vigorous winds outside her cottage home on Whisper Lane that caused all her windows to shake.

"Rena! Rena!" Her heart pounded greatly as she began to search every room, only to find them empty.

Rena was nowhere in sight, so she ran out the front door and stopped instantly, holding tightly to the porch railing. It was then when she noticed, over the cottage rooftops, the heavy, swirling winds down at Fountain Lake Park. She ran frantically down the cobblestone street.

"Rena! Rena!" she yelled.

When she realized it was a tornado, steadily swirling in one area, she stopped in her path and gasped, hearing only the sound of the pounding of her heart. She continued to run again, when a neighbor, looking outside his door window, recognized her.

He ran out to attempt escorting her back.

"Get... inside!" he yelled.

The strong winds made it difficult for her to understand and so he cupped one hand on the side of his mouth and with the other, held her arm tightly.

"There's… a… tornado… warning… you have to go… back inside!"

He tried pulling her the opposite way as porch chairs flew onto the street and garbage cans left outside, rolled away! The trees swayed and their branches broke, falling onto Whisper Lane. Both steadied themselves in the rough winds and watched.

She turned to him and tried to catch her breath, twisting her arm away from his hold, but he wouldn't let her go.

"No! My daughter, my daughter!" she pointed towards the park.

As he turned to look, his grip loosened. Then, with all her might, she escaped his hold and began to run against the untamed winds that soon after, kept her and the protective neighbor from moving further.

"Get… inside!" he pointed to his cottage, hoping she would realize it was out of her hands.

She nodded with a grave expression, just before a strong gust of wind pushed her back towards her cottage.

The neighbor steadied himself against the strong winds until she was safe inside her home, before entering his own.

*   *   *

Rena realized it was time to enter into another dimension, into a new world with a new friend, the only choice she had to survive. Nevertheless, she continued to think about other options up to the final second, not coming up with one.

"If we try to leave your way, Rena, the tornado will follow us. I know it sounds crazy, but I think it wants us. There's no way out now anyway. We need this tunnel so I can go home and for you to have a chance to come back."

Rena knew she was right and sadly replied, "I'm ready—to go."

"Before we go I have to tell you what to expect, so you're not surprised. There will be a magnetic feeling, pinching your skin. It will make you weak and a little sick. Don't be afraid and change your mind when we go through, if you do, you could be lost in between two worlds separating us into different dimensions. I'll be right beside you the whole time, Rena. Oh, and keep your eyes closed."

Rena kept quiet the whole time she spoke and not because she had nothing to say, she was frightened and with good reason.

"M-maybe the storm will stop," she thought aloud.

Avanna heard her and shouted, "Rena, there's no other way! The tornado is coming!" She pleaded, "Please, let's go… now!"

"OK!"

The trees barricading the exit shook. The tornado was changing its' path, onto theirs. Avanna held on tightly to Rena's hand and Rena held on to the crystal ball. A powerful, gleaming light appeared. They closed their eyes and lowered their heads, as they walked further inside. Within moments, they had become extremely weak, dragging their feet through the magnetic sensation Avanna described earlier.

'It has to end already!' Rena's thoughts screamed as a heavy humming noise filled her ears.

"Rena, I know how you… are feeling… and it's almost over… we're almost there!"

Rena heard her, but was unable to give a reply. Soon after, there was a sudden silence. The once bizarre feeling finally disappeared, except for some leftover pinching felt all over their bodies. Both raised their heads at the same time, speechless, and noticed they were seemingly unharmed.

"Are you all right… Rena?" she asked in a weak voice.

Rena stared into her eyes and only nodded.

Avanna watched Rena's eyes open and close continuously, as if she was trying to wake from a bad dream. It brought memories from when she had gone through to another world the very first time and the thought of ever going back home seemed impossible. It was a feeling that had since stayed with her.

She led Rena outside, stepping into the world of Wanderamid.

"I feel closer to my home already," she said, hoping Rena would come to realize, without any disbelief, that they were truly there.

Behind them, a beaming light surrounded the outside of the tunnel, as it became only an outline, fading away.

Rena felt the heat on her back and turned to see what was at one time difficult to believe, the tunnel disappearing before her eyes.

"Rena, are you all right?"

She only stared, fascinated by the sight.

Avanna shook her before she finally turned and responded with eyes slightly widened. "Yes, I am."

Rena had always wanted to be independent, but when she made that magical wish the day before, she had no idea it would come true the way that it did.

'I should have never made a wish on that dandelion,' she thought regrettably. Soon after, she realized there was no time to wallow in her mistakes, only concentrate on helping Avanna find her way home and then back to her own.

"I'm ready to help find your tunnel, Avanna. Are you ready?"

"I've never been so ready, and so weak. Do you think I'll make it, Rena?" She looked at her with tired, aging eyes.

"Sure… you'll make it… and I'll be with you when you do. That's why we're here, to get you home."

Rena took on a lot of responsibility, more so than she had ever imagined. Avanna was weak and growing weaker. There was no telling how far their journey would take them. Her strength had to be strong for the both of them.

"Look over there, Rena its Errantry forest." Her finger hung over as she pointed to a wide spread of tall trees.

Rena turned and saw the vast forest ahead, filled with enormous trees and thick branches covered with large leaves, swaying back and forth steadily, gracefully in the calm wind. Then, Avanna turned and pointed where the tunnel used to be.

"Look over here. It's gone. There's no turning back now."

Rena looked back, speechless; it was completely gone.

"When I came here the first time, I met two witches. One told me that no matter how much time I was away from home, I had to keep the faith that one day I would return. I almost lost hope in Whilom, but then you came with the crystal ball," she smiled gratefully.

"I won't lose hope," Rena assured as she looked around. "Where did you see… witches? We got away from one in Whilom. I would have stayed there if I knew we were going where there are two of them."

"They aren't… bad witches…. At least one of them isn't." She shrugged her shoulders and slowly turned away.

Rena lowered her head in despair and thought about what she had gotten into. When she gradually looked back up, Avanna was facing her, showing more wrinkles and her hair turned grayer.

"We better get started," she suggested. "Let's get you home."

"Thanks, Rena," she replied sincerely. "But, I have to tell you something first."

Rena thought, 'Not again'.

"Remember where the tunnel was?"

"Yes," she replied, unsure she wanted to hear the rest.

"You can't come back here when it's time for you to go back home. The tunnel already moved somewhere else. That's why I haven't found the right one to Wishing Willow. If you change your mind, I'll understand and help you get back first—if that's what you want."

Avanna hoped that was not what she wanted and Rena knew Avanna would never make it if she returned to Whilom first. However, they both meant what they said and to succeed in each other's goal they had to continue with their original plan.

Rena let out a big heavy sigh. "I believe we'll get through this, I really do," she responded with a positive attitude.

They both walked towards the tall trees, everywhere else was only endless green pastures under an enormous, clear, blue sky. Surely, the only way to travel was through Errantry forest. As they took their very first step, they had no warning before the ground began rumbling, strongly and rapidly cracking under their feet. Trees began to grow through the pastures at a fast speed all around them. The only space untouched was where they stood in their trembling bodies, with eyes once restless, wide with fear.

"What do we do now?" Rena stood stiffly. "I'm scared to take another step. What if a tree grows right underneath us and carries us up to the sky?"

"We w-will have to run into the forest," she pointed with her shaky finger.

"I c-can't move and you want me to run?"

"OK," Avanna replied calmly, when actually, she was terrified. "Let's just wait here, until... y-you feel a little b-better."

"All—right," Rena responded bug-eyed and still, not giving any attention to her stuttering reply.

CHAPTER SIX

IN WANDERAMID'S SKY

Rena would have rather been in between the crowded trees than in the middle of broken open space. She whispered anxiously to Avanna, "Are you ready to go?"

"I think so," she answered in a quiet voice. "Walk with me, slowly."

"OK, but when we're half way there... start running." Rena whispered strongly.

They began to walk carefully towards the forest when unexpectedly, they heard the sound of wings flapping along with a heavy swoosh which created a strong wind that swiftly swept over them.

As they ducked down, they saw each other's troubled eyes and then hesitantly raised their heads, petrified what they would see. An indescribable creature blocked their view of the sky with its gigantic wings opened wide, circling above them.

"Hurry, it's a pterodoc!" Avanna urged. "Run inside as fast as you can!"

Rena ran as fast as she could over the wide cracks beneath her, away from the monstrous sight resembling nothing she had ever seen. When she made it inside, she turned around quickly, only to find herself—alone. Avanna was not with her.

A faint call for help came from where she stood moments before. It was Avanna, barely moving with the pterodoc headed her way. She stood in fear, watching helplessly as Rena ran towards her with the crystal ball held by her side.

"Avanna, grab my arm!" She hurriedly approached her, the pterodoc directly above them.

Avanna grabbed on to her with a weak grip and then they both ran just as it dived again with the tip of its mouth breathing inches over their heads.

"I'm sorry, Rena, I'm too weak."

"Don't apologize… just keep running!" She anxiously pulled Avanna along with her.

They were only seconds away before finally entering Errantry forest. A powerful thump behind them caused their feet to lift off the ground. They shuddered to look back, but knew they had to and with each second, the pterodoc gradually came into full view. It tried to squeeze in between the trees, but its shiny, wrinkled body was too large to enter. Its human-like eyes stared at theirs, as they stood motionless and frightened. One more breath of its scent would surely knock them over.

Just when they thought it might force its way to them, it slowly stepped back and then flapped its gigantic wings, lifting up and away, gliding into the cloudless sky from which it came. The once stench atmosphere, slowly became breathable again, however, before it did, Rena took a deep breath and became suddenly weak.

"I'm going to sit by that tree for a while. I think you should too," Avanna suggested when she noticed her not looking well.

"Yes… that's a good idea," she agreed.

Relieved the chase was over and the pterodoc gone, they rested against the uneven surface of a huge oak tree. The forest darkened with only a slight of sunlight passing through the branches with huge leaves that hung over their heads. They were exhausted from panic, and even though Avanna was the weakest, Rena's eyes were the first to close.

Avanna quickly tapped on her shoulder before she had the chance to fall into a deep sleep.

"Rena, we have to get up now. We have to keep going."

Even though she discreetly rolled her drowsy eyes, she understood why Avanna was anxious.

"I'm ready," she replied tiredly.

Both stood up and brushed the grass and dirt off their clothes, only the musty scent of the forest remained. They began walking through a trail filled with plants, with leaves resembling that of a candle flame, glowing all around them. Just like the dandelion, Rena was captivated and reached down to touch one, her fingers only inches from their soft and fuzzy texture.

"Stop, don't touch them!"

Avanna alarmed Rena with her sudden outburst and swiftly pulled her hand away from it, falling backwards onto the ground.

"Why did you do that?" she shouted angrily and lifted herself up from her surprised plunge. "You scared me! They're only plants!"

"I'm sorry. I didn't mean to scare you. Are you all right?"

"Yes, I'm fine," she shook her head, exhausted from her own shouting.

"This world is not like the ones we're from Rena. Many things look pretty and different here, but they'll fool you," Avanna alerted. "The plant you almost touched is a mullein plant. I should have told you that before, but I didn't remember until I saw you reaching for it. If you touch them, they'll burn you, and if you smell them up close, you'll lose your memory for a long time. They come in handy though when you need light. Try to remember everything I tell you, Ok?"

"I will." She brushed off the grass and dirt from her clothes—again. "Thanks for looking out for me and I'll try to be more careful next time." She pushed her hair away from her eyes. "It's hard to believe we're really here… in a different world. So far, I've seen a pterodoc, and now mullein plants. How did you find out the name of this world?"

"Well, when I first came here I read a riddle on a huge statue of a lady with wings. Her arms hung down in front of her with cupped hands. I was thinking, 'What was she holding?' I don't remember where the statue is, but I do remember what it reads. *"Here is good and here is bad, it could be worse, so don't be sad. The faith is not gone, only far away. To stay out of havoc, you must want to stay. Welcome to Wanderamid, a world among many.* I don't think I'll ever forget those words, no matter how old I get."

Rena repeated the words in her mind and then sat down in the tall forest grass as though she were in a trance.

"Ahh, I know what it means! It would be easier for me or us, to choose to stay here in Wanderamid, than to find our way home. Am I right?"

"You're right," Avanna responded gloomily.

"Well, I won't let those words stop me from helping us get home."

"I won't either," she replied with a weak grin.

"Let's get some sleep," Rena suggested. "I think you'll get stronger if you do and I'll feel a little better."

"OK," Avanna agreed. She felt she at least owed her that much.

Rena had no idea what other encounters, they would come face to face with, and neither did Avanna. Any worries they had they kept to themselves. They chose a spot empty of mullein plants and rested their tired bodies. Within seconds, their heavy eyelids covered their big weary eyes. Avanna took a moment, reopened hers, and saw a little bit of gray in Rena's hair, just as she suspected there would be, and then fell fast asleep.

*　　*　　*

Ms. Winterton frantically reached for the phone and dialed 911. She was unable to imagine Rena caught in the area where she saw the tornado. Her body cringed at the thought.

"This is the Whilom police station. What's your emergency?" the dispatcher asked calmly.

"Hello! I can't find my daughter! There was a tornado and I don't know where she is!" she cried out.

"What is your name?"

"Rylia Winterton!"

"When did you see your daughter last, ma'am?" she asked, chewing her gum loudly over the phone.

"Almost an hour ago, I'm not completely sure. She was only going for a short walk. I heard strong winds and when I went down the street, I saw a tornado down by the lake! I tried to... The winds kept me from going down there! I think that's where she went!"

"Try to calm down, ma'am, maybe she didn't go to the lake, and she's on her way home. Where do you live?"

"23 Whisper Lane! Please, send help!"

"A police cruiser is already on their way, ma'am. You should see it arriving any moment. Ms. Winterton?" She waited patiently for a response.

"Yes," she answered. "I'm still here. I'll be waiting."

When they ended the call, she sat nervously in her varnished, wooden kitchen chair with her hands folded, twiddling her thumbs, and waiting for the police to arrive. Only a few seconds passed before she walked to her front door, hoping to see Rena walking up on her perfect lawn, however, she was nowhere. Then, she stepped out on the front porch and called out, "Rena! Rena!"

The neighbors, outside checking damages from the storm, turned their heads when they heard her.

"Have you seen Rena? She went for a walk and I haven't seen her since!"

"No, Rylia, I didn't see her. I just came outside," replied an old neighbor.

"If you see her, please tell her to come home!"

"Sure. We'll keep an eye out for her."

"I would appreciate that, thank you!"

He nodded to the other neighbors and then looked back at her. "Don't worry, she'll come around!"

The neighbor who led her back home during the storm stood on his porch and shouted, "Hey! Did you find your daughter?"

"No! I called the police!"

"Let us know if you need our help!"

"Thank you!"

She stepped off her porch to get a clearer look down the street and then the opposite way when she noticed a police cruiser turned onto Whisper Lane.

"Over here, over here!" she shouted and waved her arms high in the air, directing them to her.

They pulled over to the curb in front of her home. The neighbors watched and then eventually went about their business.

"Are you… Ms. Winterton?" the officer asked with a deep rugged voice, as he looked at his notepad where he had written her name.

"Yes, I am," she answered, bending at eye level next to his opened window. "My daughter told me she wouldn't be far. I heard strong winds outside and went to see how the weather was. That's when I saw a tornado down by the lake! I called her name, but she didn't answer me." She burst into tears.

"I know your upset, ma'am, but could you please calm yourself down? We need to ask a few questions before we can even begin to search for your daughter," he responded coldly.

Ms. Winterton nodded and stepped away when he opened the door. Her head leaned back as he gradually stood tall. His huge hat, added to his height.

"I'm Officer Morley," he announced, straightening his hat. "I'm sorry; I should have introduced myself before I asked your name."

Ms. Winterton was too upset and only nodded.

The second officer walked over beside him. His hat was too big for his head and his open ear-to-ear smile showed his large set of teeth.

"I'm Officer Wodderspoon. Is this where you live, ma'am?"

"Yes," she wiped the tears from under her eyes.

The two officers began walking towards her cottage while she stayed by the cruiser, wondering what they were up to.

"We should be going to the park to look for my daughter. I told the dispatcher that's probably where she went. Did she tell you... what I said?" She spoke loudly as they kept walking away.

"Ms. Winterton," Officer Wodderspoon responded with his oversized smile, walking back to the cruiser where she stood with a bewildered look on her face. "We would like to look inside your home before we go down to the park. It's normal procedure, ma'am, and it won't take long, I promise.

"But I don't understand. My daughter hasn't come home. That's why I called the police," she replied firmly. "There's been a tornado and you want to look inside my home?"

Officer Morley walked up to them as they both stood speechless.

"Ms. Winterton," he responded calmly, "Please, let's go on inside and then we will go to the park."

Ms. Winterton walked in between them and they followed her.

After they all entered the cottage, he did not hesitate to ask any questions.

"So, Ms. Winterton, how did—I'm sorry, what's your daughter's name again?"

"Rena, my daughter's name is Rena," she answered while his uncaring attitude began to irritate her.

"How did, Rena, seem before she went out? Was she upset with you? Did you both argue?"

"No, we didn't argue about anything."

"Um, where's the father? Is he here?"

"No, Rena's father left a long time ago. He couldn't have anything to do with this," she answered surely.

"What makes you so sure," he asked suspiciously.

"Because he's not here, he's a journalist, always in some other country. We haven't seen him since Rena was four years old."

"We'll get back to him later," he said in a rushed manner.

It had become clear to Ms. Winterton that the officers believed she had something to do with her daughter not being home. When she noticed Officer Wodderspoon was not in sight, she became increasingly annoyed.

"Either we all go down to the park right now, or I will call the sheriff and ask him to send me officers, who are willing to help find my daughter."

Ms. Winterton's firm words expressed she had enough.

Officer Morley thought then that maybe something did happen to Rena and Ms. Winterton was telling the truth.

"Wodderspoon, let's go!"

Officer Wodderspoon rushed from the top of the stairs, back down to the kitchen. "But, I didn't search all the rooms," he said, and then turned and smiled at Ms. Winterton.

"There isn't anything in here to search for. We're going down to Fountain Lake Park," he turned to her with a sincere, apologetic grin, "to search for Ms. Winterton's daughter."

She was relieved he finally listened to her. They walked outside to the cruiser and he opened the back door for her, at the same time Officer Wodderspoon entered the passenger side. They drove down Whisper Lane, swerving around the fallen branches that practically filled the cobblestone street. Minutes later, they arrived and exited the cruiser, staring at the damage from the tornado. Huge trees had fallen everywhere and left much doubt Rena was safe. Then, he reached into his open window for the radio microphone.

"This is Officer Morley, 10-9 with possible 10-55. I repeat, this is Officer Morley, 10-9 with possible 10-55. Please respond."

"What's your 10-20, Officer Morley?" asked the dispatcher.

"We're at Fountain Lake Park, in the process searching for a young girl." He turned and asked Ms. Winterton, "How old is, Rena, and what was she wearing when you last saw her? I also need to know the color of her eyes and hair."

Ms. Winterton looked at him with eyes full of sorrow and her heart began beating rapidly.

"She just turned thirteen. She's wearing green jeans and a yellow shirt that has a… butterfly print in the front. She has big, dark brown… eyes and long, dark brown, wavy hair."

Officer Morley repeated the description she gave to the dispatcher, and then added, "We'll call if we need assistance, 10-04."

"I'll put out an APB. 10-04." The dispatcher ended the call.

Ms. Winterton could not accept what was happening. She kept repeating in her mind, the last conversation she had with Rena. If only she could turn back time.

"If you want, you can wait here and Officer Wodderspoon and I will go into the woods to search for Rena," he suggested.

"No, I need to go with you. Please, we have to go—now," she urged, trying to hold back her tears.

"That's fine with me," Officer Morley replied. "Are you ready officer?"

"Ready," he responded.

"Let's go in."

The search for Rena had officially begun.

Ms. Winterton walked, along with the officers, through the rumble, in search for her daughter. Each shouted her name, desperately listening for a reply. When she looked over where the dock and bridge used to be, she tried not to let the ruins from the storm affect the strength she had.

"I'm going this way." Officer Wodderspoon took a path of his own while Ms. Winterton and Officer Morley stayed together.

Although they went different directions, their calls for Rena were the same, through the eerie silence.

"I think I found something! Walk over here! Over here!" Officer Wodderspoon yelled out.

They looked to see where he was, and then caught sight of his arms waving, crisscrossing high over his head. Carefully, they walked over the rumble, through the still, misty air, towards his direction. When they approached him, they noticed he had come across an old storm drain tunnel, made from concrete blocks, its entrance barricaded with falling tree limbs.

"I remember when Rena mentioned this tunnel. She told me she and her friends never went in. It scared them," she sadly recalled.

On the right side of the tunnel, they noticed a path leading out from the woods, blocked by a huge tree, broken in half.

"It looks like it was hit by lightning. There's a burnt mark on the area that's broken." Officer Wodderspoon showed them what he was referring to and then gazed back at the entrance. "We'll have to move these limbs in order to get inside."

They all agreed and without hesitation, began moving the first one. Officer Wodderspoon lifted one end a few inches off the ground, while Ms. Winterton and Officer Morley lifted the other. Then, he looked up at them.

"If... I... saw a tornado... coming," he paused to catch his breath, "this is where I would go." He dropped his end on the ground, and right after, they dropped theirs. It was too heavy, so they rolled it the rest of the way, out of the way, catching their breath before they continued.

When they placed the last one aside, Ms. Winterton, rushed in, however, the darkness prevented her from continuing.

"Do either of you have a flashlight? I can't see! Rena, are you in here? Can you hear me?" She waited impatiently for them to respond.

The officers each had flashlights on their duty belts.

"Yes! We're coming in!" Officer Morley yelled.

Both immediately entered the dark, chilly tunnel, shining their flashlights on Ms. Winterton's face.

"OK, we're here. We need to move slowly though, so we don't ruin any evidence, if any," he advised.

"Will you please remove the light from my face?" she asked in a respectful tone.

They directed the light onto the tunnel concrete floor, circling around slowly with her close by, when she noticed something shining by her feet, resembling gold.

"Could you please shine the flashlight over here?"

She crouched down to take a closer look, her heart beating rapidly. It was a gold locket on a chain. She picked it up and held it tightly in the palm of her hand.

"This is Rena's locket," she said softly. "It has a butterfly on it. Rena loves butterflies—she would never take this off." Her hands began to tremble and she cried uncontrollably.

Officer Morley squatted down beside her and gently placed his hand on her shoulder. "Is the chain broken?"

"What?" she quickly calmed down, confused by a question she thought had no reason.

"Is the chain broken?" he repeated.

She opened her hand and he aimed the flashlight on the necklace. She saw it clasped.

"No, it's not broken. What are you thinking? What does it mean?" she asked anxiously.

Officer Wodderspoon looked down at her with an immense smile. "It means she probably put it there for a reason."

"That's right," Officer Morley shook his head smiling. "If she put it there for you to find, then she's one smart girl."

The officer's theory was that Rena left her necklace behind on purpose, as a message to her mother. She quickly stood along with them and continued searching deeper for anything to help figure out where Rena could have gone. As they combed the tunnel, Officer Wodderspoon noticed something very odd, a black straight line sparkling on the floor. He stood before it and called out for Ms. Winterton.

"Ms. Winterton, does your daughter have sequins on her clothes?"

"No—not on her clothes, but she does have them on the sides of the new sneakers I gave her last night," she replied, sniffling.

"Come here please, I have something I want you to see." He shined the flashlight over the area. "Are those from her sneakers?"

She went over and looked down where he aimed the flashlight. "No," she replied, disappointed. "They're not hers. Rena's has silver sequins on them and they're smaller. Those are colored, see—and bigger."

The colored sequins confused the officer's even more. Could someone else be with Rena? If so, who could it have been and where did they go? There was no way she could have left the tunnel, if she was still in it, because the tunnel entrance was blocked and so was the path outside. They realized they had taken on a difficult case, a young girl, missing with no clue as to where she could be. The signs found, pointed to child abduction.

"Ms. Winterton, I'll... have to ask you for... your daughter's locket, we'll return it after the investigation. This is a crime scene now, Officer Morley said regretfully. "I'm sure you understand."

She hesitantly handed over her daughter's locket and chain, the one thing that made her feel closer to Rena, besides the tunnel.

"I'll call forensics down to the site," said Officer Wodderspoon.

Ms. Winterton felt the whole world collapsing around her. All she wanted was Rena home. Officer Morley escorted her back through the woods to the police cruiser where they silently waited for police forensic workers to arrive. Officer Wodderspoon caught up to them soon after he completed the call for assistance. They never thought they would be at the core of a parent's worst nightmare and prayed for some sort of miracle, a sign to help get the answers they needed, leading to the whereabouts of Rena Winterton.

Ms. Winterton held her head in her hands, tears dripped down her face. She thought if she had only spent the day with her, Rena would have been home safe.

In the distance, the police backup and forensics team were approaching and then parked near the entrance where the officers and Ms. Winterton stood waiting. They took out their carrying bags, stocked with the necessary equipment, out of their vehicles.

"In there," Officer Morley pointed. "We need the crime scene ribbon up to block this area," he ordered. "There's another part we need blocked off in the park. Wait here."

Officer Morley and Wodderspoon were ready to lead them to the tunnel where they found Rena's necklace.

"Ms. Winterton—one the officers will bring you home. We'll let you know if we find anything new." He nodded and then walked away with the others.

She stood silently still as everyone rushed around her, planning the search. It was as if she were standing in the middle of a movie. Then, an officer walked up to her.

"Ms. Winterton?" he questioned politely.

She looked up at him with her pain-filled eyes and only nodded.

"I'll be bringing you home, ma'am."

"Thank you," she answered softly.

They walked quietly to his cruiser and he opened the passenger door for her. Moments later, they were in front of her cottage.

All she could do was wait however long it would take.

CHAPTER SEVEN

A TWINGE OF GUILT

O n the small mountain, overlooking Fountain Lake Park, Ms. Biddock gazed with piercing, green eyes endlessly out her bedroom's sliding glass window at the aftermath she created for everyone, especially herself. There had to be a way to fix it and to do that, she would have to go back down to the storm drain tunnel, where her long awaited chance to return home, crumbled before her eyes.

Her three black felines walked calmly beside her as she walked to her office. She turned on her huge, emerald lamp and walked directly to her bag where she kept her green, leather bound grimoire. She took it out and swiped her hand over it lightly, setting it on her extravagant gothic desk, she magically created from an old oak tree once outside her cottage, with picture carvings of her three dear friends. When she opened it, it gradually grew and spread over the edges of her desk, just as it had before in her school office. She flipped its poster-sized pages, searching aimlessly on how to produce a window of vision into the distant world, Wanderamid. In only a few minutes, she reached the title, Unseen Shadows and desperately read aloud the words underneath.

*"Neither eyes of the future, nor eyes from the past,
only eyes from the present bring sight to another path.
Skies from different worlds are what I seek, to follow the
trusting and the weak and before every change is forever
sealed, preventing all visions, from becoming revealed!"*

Instantly, a peephole appeared in front of her! Her
eyes stayed focused as she watched its crooked edges
open, zigzagging uncontrollably. A glossy view of
Errantry forest appeared. With each second, it had become
clearer and then showed Rena resting on the ground,
seemingly unharmed.

Ms. Biddock tried to communicate by calling out to
her in a commanding whisper. "Rena... Rena!"

Rena scooped slowly on her other side.

Could it be she heard her voice?

Suddenly, two of her three felines jumped on the
desk.

"No!" She pulled them away from the peephole just
in time.

Her concentration broke and the window to
Wanderamid instantly disappeared with a razor sharp
sound ending its vision.

The felines squirmed out of her arms and out of sight.

"It's all right little ones, you can come out. No harm
done." She looked all around for them. "I'll try again later,
only next time, you will be in another room."

When she could not find them, she prepared for her
walk to the park, to find out information they had on Rena

and her friend. Along with her felines that finally came
out from hiding, she walked out onto the bedroom balcony
and saw in the distance police officers searching inch by
inch through the woods, walking side by side.

"They must be looking for Rena and her friend," she
spoke to her felines, sitting on the vine-covered railing.
"What have I done? She wasn't at all like the horrible
Devilea. If it weren't for her, I would have never entered
Whilom. The day will come when I will take back what is
mine, magic powers and all!"

Before she left, she changed out of her damp clothes
worn prior to the storm and fixed her wild spun out hair,
easily done with the wave of her wand. Afterwards, she
walked back to her balcony and secretly peeked around
the corners, to make sure no one was watching. She
levitated over the railing gently, lightly lowering until she
floated inches above ground, then continued down the side
of the mountain. When she reached the lake, the many
police officers and crime scene workers were searching
under piles of debris, further away from where Rena and
Avanna were. Pin flags placed in the ground marked areas
they had already covered.

They had no idea their efforts were meaningless.

With the bridge gone, she had to cross over the only
other way she knew how, uttering the words under her
breath.

*"Carry me across to the other side, without any one's
notice. No need to interfere with their pointless service."*

Her body lifted, gliding across the serene waters,
landing gracefully and unnoticed behind the tunnel. She

casually walked on the side and headed towards the entrance.

An officer in the opposite direction caught sight of her while she pretended not to notice the activity around her.

"Excuse me, Ma'am!" He ran towards her and then shouted to the officer working inside, "Don't let her in!"

When she reached the entrance, the officer quickly stretched his arms out and blocked her from entering.

"You can't come in here, ma'am; we're in a middle of an investigation." Her unusual eyes suddenly surprised him.

Meanwhile, the officer who gave the order caught up to them. He jerked when his eyes met with hers, shocked, but only for a moment.

"I'm sorry, uh, you can't be here. We're in the middle of a search. I'll have to ask you to leave."

Ms. Biddock calmly looked at them and replied, "Oh, I'm terribly sorry, I'm only going for a walk, I won't bother anyone." She ducked quickly, about to go under the officer's arms, but he lowered them as she did.

"I'm sorry, ma'am, you'll have to leave—now."

Ms. Biddock wanted to avoid causing a scene, so she nodded and then proceeded to walk away. The two officers looked at one another, shaking their heads.

She arrived back to the edge of the lake, uttering the same words used before and then glided back across the calm waters running smoothly under her feet, landing lightly on the other side. One of the officers she spoke with moments before, noticed her. He stood, scratching his head, wondering how she arrived there so quickly, and without a boat. Her eyes met with his and she smiled and waved. His confused expression made her laugh aloud, "Ha! Ha! Ha!" Then, she turned away gracefully, walking on the path leading back to her cottage.

When she reached her home, she levitated over the balcony railing and entered through the glass sliding door left open. She was anxious to change back into her witch wardrobe and let her hair down. To help with her thoughts, she made herself a cup of cold black tea, and then walked contently to her office. She sat and rested in her comfortable, antique chair, covered in green velvet with wide cushioned arms, drinking her tea while predicting a new plan.

*   *   *

In Errantry forest, Rena and Avanna slept peacefully on a patch of soft green grass, resting their overstrained minds on folded arms. Apparently, they were too exhausted from the uncomfortable experience they had withstood before and after they had entered into Wanderamid.

It was the heart of the night and a rare light wind traveled on Rena's path once more. It carried voices through her shielded ears, whispering into her resting mind, compared to the mystical night on Whisper Lane.

"You must hurry before it's too late. She doesn't have much time. She doesn't have much time. Rena! Rena!"

Rena immediately rose up, out from her sound sleep, and captured a sparkling zephyr, floating above her head. She shook Avanna's arm gently to wake her up.

"Avanna, wake up," she whispered strongly, desperate for her to see, but it vanished before her eyes opened.

Avanna was not happy at all when awakened unexpectedly from a sound sleep.

"Why did you wake me up? This was the best sleep I've had since I've been away from home." She rubbed her eyes and with the light from the mullein plants, saw Rena's larger than usual.

"Avanna, did you hear anything?" She pulled the shawl tighter around her shoulders, blocking the brisk air. Her eyes scoped the unknown forest as she thought one of the voices heard resembled that of Ms. Biddock.

"Yes, I did—you," she answered sarcastically. "I was sleeping well, until you woke me."

"Maybe we should start walking, so we have extra time to look for your tunnel," she suggested.

"I guess you're right," Avanna rolled her eyes. She would have rather gone back to sleep. "Let's… go."

Strange new aches surfaced behind her legs and lower back. She thought at that time it was best not to tell Rena.

The silent forest gave Rena the jitters. She felt at that moment someone would jump out from behind a tree.

"I think we're being watched," she said, paranoid.

"Don't be silly," Avanna chuckled, while at the same time, was aware it was possible. "Come on."

They began walking down the dim, misty trail, each mullein plant brighter than the last. Surprisingly, they helped create a needed calmness for Rena.

"If the mullein plants weren't here, we wouldn't be able to see where we were going."

"Yes, we would, if we got up in the… daylight," Avanna replied, mockingly.

"Ha! Ha! Very funny," said Rena. "You know, it's not every day I end up in a mysterious world."

"I know—look! Do you still feel you're being watched?" Avanna pointed up into the trees where two owls sat on an enormous branch. They hooted above their heads, while their gawking eyes watched their every move. "You were right, we were being watched."

They both laughed and walked further into the forest.

The sound of bird's wings fluttering from tree to tree brought their attention to a clear view of the sky, further down the path they walked on.

"Look up ahead, Avanna," Rena pointed to show her and then from the corner of her eye, captured the sight of abnormal sized spiders, as big as her feet, crawling upside the trunk of a tree. She stopped immediately and held her arm out in front of Avanna to prevent her from taking another step. "Avanna, look," she whispered frantically, crossing her legs, afraid they might climb up her jeans and squirming at the thought.

Avanna was too weak to react. Her only thoughts were about getting back home.

"Let's walk faster," Rena said anxiously.

"Okay, right… away," she rolled her eyes tiredly.

Rena detected a weakness in her voice.

"Oh—I'm sorry, Avanna. I forgot. This pace is fine. I got a little scared."

Avanna pressed her lips tightly together to keep from saying something she would later regret and walked her own speed, which was slow.

Their appetites increased with every step, keeping their desire for food to themselves. Neither of them wanted to be each other's burden.

"Do you remember any fruit trees being around here?" Rena asked, hoping she did.

Avanna's head became too heavy to hold up. She answered tiredly, "Yes, but I don't remember where they are."

"You'll remember. I know you will," Rena replied with certainty.

The clear view of the sky revealed a break in the trail, the beginning of two roads. Soon, they would choose which one to travel and wishfully the one chosen would lead them to food. Rena continued to hear the unfamiliar sounds in the forest while Avanna's hearing and eyesight steadily faded along with her strength.

Avanna turned slowly to look at her and said, "I don't mean to sound like I'm giving up, but, I feel really weak. I don't know if I can walk anymore."

"We're almost at the end of the trail, Avanna, hold on, OK?"

For the first time in Wanderamid, she felt alone. Avanna's weakness was growing and so was Rena's doubt about Avanna surviving the rest of the trail. She held Avanna up the best she could with her eyes fixed on her every step. Then, she noticed a change on the ground, slowly raised her head, and found they were standing in front of two roads.

"Look, we're here!" Rena said aloud, excited and relieved at the same time.

However, Avanna's head remained hung low, too weak to respond. She began to accept the fact, Avanna's journey would end there, and the thought devastated her. 'Anything's possible', her mother's words came to mind, giving her renewed hope.

"Avanna, I'll describe the roads to you and you choose the one we should take," she said holding back her tears. "The one on the right has a tall… wooden pole, with a street sign higher than regular one." Rena placed the palm of her hand under Avanna's chin and lifted enough for her to see. "The sign reads… Amble Road. Do you see the letters? They sparkle, too!" she smiled and then turned Avanna's head to show her the other. "That one doesn't have a sign at all. Do you want to go on Amble Road?"

Avanna answered with lips that could barely move. "Amble… Road."

"Yes, let's take that one," Rena agreed happily, removing her hand slowly, away from Avanna's chin.

Amble Road was the chosen one to lead them to their journey's end. Rena held on to Avanna's arm while they took their first step on the glittering pavement. Immediately after, she felt Avanna pulling away from her hold. When she turned, Avanna's face lit up like the road they were walking on. While she still looked like an old woman, it seemed her energy was that of her true age. The pain in her legs and back disappeared and she had a sudden urge to run and kick her heels up in the air.

Rena was amazed.

"Where did you learn that?"

"Here!" she laughed and swirled around with her arms stretched out.

It was the first time Rena had seen Avanna's true self. Truly, it was a sign things would get better. While they were having fun with Avanna's new found energy, the sun appeared, dimming the once glittering pavement. It was then Rena noticed the long, shiny, flat stone trails in between lines of huge oak trees, on the sides of Amble Road, curious as to where they led.

"Let's go down one of these trails," she suggested anxiously.

"Not now. Let's keep going." Avanna ran and kicked up her heels once more. "I don't know how long I'll have all this energy. It must be Amble Road!"

Rena let out a big sigh. "All right, but let's keep an eye out for any tunnels, when we kick up our heels!" she giggled.

They had no idea how long the glittered pavement was and there was no telling how much time they had before they would reach another. Avanna took advantage of her magical experience for as long as she could.

Meanwhile, their laughter traveled through the warm wind over a hill and into a village, where the two witches' lived, Clemedeth and Devilea. Devilea's ears twitched and her eyes widened when she heard the startling sound of laughter. Her eyebrows rose up and seesawed, as her face gradually cringed, walking over to the window.

"What is it, Devilea?" Clemedeth chuckled.

Devilea said not a word. She was a miserable little witch with an evil demeanor, not at all like her guardian, Clemedeth. Her devious attitude provoked a curse upon them both, yet Clemedeth never held it against her. She continuously guarded her, minus any bitter feelings. Wanderamid's powerful witch, the queen of witches good and evil, bewitched them. Devilea had always admired the great powers she owned and was determined to be greater than she ever was. It had been a long time since they or anyone else had seen the witch of Wanderamid, she disappeared. Neither knew her whereabouts, although Devilea believed she was gone from Wanderamid forever.

Her immature mind began to stir and from the expression on her face, Clemedeth knew she was irritated. Whatever she had in mind, would surely become known.

"I'll be back, just… going out… for a walk," she finally responded.

"Oh, I'll go with you," Clemedeth smiled as she invited herself.

"No!" Devilea shouted.

It was a sure sign she had no good in mind, just as Clemedeth thought.

"I'm going by myself!"

"I'm going with you," Clemedeth said calmly, ignoring her little outburst. "We never walk on the trail together. We'll have a good time."

Like always, Clemedeth interfered with her plans. She walked out of the cottage after her, strolling through the mystical Tarot's trail, close to her side. Luckily, the magic powers given to them were equal, but the changes in their features were not. Clemedeth's hair became wavier and turned lighter, while Devilea's nose grew crooked and her lips, uneven. Over the years, even her pearly white teeth were no more. When Clemedeth noticed extreme changes in Devilea's appearance, she never acknowledged them, nor did she.

"I'm glad you thought about taking a walk. We should do this every day," Clemedeth smiled.

Devilea rolled her eyes, having no interest in talking, only in finding those she blamed for ruining her day. Despite her rudeness, Clemedeth continued to enjoy the serene walk. The view of the cottage gradually disappeared behind the crooked trees and the sounds of crows cawing and owls hooting, seemed to enhance. The rabbits on the witch's trail resembled that of a rat, preyed upon by one-eyed snakes, hissing strongly before their capture to devour them. Although, having only one eye gave the rabbits extra advantage to escape—usually, and then turning into a one-eyed snake with a head of a rat.

Clemedeth was also curious as to who was new in town and knew it would not take long to find out. Up ahead the small hill leading down to Amble road was in sight and they were practically there.

"How far will we be walking?" she curiously asked.

"I don't know," she answered scrunching her shoulders, "maybe just to the hill to look down on Amble road, you know, since we're close to it."

"Sounds like a plan to me!" Clemedeth replied happily, hoping her cheerful attitude would rub off onto her.

Clemedeth was three years older than she was. They were cursed when Clemedeth was only thirteen years old, that was three years ago. At the age of ten, Devilea had been already a selfish child and her powers since then had increased during those years, adding to her devious ways. Clemedeth realized it and had since monitored her every move around others, including herself.

"You can go first," Devilea said impatiently, as they arrived at the foot of the small hill.

"We can climb at the same time, that's big enough for the both of us," replied Clemedeth.

Without a hint, Devilea scaled to the top of the hill. Clemedeth followed close behind. They saw it was a long way down, at least 20 feet. It was no bother to Devilea; she planned to use her magic.

"Wait!" She noticed Devilea's arms ready to take flight. "What are you doing?"

"I'm going down the hill."

"No! We're supposed to be taking a walk... not a flight. Let's walk. Come on, put your arms down."

Once more Clemedeth irritated her with her mortal ways and when she turned away, observed two people, walking in the distance. Without saying a word, she was the first to slide down the hill, Clemedeth immediately followed, racing towards Amble Road.

As they neared Amble road, Clemedeth lost control and ran into Devilea, landing her swiftly face down in the dirt. She stood looking down at her and shouted, "Devilea, are you all right?"

Devilea lifted her head, moaning, "My nose."

"Give me your hand and I'll pull you up."

She reached for Clemedeth's hand, her nose throbbing to the beat of her heart, "My nose. Is it crooked?"

"It's been crooked for three years, Devilea! Don't you look in the mirror?" she asked and then right after, regretted her choice of words. "Let's go back and put some ice on it."

"No!" she quickly stood, "I feel better now. Let's keep walking."

"Are you sure?"

"Yes, I'm sure. Let's walk down the road. You can go back if you want."

Meanwhile, Rena slowed down her pace when she saw two people walking opposite their path.

"Do you see those people walking towards us?"

"Yes, I guess we'll find out who they are soon," Avanna answered as she walked ahead of her.

Rena caught up to her. "But, what if they're dangerous?"

"We could hide behind one of those trees and wait until they pass by."

Rena instantly thought it was a good idea. "Hurry, they're getting closer!"

Before Avanna hid behind the oak tree, where Rena already was, someone called out her name.

"Avanna, is that you?" Clemedeth shouted.

She turned quickly to see who it was.

"Clemedeth!" she shouted back, and then walked briskly towards them with her new found energy.

Rena remained hiding behind the tree.

CHAPTER EIGHT

A LONG-AWAITED SIGHT

Rena peeked around the tree and saw Avanna talking with the two strangers, happy to see each other, which gave her reason to believe it was safe to come out from hiding. As she began running towards them, Devilea was amazed to see she had the crystal ball, a sight she had been waiting a long time to see.

Clemedeth was surprised to see her again.

"We thought you found your way home. Where were you all this time?"

"I went through another wrong tunnel and ended up in a town called, Whilom, where the crystal ball was stolen from me and I couldn't get it back. Rena found it." She turned to see Rena standing next to her. She smiled. "This is Rena."

"Hi, Rena," Clemedeth greeted her and then asked with a puzzled look on her face, "Why did you go through the tunnel?"

Avanna answered before she had a chance to respond.

"A tornado came and blocked us from leaving the tunnel. Oh, and there was a witch, too, who wanted the crystal ball! We had no other choice but to go through together. Now she's helping me find my way back home."

"Did you say a witch wanted the crystal ball… in Whilom?" Devilea asked with raising eyebrows.

"Yes, but she's still there," Avanna assured them.

Devilea wondered, 'Could it be, Emera?'

She noticed how much Avanna aged since she saw her last. At the same time, Avanna noticed Devilea's nose grew more crooked.

"Hello, Rena," Devilea greeted her with a small force grin. She had no interest in meeting her; it was only an excuse to get a closer view of the crystal ball.

"Hello," Rena replied.

Avanna leaned over to her and whispered, "These are the two witches I told you about."

Rena remembered her saying one witch was "good" and the other was not. She knew which witch was not.

"So, what are you doing on Amble Road?" Avanna asked.

"Oh, we were just taking a walk that's all," Clemedeth briefly looked over at Devilea and then back at them. "Are you hungry? Did you eat anything yet?" She noticed Avanna thin.

Rena's eyes widened. They were both starving!

"Yes, we're starved," nodded Avanna. "I haven't had anything to eat since yesterday."

"Then come with us to our cottage. It's right over the hill, in Hemlock Village," she replied with a welcoming smile. "We have plenty of food."

Once again, Devilea had become irritated with her surprise invitation. Rena could tell she was not as welcoming as Clemedeth, however; she was not surprised.

Without any hesitation, they both accepted.

"Sure, that would be great," Avanna smiled gratefully.

Off to Hemlock Village they went, venturing once again, into the unknown.

There was a boy sitting on a branch above them in an oak tree. He waited patiently, watching until they walked further down Amble Road, then gently climbed down to the branch closest to the ground, before taking a short jump. Although, Clemedeth's invitation was sincere, he had to protect them from Devilea. As he ran quickly down the flat stone trail to his home through the woods, he thought about how to prepare for his travel.

When he reached his cottage, his goats were grazing in the front yard and then swiftly spread apart, creating a path leading to the front door. He went straight to his bedroom to fill his backpack with things needed in case he was gone longer than expected. When he finished, his grandmother Oula unexpectedly showed up by his bedroom door with a puzzled look on her face.

"Micah, where are you going with your backpack?"

"Just over the hill, I shouldn't be gone long," he said to comfort her.

"You mean where the two little witches live? No, you can't go there, it's dangerous. The one with the crooked nose, she isn't right. I think she's the reason we can't find your mother. I don't want to lose you, too. Please, Micah, don't go."

"I'll be OK. There are two girls on their way to the witch's cottage and I have to protect them from the witch, with the crooked nose," he chuckled." Everything will be all right, I promise. Just don't look for me if I'm gone too long. Promise me."

"Please, Micah, don't go," she repeated, blocking the doorway.

He placed his hands on her shoulders. "I have to do this. I'll be back and Mom will, too, you'll see. Promise me, you'll stay here. I don't want to have to worry about you, too."

Grandmother Oula's sad eyes glistened. She was convinced her grandson was leaving, to guard those girls from harm and there was no way of stopping him. Finally, she gave in and moved out of his way.

"I promise, and please hurry back home."

"I will, and don't worry! I'll be back! Even if it seems like I won't, I will! Don't forget that!"

Too much time had already gone by. Micah ran out of his home back down the flat stone trail, leading to Amble Road. His grandmother watched through the screen door until he was out of her sight.

Meanwhile, the girls arrived at the foot of the hill and without stopping, began to climb. As they were approaching the top, Rena immediately noticed the thick branches on the most crooked trees she had ever seen. They completely blocked the sky like the ones in Errantry forest, only they hung much lower.

When they all made their way to the top, Rena pointed out, "This trail looks spooky… I mean… different."

"What do you mean by… different?" Devilea curiously asked.

"Then the Errantry trail," she quickly replied.

"Devilea will walk beside me and the two of you walk together behind us," Clemedeth suggested before leading the way.

As they began walking on Tarots trail, Rena saw what resembled mullein plants, only they were deep purple in color. From the looks of the trail, Rena could only imagine what the witch's cottage would be like.

"Avanna, look," she pointed at the plants to show her.

Avanna was not at all interested. The energy she received on Amble Road rapidly began to fade on Tarot's trail. Rena noticed and it made her nervous.

"You look tired, Avanna. Would you like us to slow down?"

Without any verbal reply, Avanna only nodded.

"We're almost there," Clemedeth turned with a smile. "We don't have too far to go."

She continued to lead the way while Devilea kept quiet, impatiently waiting for the perfect time, to steal the crystal ball.

In the meantime, Micah reached the end of his home trail, quickly searching down Amble Road, until his eyes saw the hill that led to Hemlock Village. He fast-walked to the foot of the hill and before climbing, straightened his backpack, then scaled all the way to the top as fast as he could and then slowed down to listen. It was best he remained hidden in case the girls needed his help, so he kept his distance. He stopped for only a few seconds when suddenly, he felt something slithering around his ankles. It was a snake! Thinking quickly, he leaped on top of a large rock he spotted next to an oak tree, his teeth pressed tightly together, trying hard not to make a sound. For a moment, he thought he was safe, until there was a heavy swoosh sound above his head, over the withering branches. Although he could not identify the sound, he knew whatever it was, had to be huge. It had gone away as fast as it came, like the slithering snake on the ground. He waited on the large rock, until he felt comfortable enough to move on.

The same time Micah heard the strange sound above him, Avanna and Rena caught first glimpse of a witch's cottage, guarded by crows resting on its' broken gutters.

"This must be it," Rena whispered under her breath.

"We're here!" Clemedeth announced excitedly.

Rena stared at the dead overhanging branches that covered the roof, watching as huge black bats flew out with dark, red glaring eyes, creating tremendous flutters that blocked any surrounding sounds, sending a sudden chill up her spine.

"Avanna, watch out!" she shouted as they flew over them, barely touching the top of their heads, then quickly headed back to hiding after they sensed Devilea's presence.

"They won't bother you," she assured them, eyeing the crystal ball that would soon be inside her home. "Not while you're with us."

More unfamiliar sounds became apparent from under the black misty path as they walked closer towards the front door, covered in thick spider webs, empty of spiders.

"Eww!" quivered Rena, as a thick web, clung to her hair and shawl, from one of the branches that hung low over her head.

"Don't worry, I'll open the door," Clemedeth said to help calm her fears.

Rena grew tense, standing in front of witches' home and in the same moment, fascinated. It was what she imagined it to be and then some. It truly was a witch's cottage.

CHAPTER NINE

THE MIDDLES END

At Fountain Lake Park, forensics and police officers kept searching for more clues that would lead them to Rena Winterton. They used the boats in the lake to search for any remains; everyone silently prayed there would be none. Volunteers arrived eager to assist with the search. They began walking through the woods, inches apart from each other, to avoid missing any new finds, searching the tunnel every thirty minutes with a new set of eyes.

The three boys, who took the crystal ball away from Avanna, walked up to the entrance of the park and stood behind the yellow crime scene ribbon, curious as to what happened. One of the boys wanted to ask about the old woman in the tunnel, but was fearful. He hesitantly turned and walked away with the others, then stopped dead in his tracks.

"Let's go back and ask the police if they found the old woman, just to know she's all right."

"Are you crazy, dude? They'll be all over us asking questions," his friend replied anxiously.

"Yeah, and I don't want to get involved!" the other responded.

The two boys strongly voiced their opinions, and then continued walking; he followed. Neither spoke another word about it.

The police officers finished setting up the tent, and the volunteers helped placed the tables and chairs inside. Neighbors brought flashlights to the entrance to prepare for nightfall and coffee shop owners donated fresh coffee for those involved with the search. All who heard of Rena's disappearance offered their assistance in every way possible.

"I need somebody to move some of these fallen limbs back! They're still too close to the entrance!" yelled an officer who just started his shift.

He went inside the tunnel and stood along the entryway to Wanderamid, looking around the area where they had discovered color sequins, lined on the floor. Suddenly, above his head, he heard an unusual and frightening heavy swoosh sound, over the roof, followed by a sound of wings flapping, just as Micah experienced on Tarot's trail.

"What the heck!" He ducked his head slightly.

The only thing he could come up with that would make such a noise, or any sense, was that there had been another storm brewing outside. Nevertheless, when he found the weather calm, he became extremely nervous. There was no other logical explanation.

Were the sounds coming from Wanderamid, in the core of the tunnel?

"It must be my imagination," he murmured nervously.

*   *   *

Back at Ms. Winterton's cottage, she sat at her kitchen table with her head held down in her hands. She had not heard anything since she returned from the park.

Officer Morley and Officer Wodderspoon were still at the precinct finishing their report. After they handed it in, they walked back to their police cruiser without saying a word. Both felt the investigation would be a long one, not like the others they had in the past.

The silence broke between them.

"So, Trent, what do you think about all this, off the record that is?" asked Officer Wodderspoon as he opened the passenger door.

"I don't know, Flynn. I just don't know. It's all too strange. We have to ask the neighbors questions and take it from there."

He only nodded.

They had fifteen minutes before arriving on Whisper Lane, fifteen minutes of pure silence.

Ms. Winterton felt she had been waiting too long. She was curious how the search was going and called the police station.

"This is the Whilom police station. Is this an emergency?" the dispatcher asked calmly.

"Yes. It's Ms. Winterton. I'd like to speak with Officer Morley, please."

"Officer Morley is not here. He just left with Officer Wodderspoon," she said.

"Please, tell them I called. I need to know if they found anything about my daughter, Rena Winterton."

"I'll send your message out to them, ma'am."

"Thank you," she replied.

They both ended the phone call.

Anxiously, she peered out her kitchen window and saw a police cruiser driving down the street, then parking in front of her cottage. It was the officers! Officer Wodderspoon walked directly across the street, towards the neighbors standing outside. Officer Morley walked towards her as she stood inside by the front door looking out, eagerly waiting.

As he stepped up on her porch, he tipped his hat to her, "Ms. Winterton".

She gazed with sad eyes through the screen and gave a simple smile when she opened the door.

"How are you holding up, Ms. Winterton?" he asked not feeling quite right with his choice of words.

Ms. Winterton realized he meant well.

"Since I came home, I haven't held up well at all. Thoughts of Rena, before the storm, have been running through my mind, what I should have done, what I should have said. Tears came from deep within me, I thought never existed. I started to feel like I accepted grief. I don't want to accept grief. I want to stay strong to find my daughter."

He finally understood and for a moment, kept silent.

"Officer Wodderspoon and I are going to the park. Would you like to come with us?"

"Yes...I would," she tried to keep her tears from falling.

He realized it was the only place Ms. Winterton felt closer to Rena.

"Come on, Ms. Winterton, and lock up."

"No. I want it open... in case she comes home and doesn't have her... key."

He nodded and they both left. At the same time, Officer Wodderspoon walked back across the street and bowed his head to her. He too had a loss for words.

"Ms. Winterton will be coming with us to the park," he said, as they all walked to the cruiser.

During the drive down, they were silent the whole time. When they arrived, they immediately noticed the search tent surrounded by a crowd of people waiting to help find Rena. Officer Wodderspoon held up the crime scene ribbon for Ms. Winterton to enter before them.

It was around six o'clock in the evening and fifteen members of the police crew were going home while the other fifteen remained, keeping the investigation ongoing. Ten forensics crew members were also working, along with the one hundred volunteers who were not leaving anytime soon.

Officer Morley led the way to the tent to speak to the other officers.

"Did anything happen while we were gone, like maybe someone suspicious hanging around?"

They all shook their heads no and then one of them walked up to him.

"I'm Officer Liam, sir," he shook his hand.

"I'm Officer Morley, and this is my partner, Officer Wodderspoon. This," he placed his hand gently on her back, "is Ms. Winterton, the missing girl's mother."

"Pleased to meet you, ma'am." He nodded, gave a soft grin, and then proceeded to answer the officer's question. "We didn't see anything except for three boys standing at the entrance talking. One had a worried look on his face that made me a little suspicious. They left quickly after, but I wouldn't be surprised if they come back."

"Is that so?" he replied in a suspicious tone. "Hmm, if you see them again, let me know. I'd like to speak with them."

"I'll keep an eye out for them, sir," he assured him.

They walked away and continued towards the tunnel where there was an officer working inside.

"Officer," he called out as they approached the entrance. "Have you found anything?"

"No!" he replied with a shaky voice and then dropped his flashlight, seemingly disturbed.

Officer Morley was concerned with his behavior and asked, "Is everything all right in there?"

"Yeah, yeah, just a little confused about something, nothing important, it was nothing." He nervously picked up his flashlight and tried to hold it steady.

They all walked warily to where he stood.

"Tell me, maybe it's something." He and the others stood, curious to hear what he had to say.

The officer moved closer to them and with eyes wide open described, "Well, there was an unusual sound, nothing I ever heard before. It sounded like… something huge flying over this tunnel, with… big wings. I went outside, but didn't see anything. Nobody else seemed to notice, so I kept it to myself. Please, will you keep… this… off the record?"

"Sure, uh, no problem," he began to wonder about his state of mind. "Where were you when you heard—wings—flapping?" He glanced over at the others with raised eyebrows, rolling his eyes.

"I was standing right here." With shaking knees, he stood where they discovered colored sequins, right in the middles end of the tunnel.

They all looked at each other, and then back to him.

"You can take the rest of the night off. I'll sign you out. Get some rest and keep everything you told us, to yourself. You can come back in the morning. Oh, what's your name?"

"Derwintwater, sir, Officer Derwintwater," he answered, and then without hesitation, walked out; relieved he was dismissed for the night.

Officer Wodderspoon watched as he left quickly out of the tunnel and then turned and looked at Officer Morley in awe.

"What was that all about, Trent?"

"It means he's working too hard! I have not seen any big birds flying around here! What else could it mean? Let's look in here some more." He turned to Ms. Winterton and in a softer tone of voice said, "Please stay over by the entrance; we'll only be a few minutes."

She walked out while the two searched around inside, aiming their flashlights at the middles end of the tunnel, where he heard the strange noise. They stood at the exact spot he said he was. Not long after, a heavy swoosh sound above them followed by the sound of flapping wings that seemed to have touched the roof. They ducked down and instantly bolted out of the tunnel, scoping around the area.

"Did you see anything?" Officer Morley shouted out to her.

Startled by their exit, she was unable to move a muscle. Then lastly, she answered aloud, "No, I didn't see anything! What happened in there?"

He stood still and shook his head, "I can't explain it."

"It was a sound like w-wings... f-l-lapping. I-I never heard anything l-like it," added Officer Wodderspoon. "Just l-like he described."

"Are you all right, Officer Wodderspoon?" she asked, seemingly concerned with his odd behavior.

He twitched his head to one side and responded, "Uh, y-yeah, I'm OK."

"Hey, pull yourself together!" yelled Officer Morley. "There has to be a logical explanation for what we heard in there!" Although he believed there had to be, not one came to his mind.

"OK, T-T-rent," he replied, still trembling.

"Officer Morley!" shouted Officer Liam, "Come on over!"

He began to walk over to him. Officer Wodderspoon followed.

Ms. Winterton chose to remain by the tunnel.

"Yes," he replied and then looked down at three young visitors, with petrified expressions.

"These are the boys I told you about."

The three boys stood frozen as though they had seen a ghost, their eyes fixed on Officer Morley's, knowing he would be asking them questions.

"What are your names?" he asked firmly as he looked down at them.

"My friends call me, Big Red," answered the first boy with curly, fire-like hair and a body as skinny as a twig.

"I don't mean what they call you, son. What is your real name?" he asked, trying not to laugh and thinking they should have just stuck with "Red".

He seemed as though he had to think about it. Although he stood stiff, he was truly nervous, apparently shaking inside.

"My real name is… Alroy."

Officer Morley proceeded to ask the next boy, "What's your name son?"

He looked up at him with his bright, blue eyes. His hair was blond and straight like a horse's mane.

"Caden, sir!" he responded with a firm voice.

"And," he gazed over to the last boy, "what is your name?"

"My name is, Elon, Officer."

Although his voice was more relaxed than the others were, his right foot tapped continuously on the ground.

"I want to thank you for being—cooperative," he said gratefully. "I just wanted to speak to you. I heard you were here earlier and was wondering if you know anything about— what is going on here. Do you think you could help us?"

"Help you with what, sir?" Caden asked.

"Well, there's a missing girl, Rena's her name. We think she was here last, before she disappeared. Did any one of you ever see anyone strange hanging out in the park?" He watched as they looked at each other, before giving their attention back to him.

"We didn't mean to take her glass ball, we didn't keep it!" Caden shouted.

"What do you mean by a glass ball?" Officer Wodderspoon asked, confused, "Whose glass ball?"

Caden's friends were surprised he said anything. He surprised himself and then tried to talk his way out of his words.

"Nothing, sir, I… don't remember what I just said."

"Now listen here, you started it. I want you to explain what you just said so I can understand. Go on, explain." He stood patiently waiting.

The other boys realized there was not anything they could say to escape the situation. They nodded, giving Caden their approval to tell the officers what happen on the day they stole the crystal ball.

"Well, sir, one day we were walking down here and saw a woman, an old woman, hiding in the tunnel, the one over there." He pointed towards the tunnel Rena was supposedly in. "She was sleeping inside with a glass ball in her arms. I pulled it away from her and she woke up! She looked old and at the same time seemed my age. I got scared and ran out." He shook his head, ashamed what he had done. "She couldn't run after us. When I looked back, she was only at the entrance. Then all of the sudden, she yelled out to give back the crystal ball. That's what she called it, a crystal ball. Right after, a bright light came out of it and it scared us, so I dropped it and we kept on running. I feel… we feel really bad about it now." He lowered his head down in despair and then looked back up, "Did you find her, sir, the old woman?"

Ms. Winterton had since moved closer, away from the tunnel. She heard everything the boys admitted.

Officer Morley turned, not surprised to see her behind him, and then returned his attention to the boys.

"No, we didn't find her. You can go home now. Give Officer Liam your full names, in case we need to speak to you again, and don't forget to give your phone numbers and addresses, too."

The investigation was definitely one out of the ordinary. First, there were swooshing sounds with flapping wings and then an old woman with a crystal ball, who seemed like a young girl.

"Officer Morley, do you think the old woman they saw is with Rena?" Ms. Winterton asked, curious to hear if the same thought crossed his mind.

"There's a good possibility, after all, Rena's necklace was found in the tunnel where the boys saw her."

She was not sure whether to be worried the old woman they spoke about was with Rena, or relieved.

"By the way," she added, "you didn't ask the boys what the old woman was wearing, if she had colored sequins on her clothes."

"You're right, Ms. Winterton. Wodderspoon, hurry and catch up with the boys! Find out what the old woman was wearing, and ask about the sequins, too!" he ordered, embarrassed he and the others neglected to ask.

"Right on it, Trent," he replied, wondering why he was shouting. They were only a few feet apart.

Ms. Winterton had thoughts of her own, about the tunnel, the crystal ball, and the strange noises, that petrified four people. Something mystical was happening in Whilom and her daughter seemed caught in the middle of it.

Officer Wodderspoon rushed back after his talk with the boys.

"Trent! Ms. Winterton!" he shouted out of breath. "The old woman—she was wearing a shawl—with colored sequins!"

Officer Morley and Ms. Winterton looked at each other in awe. The news gave greater possibility that Rena and the strange old woman were in the tunnel together at the time of her or their disappearance. She believed something in there was a way to bring her daughter back and was convinced it had some kind of mystic exit. However, until she had proof, she kept her unimaginable theory to herself.

"Maybe you should go home now, Ms. Winterton, to get some rest," Officer Wodderspoon suggested. "There's nothing you can do right now."

"But I don't want to leave," she responded with sad, worried eyes.

"You have to let everyone do their job. We'll contact you in the morning or if anything should turn up before then," he assured her.

"We'll give you a ride home," Officer Morley offered. "Come on."

They walked her to their police cruiser that filled once again with silence as they drove her home. When they arrived, Officer Morley got out and opened the door for her. She walked up to her porch, deeply saddened, unable to thank them for the ride. They stayed behind and waited until she reached the door.

"Good night, Ms. Winterton!" Officer Wodderspoon shouted through the open window.

She entered inside, turned with a sorrowful grin, and slowly waved as she gazed through the screen door.

"We'll let you know if we hear anything!" yelled Officer Morley. "Try not to worry; we will find her!"

She closed the door slowly and then walked to the staircase, where she last heard Rena's footsteps, resting her head on the railing as she wept.

CHAPTER TEN

THE GOLD BUTTERFLY STAND

Rena and Avanna entered inside the witch's cottage in Hemlock Village and were instantly amazed. There were shelves built inside the walls, filled with old, leather bound books, complete with black magic and recipes for potent potions. Each title was scripted with unique lettering, which would increase anyone's interest.

Clemedeth saw the expressions on their faces.

"Feel free to look around," she smiled.

"Let me hold—" Devilea had begun to say when she approached Rena.

Rena pulled her arm away immediately, protecting the crystal ball in her arms. "I'll hold it."

"I was going to—"

"No, it will stay with me." She forced a smile, "Thanks anyway."

Devilea nodded and forced one in return. "Go on, look around. We'll be in the kitchen."

They followed her into the kitchen where Clemedeth had already begun preparing their meal. There were glass cabinets showing glass jars filled with herbs; mice tails; pigtails and crow's feet. In an instant, they thought of that room as their least favorite, then quietly turned around without them noticing and continued separately to other areas of the cottage filled with indescribable aromas emerging from burning incenses.

Avanna grew wearier as her weakness fully returned and wanted to relieve her feet from any further tours of the witches' home. Her eyes caught sight of a wooden rocking chair further inside a room and walked towards it to rest in its comfortable tan, silk cushioned seat. As she leaned back, she admired the window, topped with a sheer, lavender valance. Then, immediately after, noticed outside the window, a unique spider web, its size at least twenty times thicker than a common one. She stared, excited to see its creator.

Rena was attracted to everything in view, mainly the wall opposite the one filled with old, leather bound books. Sitting on a floating red shelf, were two crystal balls, one larger than the one held in her arms, the other smaller. Between them was an empty gold butterfly stand. Due to her love of butterflies, it captured her full attention, drawn to its' design of yellow and purple gemstones. Her eyes roamed, searching for the crystal ball separated from the mount, but it was nowhere in sight. She could see the one held in her arms would be a perfect fit, making a complete set, though she was not positive. With both hands, she raised it towards the stand to confirm they measured the same and then unexpectedly felt it pull away from her. The force jolted her and she tugged the crystal ball back quickly, separating from any control. Rena realized at that moment Devilea's interest in their crystal ball; she wanted it for the empty stand.

What would it mean to her if she owned a complete set? Would it give her greater power?

Although they were starving and looked forward to having a home cooked meal, Rena believed something terrible would happen if they stayed and immediately began searching for Avanna. The first room she walked into had tarot cards on an old wooden table, ready to predict one's curiosity for their future. On the floor, voodoo dolls dressed with scraps from old clothing, stood against a dark, empty wall. She casually walked further inside and saw Avanna, resting near a wooden table with magic wands on top, accented with gemstones of every color. Her eyes stayed fixed on the spider web.

Devilea caught Rena quietly moving towards Avanna and walked out of the kitchen, sneakily following her.

"We should be going. I don't trust Devilea," Rena whispered into Avanna's ear, hoping she heard her, but she did not move once. Her eyes stared out the window in a daze.

Devilea heard her every word and quickly shouted out, "Dinner won't take long, right Clemedeth?"

Rena swiftly turned her head, shocked to see the back of Devilea's inches from her face.

Devilea casually turned to her two guests with the strangest grin. "Rena, why don't you put that beautiful crystal ball down and relax?"

Rena was speechless. Her eyes anxiously searched for Clemedeth, and then saw her in the kitchen, dropping crow's feet one by one into a boiling pot of water. The awful sight caused her stomach to turn and her craving for food instantly ended.

Moments after, she turned to Avanna once more and spoke louder. "You know, we really should be going."

Avanna was not able to see the full expression on her face, however, she could sense from the partial tone in her voice that she wanted to leave.

"I think we should go now, we have a long way to travel."

"Clemedeth!" shouted Devilea. "They have to leave!"

"But I'm making a delicious crow stew! It will be done in about forty-five minutes!"

Avanna heard part of what Clemedeth shouted and recognized Rena's reason for strongly suggesting they end their visit. 'Crow stew?' she squirmed.

Their appetites would definitely return later, so when Clemedeth entered the room soon after, she kindly asked, "Do you have anything we can bring with us to snack on?"

Rena helped her up from the chair.

"Sure, I'll find something for you." She smiled and went back into the kitchen searching the cabinets and refrigerator. "I have some crackers and cheese you can take. Will that be all right?" she asked loudly.

"Yes, thank you," Avanna replied as they were almost to the front door.

Rena was relieved knowing they would get something in their stomachs, besides crow stew.

"Could you put it in a bag, too?" Avanna added.

"Sure," she replied while wondering why they had to leave suddenly.

They slowly reached the witches' cedar arched door, with broomsticks on each side, ready for an immediate flight and waited. Devilea's face shriveled when she realized her plan was not going her way.

What would she do to get crystal ball?

Clemedeth finally finished packing their bag of snacks and brought it to them.

"Thank you," Avanna smiled gratefully and then asked, "Oh, by the way, have you seen a pterodoc flying around?"

Devilea unexpectedly answered nervously, wiping the sudden sweat dripping off her forehead, "I d-don't remember seeing one. No."

*   *   *

Devilea thought back to the day when a young boy arrived in Wanderamid through one of the tunnels with the crystal ball. She ordered him to give it to her, but she frightened him. When he tried to run back inside, he fell and the crystal ball left his hold, rolling away, disappearing before their eyes. Devilea snapped and without a second thought, cast a spell on him, turning him into a monstrous creature with wings, a pterodoc. Clemedeth was unaware, Devilea never told her.

*   *   *

"Are you sure? How did a pterodoc come around here?" Clemedeth asked surprised. "I never saw it; then again, I don't go out much. I wonder who that poor soul could be. It's a witch's curse, you know, otherwise they don't exist."

She turned and noticed the odd look on Devilea's face; an expression that instantly caused a sick feeling in her stomach. Something was not right and she felt Devilea was somehow involved.

"Well, I hope you find your way home Avanna, and you too Rena," she said hurriedly, rushing them out of the cottage. "If I could help you find the right tunnel I would, but our powers are limited when it comes to the tunnels. The crystal ball will help you get back home, more than we ever could."

"Thanks, for everything," smiled Avanna.

"Yes, thanks," added Rena before she hurriedly walked out.

They left from the witches' cottage and Clemedeth quickly closed the door behind them.

"Devilea!" she yelled and then noticed her already in the kitchen, "I think we need to talk!"

"Sure, wait till I pour us some goat's milk. Sit down and I'll bring it to the table, we can talk there."

Clemedeth sat at the table, waiting for her, unaware she was slipping sleeping potion into her glass. Devilea knew she would be asking her about the pterodoc, a subject she did not care to discuss. She casually set the glasses down, one for herself and the other for Clemedeth, who drank from it right before she was about to speak.

"What did you want to talk about?" she asked, knowing the potion would take effect at that very moment.

She was right. Clemedeth barely had a chance to respond when her head slumped down on the table and immediately began to snore. Although Devilea tricked her, she made a caring move by placing a pillow under Clemedeth's slumbering head. Her next move was to bring about the start of a new plan.

Meanwhile Rena mentioned how Devilea acted odd when they spoke about the pterodoc. Avanna was too weak to respond and only shook her head. Rena realized she was unable to keep up with a conversation and kept quiet, as they walked on silently wondering where the next stop in their journey would lead them. Suddenly, Rena heard someone or something from behind. Who or what could it be? Shaken from the constant sound of the rustle of leaves, she was unable to ignore it any longer. She turned swiftly and gasped. Standing inches away was someone she had never seen. She frantically tugged on Avanna's arm. Avanna was too weak, nevertheless, she turned around slowly and faced the stranger.

He stood still, staring at Rena's alarmed expression.

"What do you want?" she yelled and took steps back, pulling Avanna along with her.

"Nothing, I don't want anything," he tried to assure her. "I was just looking out for you."

"Oh," Avanna replied briefly, relieved by his answer.

"I heard you talking with the witches on Amble road. I wanted to be around in case you needed my help, that's all, really," he explained innocently, hoping he had eased Rena's clearly worried mind.

"We're not with the witches anymore, so why are you still following us?" she looked at him with squinting eyes.

"I'm curious to see where you're going through these woods. It will be dark soon. You're new around here, right?"

"Yes, but she's been here before. I'm here to help her get home." She looked behind him to make sure there was no one else around and then asked, "What's your name?"

"My name is Micah," he responded with a sincere smile. "Where are you headed?"

"We're trying to find the tunnel that will bring her back home. She's Avanna, and I'm Rena."

"I know, I've known since Amble Road. It's nice to meet you."

"Nice to meet you, too," Avanna smiled tiredly.

Micah nodded and smiled in return. He remembered Avanna had more energy on Amble Road and did not seem to be as old as she looked. He realized Rena would need some help with her.

"Would you like some company? I might be of some help. Like I said before, it will be dark soon."

"Sure," Avanna quickly responded.

Rena was surprised by her quick reaction when only moments before she was too weak to respond to her. She looked at Micah and hesitantly replied, "I guess—it would be all right."

"Great. Let's start walking. I'll help you find what you're looking for and protect you."

"Do you have any idea where we can find a tunnel?" she asked, hoping he would say yes.

"To tell you the truth, I've never been in Hemlock Village. This is my first time. Don't worry, though, we'll find one," he replied with confidence.

They continued to walk through the misty trail of Hemlock Village.

"Woe!" Micah fell directly under the thick mist on the ground.

"Where are you?" Rena shouted, waving her hand over the area he disappeared and then smacked the back of his head.

"Oww!" he yelled and then turned to look up at her, "What did you do that for?"

"I'm sorry, I didn't see you."

"Move your hands. I'm getting up."

"Are you all right?"

"Yeah, I'm OK." His face scrunched up and he asked, "What was that?"

"It was my hand, I didn't mean to—"

"No—What did I trip over?"

"I don't know," she answered, clueless.

They were curious, gathered around the area he fell, staring down through the thick mist on the ground, and saw what appeared to be a plaque sticking out of the edge of the trail, with writing on it.

Avanna looked at Micah with wide eyes. "Read it. What does it say?"

"Let me get the flashlight from my backpack first."

Although there was little daylight, the thick mist on the ground made it difficult to read.

"Hurry!" she became more impatient.

Micah looked at her and rolled his eyes, shaking his head as he knelt down to read it.

"Read it out loud!" they shouted together.

Micah looked up at them. "Sor-r-y!" He aimed the light and lowered his head closer to the plaque and read, *"Long lost voices you will hear, will lead you to a passageway of steel."*

Avanna's face lit up with excitement.

"The passageway of steel means a tunnel! It's made of steel and it's a passage! There must be one nearby!"

"Avanna, the tunnel we came through wasn't made out of steel, it was made out of concrete," Rena reminded her.

"The one from Whilom was concrete, but there have been others I've gone through that were made of steel," she quickly explained.

Now they were all smiling. The hope they had been waiting for finally arrived.

"Let's keep going," Avanna said. "It can't be too far from here."

They all agreed and traveled through the long and dark mystic trail when she heard a voice in the distance, but kept it to herself. Rena and Micah stayed close to her, to keep her from falling as Micah did. Even the shortest fall would hurt her greatly. Then, she heard it again. It could not have been her imagination; it had to be real because she heard it twice!

Avanna immediately stood still and with widened eyes looked at them, "Stop! Did you hear a voice?"

They both stood frozen in their tracks and then Rena asked with a puzzled expression on her face, "What voice?"

"I heard a voice—two times. The first time was when we were walking away from the plaque, and then again after. I know I'm not imagining it."

"I didn't hear anything," Rena regretted calmly and then looked over at Micah. "Did you?"

"No, I didn't."

"I know I heard something! It was very faint! We must move closer to the direction it's coming from."

She walked ahead of them. Her determination to follow the voice and to find the passage of steel made her stronger.

Rena and Micah thought she had been through too many tunnels.

They walked faster to catch up with her when all of the sudden, they all heard the alarming sound of the pterodoc.

Avanna turned to Rena and Micah.

"We have to run and get out of its sight! We can't let it see us!"

"What are you talking about? So what doesn't see us?" Micah asked confused.

"It's the pterodoc—a monstrous creature," Rena described.

"It's a what? How do you know?" He still did not fully understand.

Rena answered quickly with little time to explain.

"We saw it when we came through my tunnel and it chased us into the forest. We have to run—now!"

They both grabbed Avanna by her arms and searched for a nearby shelter. When Micah offered his help to prevent any harm from Devilea, he never imagined he would be protecting them from a monster, too.

Through all the excitement, Avanna continued to hear the voice in the distance while the others continued to show no response. Clearly, their attention was on the pterodoc, flying over the crooked trees of Tarot's trail, flapping his gigantic wings. They had to make it to a safe hiding, before he neared the opening ahead of them, giving him entry to the trail.

"Where is it? Do you see it?" Micah's eyes searched around aimlessly.

"No!" Rena stopped and listened. "I hear it… over the trees."

"Over there, by that tall bush," he pointed.

They both ran with Avanna carried between them.

"Why didn't it go through the trees?" he asked nervously.

"Oh, no," she realized, "It's trying to find us for Devilea!"

"Well, it didn't see us hiding here," Micah assured them.

While they were talking, Avanna heard someone calling her name, "Avanna!"

"What!" she shouted.

Rena and Micah stared at her with eyes surprised.

"What?" Rena asked her, confused.

Avanna kept hearing the voice, and it sounded like her mother.

"Oh, nothing," she replied nonchalantly. "Rena, could you get us something to eat out of the bag?" She was beginning to think she was hearing voices that were not real.

"Yes. Are you OK?" she asked concerned.

"I'm fine. A little hungry," she hinted anxiously.

"Oh… right."

She opened the bag Clemedeth packed for them and handed out crackers and cheese. For the time being, it took their thoughts away from the pterodoc and the voices only Avanna heard.

CHAPTER ELEVEN

BITTERSWEET REUNION

In the witch's cottage, Clemedeth was deep asleep. Finally, Devilea had the opportunity to carry out her plan, to take the crystal ball away from Rena, and without any interference from her meddling guardian. She had no idea they befriended a stranger willing to protect them—from her.

All were unaware about an annoying surprise, which was about to happen.

Devilea decided to walk rather than using her broomstick, since it would cause for a difficult flight through a tight and crooked trail. She knew they were not far away since Avanna was too weak to travel, so she left unhurriedly, walking the same path they had taken.

Meanwhile, the pterodoc reversed, towards Amble Road, opposite from where Micah and the girls were unseen, in their newfound hideaway. When he looked down through an opening of the crowded and crooked trees, he caught sight of Devilea and imagined she was up to no good. He directed back swiftly to where Avanna and the others were hiding. Devilea felt a strong gust of wind as he did, and then thought he would disturb her plan.

"I should have turned him into an ant, or better yet a rabbit to be chased by one-eyed snakes!" she muttered angrily to herself.

In the meantime, he reached Micah and the girls, roughly circling purposely above them, diving through the air with great force.

Rena swiftly turned and faced Micah, "I thought you said it didn't see us!"

He jerked back with surprised eyes, "I really thought it didn't."

They stood suddenly and the snacks dropped from their hands before guiding Avanna closely as they ran away from a place they thought to have been safe.

The only way to get them off Devilea's path was to scare them, and that is what the pterodoc did.

Micah spotted what appeared to be a tunnel, hidden partly under thick, leafy vines, hanging in front of its entrance. His goal was to get them safe inside, as quickly as possible.

"We have to go inside that tunnel, straight ahead!"

"OK!" Rena nodded nervously.

As they approached the tunnel, Avanna heard the voice she thought resembled that of her mother's. Surprisingly, Rena and Micah heard it, too, confirming what she had been telling them.

Avanna caught the surprised expressions on their faces.

"You heard it! This is the tunnel of steel!" she shouted, relieved, while at the same time frightened by the pterodoc, seconds away from them.

They all scrambled through the overhanging vines and quickly entered inside where they heard Avanna's name echoing, along with her brother's, Jack. All of them looked at each other in disbelief. The look on her face told them it was someone she knew. It was definitely her way back home.

"It's my mother," she confirmed nervously. "But, she's calling for Jack. That means he wasn't found."

There was a heavy thump at the entrance, which caused their hearts to beat even faster. It was the pterodoc! They stood terrified not knowing what he would do.

"It can't see us," Micah whispered.

"Look at it," Avanna spoke in a hushed voice. "It looks like it wants to say something."

"What?" Rena replied with raising eyebrows. "It's a pterodoc. It can't talk."

Suddenly the pterodoc felt an evil presence nearby and when he turned to his left, was not surprised to see Devilea! To prevent her from getting any closer, he flapped his gigantic wings and lifted up, flying over the trees.

"You were right, Rena," agreed Avanna. "It was finding us for Devilea. It flew away."

Devilea paid no attention to the monstrous creature; she would take care of him later. Her main concern was only to retrieve the crystal ball. She yelled from the top of her lungs, "Avanna—wait, I need to talk to you!"

She knew where they were and was aware there was not much time left. With the crystal ball in their hands, they were able to leave at any moment.

"Don't answer her," Rena whispered firmly. "She wants the crystal ball!" She turned to Micah, "You have to come with us now. You can come back later. There's no other way to leave except with Avanna."

"All right, but we have to go now," he responded, while securing his backpack. "Devilea will be here soon, if she isn't already."

They had no idea how close she was, although her voice hinted she was close enough and the pterodoc—long gone. They continued further inside the tunnel. Rena held out the crystal ball carefully in front of her.

"Micah, I don't have time to explain, just hold on to us and no matter what, don't let go."

Devilea stood motionless outside the entrance, looking in with a dead stare. She was not about to let the crystal ball leave her again. Her blood began to boil throughout her veins as she furiously raised her wand! Lightning bolts shot through the crowded trees around her, into the darkened sky! The loud cracking sounds of thunder and lightning confirmed their worst fear; she had arrived. The sky lit up with heavy winds, moaning loudly outside the tunnel walls. They all turned towards the alarming sounds and saw her, lowering her arm slowly, about to aim at them.

"Oh no, what is she doing?" Rena shouted.

"I don't know, but get ready to duck!" warned Micah.

They were unable to see the pterodoc directly above her. With his tear-filled eyes, he struggled to let out the words he wanted to say while trying to block them from her wand. He was not able to see clearly and rammed into her with his webbed feet, landing on her legs and she on her wand, breaking it in half.

Avanna shouted, "Look! The pterodoc is back!"

"It landed on Devilea!" Rena watched, surprised. "I guess I was wrong about it."

"Get off of my legs you overgrown bird!" Devilea struggled to free herself.

The pterodoc ignored her order. It was safer for everyone she stayed right where she was. She remained trapped as he lowered his head, peeking inside the brightly lit tunnel. From deep within, he forcibly released a sorrowful roar, as they prepared to enter into yet another dimension, unable to find, within his human soul, a voice they could understand. Then, the thundering sky quieted and the moaning winds stopped.

"Start walking!" Rena urged.

Sadness grew inside the monstrous creature, watching Avanna slowly walk away into the magnetic light. His only chance to let her know the truth was slipping away. Then, another strong roar came from the pterodocs mouth, calling out her name!

"AVANNA… AVANNA!"

Devilea could not believe what she was hearing. Why would he be calling her?

Avanna and the others stopped and turned to see him gazing into Avanna's huge glassy eyes. She realized at that moment, it was her brother, Jack. However, it was too late for them to turn back.

"Avanna, don't break away from us. It's too late!" Rena held her hand tightly.

"But it's my brother!" she yelled. "JACK! I'LL BE BACK FOR YOU! I PROmise...."

He watched as they disappeared into the light and into Wishing Willow. His sister was gone and he hoped she arrived safely, back with their grieving mother.

Finally, his tears broke from his pterodoc eyes and drenched Devilea's head.

"Now look what you've done!" she shook her soaked head. "They're gone, and so is the crystal ball!"

Jack looked down, stared into her eyes, then lifted off her legs and flew away, before she caused him further beastly damage while at the same time, she was his only hope of becoming human again. Although his heart was sad, he felt satisfied his sister found out who and what he had become.

When he reached his secluded mountain cave, he rested, wondering if his sister would return and if he was forever, damned by Devilea's ill-fated curse.

Although Devilea was furious Jack interfered, she kept from inflicting any harm on him, knowing Avanna would eventually return to try to save her brother.

'They have to come back with the crystal ball sometime,' she thought and then walked back to her cottage, using the extra time to figure out answers to Clemedeth's questions.

*　　*　　*

At the witch's cottage, the potion wore off, Clemedeth awakened—slowly. She knew right away Devilea tricked her and waited patiently for her return.

*　　*　　*

Near Amble Road, Grandmother Oula stood at the end of the trail while a starry night formed before her eyes. She looked in every direction for Micah. Thoughts about what he said before he left remained in her mind. It gave her hope he would return safe and unharmed. When she walked back to the cottage, she sat in her chair and covered herself with a blanket, before falling asleep soon after.

*　　*　　*

Rena and the others entered into Wishing Willow, Avanna's hometown. Her mother raised her head slowly and then held her hands out in front of her to block the bright light that had suddenly appeared. Then, she noticed what seemed to be the answer to her prayers, Avanna walking towards her. Rena and Micah were by her side.

"Avanna, you've come back!" her mother cried as they embraced.

"Mom," she cried with her.

Rena and Micah noticed Avanna was back the way she used to be, young like them. Then, Micah noticed Rena with more gray in her hair, Avanna noticed, too, but was not surprised, after all, it was the second tunnel she had gone through.

"Mom, these are my friends, Rena and Micah. They helped me get home."

"Hello, I'm Ms. Marsail, Avanna's mother, but you already know that! Thank you for bringing her home." Her eyes gleamed with happiness and then she asked, "Do you need to call your parents?"

"No, Mom," Avanna quickly responded. "They have to stay with us."

"Are you lost? You can use our phone," she kindly offered.

"Mom, I'll explain later." She looked at them, shaking her head, embarrassed by her mother's questions.

"Oh, all right. What is that you're holding Rena?" she leaned closer as she wiped the tears away from her eyes to see clearly. "It looks like a glass ball."

"It is," Rena replied softly.

"There's a lot I have to tell you, Mom. I'll wait until we get home."

Her mother was surprised she had not asked about her brother and tried holding back the tears she held for him. They walked arm in arm. She was afraid to let Avanna go. Rena and Micah followed, silently admiring the serene view of Wishing Willow. Avanna stopped suddenly and turned to look at her mother, unable to keep to herself what she knew about Jack.

"I know where Jack is!" she blurted out.

Her mother stood speechless and began to tremble when she heard those words. Rena and Micah stood still, their eyes widened in shock.

"I have to go back, Mom," she added more confusion to her already frazzled mother.

"What? Back where?" she asked before fainting onto the soft grass.

Avanna was surprised by her sudden fall and began patting her mother's cheeks to wake her.

"I thought you said you would tell her when you got home. That's what you told her!" Micah said, shaking his head, as he was unable to catch her in time.

Avanna felt guilty. She gave no thought about what her mother had been through while she and her brother Jack were gone. She cried out, "Mom, wake up!"

Rena and Micah knelt down and lifted her head.

"Is she alive?" Avanna asked, thinking she had killed her with her words.

"She's alive," he responded, seemingly calm. For a moment, he even thought she was dead.

Avanna was relieved, and then started to pat her mother's cheeks again, "Mom?"

Suddenly, Ms. Marsail began to moan, her eyes opened gradually, her first vision being Avanna.

"Oh... hi, Avanna," her voice slurred, and then right after, her eyes shut.

Avanna immediately placed her finger under her mother's nose to make sure she was breathing when her head began moving along with her body and her eyes opened once more. She gazed into Avanna's eyes and then up to Micah and Rena's eyes. Without saying a word, she slowly lifted herself up, with their help, until she stood. They took little steps as they all walked towards Avanna's home.

"Hang on, Mom. We're almost there."

"The keys… are in… my… pocket," she spoke faintly.

As soon as they caught sight of Avanna's home, Avanna reached in her mother's pocket for the key to the front door. She ran to open it as the others increased their pace the rest of the way. She held the door open as they walked Ms. Marsail into the living room and laid her down on the couch, where she rested her head with eyes lightly open, as if in a daze.

"Let her rest for now. I'll tell her everything when she wakes up," Avanna inform them.

"Let me first offer a few words of advice," said Micah. "Make sure she's sitting when you do." He then added, "Do you have anything to drink? I'm really thirsty."

"Come in the kitchen and I'll get us something to eat too!" she offered. "We can figure out what to do later."

"Avanna, I don't think your mother will let you go back to Wanderamid," Rena assumed. "Micah and I will help your brother."

"I'm going back with you. He's my brother and he needs to see me. I promised him," she responded firmly.

Rena and Micah looked at each other. They knew they would not be able to change her mind. Her energy was back and she was ready to take on whatever stood in her way.

"If you need to wash up, the bathroom is upstairs to your left. I'll look in the refrigerator to see what I can fix for us to eat."

"Rena, you go first," Micah smiled.

"Rena your clothes are still a little wet. We can dry them downstairs in the dryer. I have something you can wear until they dry."

"Thanks," she replied.

"Well, it's the least I can do. I'll be up in a minute."

"Go up with her now," said Micah. "I'll find the plates and glasses."

Avanna turned to him and gave a soft smile.

"Thanks for all your help."

"No problem," he replied red faced.

Avanna checked on her mother, who was resting on the couch and then headed up the stairs to get Rena a change of clothes, after changing hers. Then, she went back down into the kitchen where Micah was waiting and began to make chicken sandwiches.

A short time later, Rena came back.

"I'm done," she said, holding her damp clothes. "I left the crystal ball on your bed."

"It's safe up there," Avanna assured them and then chuckled, "My clothes fit you." She took the damp clothes from her. "I'll put these in the dryer."

"I'll get us something to drink." Micah reached in the refrigerator.

"They look good," Rena stared at the sandwiches Avanna made.

Soon after, Avanna walked back in and whispered strongly, "Let's dig in!"

They all sat down and began filling their faces when all of the sudden, they looked up and saw Ms. Marsail standing at the entrance. She stared, smiling at her daughter, finally home and unharmed.

"Mom, you should be lying down." Avanna stood from her chair and took hold of her mother's arm, leading her back to the couch.

"I'm fine, I'm fine," she pushed Avanna's hair away from her face.

"Please, rest for me."

"Go back in the kitchen and finish eating with your friends," she ordered with a smile. "I'll rest if you promise to finish. We'll talk after you're done."

"OK, I will," she smiled.

Ms. Marsail went back to rest while Avanna finished her meal with the others. She started to remember what she told her on the way to the house, about Jack.

"This is just what I needed," Micah held his sandwich in front of him and took a huge bite.

"Same here," Rena agreed.

"Thanks, if anyone deserves a good meal, it's you two." They both smiled at her with full mouths and then she asked suddenly, "Rena, where's the crystal ball?"

"Mm, I left it on your bed," she replied with her mouth full and then swallowed. "I told you before."

"Oh. I forgot," she said, relieved. "We can't leave without it."

Ms. Marsail was listening to everything they were saying. She rose up from the couch and sneakily walked up the stairs and into Avanna's bedroom, where Rena left the crystal ball. She brought it into her bedroom and opened the jewelry box she kept the key to her safe, hidden in her closet, and then locked the magical sphere inside.

Rena glanced in the living room and noticed Ms. Marsail was gone. "Avanna, where's your mother?"

Avanna and Micah immediately stood up. They saw her walking down the stairs with pillows and blankets.

"Come inside here and get some rest. You all must be tired."

"Mom, we have to talk."

"First, you have to get some rest, I insist," she smiled nervously.

They looked at each other and then Micah agreed, "I guess it couldn't hurt."

Rena and Avanna knew they were right.

"Well, let's at least get your clothes out of the dryer, to have them ready," Avanna suggested.

"No!" Ms. Marsail shouted. "I mean—I'll get them ready for her and you can tell me everything when you wake up."

"OK, Mom," she replied.

They set the living floor and two couches with pillows and blankets. Micah rested on the floor while the girls chose a couch.

"Please, don't tell anyone I'm back," she said as she sat down on the couch.

"I won't. I'll listen to what you have to tell me."

"Thanks," she smiled with tired eyes.

They all placed their heads down on their pillows, then soon after, fell asleep. Ms. Marsail watched them close their eyes. She had no idea what to expect from her daughter and her new friends. Did she hit her head and then thought she saw Jack, or did the loss of her brother cause her to imagine that she saw him? As she walked into the kitchen, she calmly sat, knowing the crystal ball was safe, away from Avanna and the others, who could not leave without it.

CHAPTER TWELVE

THE PEEPHOLES PROPHECY

Ms. Biddock rose up from her chair after she finished her cold black tea and walked back to her desk. With rested eyes, she peeked into her grimoire, searching for a way to open a peephole, to reveal Rena's whereabouts. She came across a new and inviting title, *"Summoning Sight"* and bellowed, *"Calling for particular views, they can be many or only a few. Open this screen wide in front of my eyes, and bring forth those visions to take place what is now in sight. The previous search you showed to me is what I long for to see!"*

A peephole appeared, exactly like the one before. It opened slowly, expanding a glare view with its zigzagging edges, revealing a dark cave. Her eyes squinted and saw what she believed to be, a pterodoc. "But, what does this have to do with Rena and who could this creature be? Is it Rena?" Immediately she thought Devilea stole the crystal ball from her. Then, the picture faded, showing Micah's grandmother Oula, sitting in her living room chair as tears fell from her eyes. "Mother?" she stood, staring in disbelief. "Why is she crying?"

The picture faded like the ones before and showed yet another. It was Devilea walking on Tarot's trail and it looked as though she had been in a fight. Clemedeth appeared right after, seemingly upset, pacing back and forth in the witch's cottage. Something happened in Wanderamid and Ms. Biddock had to find out.

"Maybe Rena isn't there! If she isn't, that means she made it through another tunnel because Devilea didn't seem to have the crystal ball." She looked down at her three felines, smiling, with a surprised look on her face. "She must have gotten away!" When she looked back up, she saw Rena sleeping on a couch, and wondered, 'Where is she? What world did she enter?'

The peephole faded slowly and then sharply closed after, before Ms. Biddock sat down completely in her desk chair. She had no idea where Rena was, only that she was not in Wanderamid.

Soon after, Ms. Winterton's cries reached her ears. She wanted her to know Rena was alive and well, at least everything pointed to that. She stood up from her desk chair and walked to her window, looking down at Fountain Lake Park. Ms. Winterton was not in sight, only officers searching the wooded area. "What did they find in there? They've been searching a long time in that tunnel," she said aloud. "I must go down again, this time to speak to Ms. Winterton. She probably knows more than they do!"

Once again, with a sweep of her wand, she changed her clothes and walked out the front door, unstopping down the mountain until she reached the edge of the lake, uttering the words, *"Take me to the other side, and keep me hidden from all their eyes. Let me hear the whispers that they say, to bring new light for what is to come my way."*

As she floated across, she thought, 'It would be best to sit in a tree where I would surely be out of everyone's view.'

"Lead me to a branch that's real high; but close enough to a mother's cry."

She sat on a branch, hung over near the top of the tunnel, waiting for a chance to speak to Ms. Winterton. She listened to the whispers of many, but neither made any sense to her. Their words were nowhere near to what really happened the day Rena disappeared.

As she looked straight over the tunnel rooftop, she saw Rena's mother. Her tears were twinkling from the sun, as she walked aimlessly through the woods, seemingly distressed.

Ms. Biddock sat and observed.

Ms. Winterton spotted an officer by the lake, one she never met. He was away from the tunnel, however close enough for Ms. Biddock to hear.

"Officer!" she shouted, wiping away her tears.

"Yes, Ms. Winterton!" He began walking towards her and then ran the rest of the way.

"How do you know my name?" She looked at him with a puzzled expression on her face.

"Everyone knows who you are, ma'am. You're welcome to be here during the investigation. I'm Officer Oxnard."

"Thank you—Officer Ox-nard," she nodded and smiled. "Um, I wanted to ask you, if you don't mind, did anyone come here beside police and forensics?"

"No," he answered and then quickly after remembered, "Oh, yeah, there was one person, a lady who was walking around here yesterday. She was a persistent and an annoying... um, individual."

Ms. Biddock heard the officer and rolled her eyes, tempted to turn him into a rat, but instead continued to listen in on their conversation.

Ms. Winterton tilted her head to the side, "Why do you say that?"

"Well, the officer working in the tunnel on that particular shift told her she couldn't be there. Then, she tried to go inside. He blocked her and told her she had to leave. I had to tell her again!"

"What did she look like?"

"I'll never forget her green piercing eyes. She was taller than we were too. I wouldn't be surprised if she shows up again."

Ms. Biddock could see her suspicious expression when she turned to look at the tunnel.

There was a loud creak from a branch.

She turned back quickly to Officer Oxnard, "Did you hear that?"

"It's probably a weak branch. Watch when you walk around here. You never know when one might fall, especially after that storm we had," he warned her. "I've got to get back to work. If you need anything, just yell."

"Thank you and please let me know if you find anything."

She remained after the officer walked away and thought about the woman he mentioned. 'Why did she want to go in the tunnel?' she wondered and then quickly after, concluded the woman saw something that would shed some light on Rena's disappearance.' Her eyes wandered as she turned around slowly and then walked towards the tunnel, where she wanted to search inside— alone.

No one found any new evidence and she was not surprised, only convinced something mystical had taken her precious daughter away. The once crowded park filled with police and forensic workers, lessened in only a couple of days. Volunteers were down to about only fifty. She wasn't upset, because in her heart she was sure none of them could help. It was up to her to find out what really happened.

"Officer Derwintwater!" she shouted by the tunnel entrance.

He turned swiftly and responded aloud, "Oh, hi, Ms. Winterton."

"Hi. Walk over to the tent and get yourself a cup of coffee," she suggested. It was her only thought at that time to lure him out, for her to search inside.

"That sounds like a good idea. I'll call one of the other officers to watch the tunnel until I get back." He reached for his radio on his shoulder.

"No! I mean, um, there's no need to do that. I'll watch for you," she smiled nervously.

"I can't, ma'am. I'm not supposed to leave without another officer watching. Those are my orders."

"Officer," she responded with a nervous giggle, "I think I can watch for you. I'll stay right here."

"Uh, all right, I guess it would be OK. I won't be long."

"Oh, good!" she replied relieved. "Don't worry. I'll be right here."

"Ok," he smiled.

Ms. Winterton waited until he reached the tent and then rushed inside. She pushed against the walls, feeling for any loose cement blocks, but there were none, so she walked further inside and called out in a loud whisper, hoping Rena would hear her voice. "Rena!" She stopped at the middles end of the tunnel. "Can anyone hear me?" No one answered. She hurriedly walked back to the entrance to see if she had extra time to search, but saw the officer had already left the tent and was heading back to the tunnel.

Ms. Winterton stood back outside as if she had not moved.

"Here you go, Ms. Winterton. I thought you might like some." He handed her a container of coffee. "I didn't know if you liked cream or sugar, so I put both in."

"Yes—that's fine, thank you." Although she was truly grateful, she forced a smile, disappointed with his quick return.

"Well, I have to get back inside. If you need anything I'll be in there," he nodded his head towards the tunnel and then slowly walked away.

"Officer Derwintwater!"

He turned around and calmly responded, "Yes, Ms. Winterton."

"Are you feeling better? You know, from that strange noise you heard."

"Yes, I feel much better, thank you."

An uncomfortable feeling came over him as he thought about it and then became annoyed she brought it up.

Ms. Biddock listened to their conversation and wondered, 'What did the officer hear?'

"Call me if you need anything, Ms. Winterton," he added firmly and then cautiously entered back in.

She had a feeling reminding him of the strange noise would make him uneasy, she wanted it to; it was the only way to make him want to leave sooner. Nevertheless, as she stood outside drinking her coffee, the officer remained inside. Apparently, her plan failed, and so, her thoughts went back to the woman she was told about and kept a close watch out for her.

It was time for Ms. Biddock to come down from the tree and meet Ms. Winterton.

"Quietly lower me to the ground, without making any unexpected sounds."

At the same time she lowered to the ground, the officer was walking out. Ms. Winterton heard him and quickly moved to the side of the tunnel to keep out of sight.

Although he was unable to see her, he heard her and peeked around the corner.

"Ms. Winterton?" He was surprised to see her. "Why are you standing there? I thought you left."

"Oh, yes, I'm about to leave. I'm not feeling so good." She pretended to be sick and then walked up to him, "Is there anything wrong, Officer?"

"No, I just came out for a little air," he answered nervously and then took in a deep breath, "I was going to refill my coffee."

"Are you feeling all right?" she asked seemingly concerned.

"Oh, yeah, yeah, I feel fine, just fine."

"Good, I'm glad. I'll come back later. I'm going home to lie down."

"I'll be going back inside. I hope you feel better." He rushed back in.

"Officer!" she called out to him again and he stopped instantly. "I thought you were going to refill your coffee."

He hesitantly turned around. "I can wait. I'll get more later on. Bye, Ms. Winterton."

"Bye, Officer."

She watched him go back in and then sneakily tiptoed to the side again, knowing he would have to leave some time.

Ms. Biddock and Ms. Winterton were on either side of the tunnel, both moved back further and hid. They were, unknowingly standing behind each other. Soon after he left, Ms. Biddock let out a giggle. Ms. Winterton heard her and slowly turned around.

"Eeeek!" She covered her mouth and stared wide-eyed, startled by someone seemingly hiding like her.

Ms. Biddock turned around right after and was surprised to see her.

Ms. Winterton's hand fell from her mouth when she saw those unusual eyes the officer described.

"You're the lady!"

"You're Ms. Winterton, Rena's mother!" she imitated mockingly.

Ms. Winterton was about to call out for the officer, "Off-," but then stopped instantly when she saw her shaking her head no.

"I don't think that would be such a good idea," she advised. "You went through such extremes to get the officer out of the tunnel and now you want to bring him back?"

Ms. Winterton looked up at her, suspicious, and demanded, "Who are you and what did you want in the tunnel?"

"I want what you want. Rena."

"Rena?" she asked, surprised. "What do you want with my daughter?"

"It's more like I want what your daughter has."

"What does Rena have that you want? She's only thirteen years old! What could she possibly have that is any interest to you?"

"She has the only thing that can bring me home."

"She's has your car?"

"No!" Ms. Biddock whispered strongly. She peeked around the sides of the tunnel to make sure no one was listening and then stood back in front of her. "She has my crystal ball!"

"I know two officers, they're really nice and can get you the help you need, but right now I have to find my daughter."

She ran back inside the tunnel entrance and pushed on the cement blocks again, determined to find another exit. Ms. Biddock stood unnoticed inside the tunnel, partly crouched to avoid hitting the ceiling.

Ms. Winterton turned and shrieked, "Ekkk! How did you get in here without me seeing you? Who are you?" she whispered loudly.

"I was about to tell you before you came up with the idea that I was some kind of lunatic," she answered and then added, "You won't find another way out. At least not the way you think."

"How do you know? What do you know?"

"When you're ready to believe, let me know." She walked passed her and out the tunnel.

Ms. Winterton ran after her.

"I'm ready—I believe!"

Police forensic workers were heading towards the tunnel.

Ms. Biddock turned swiftly, looked down into her desperate eyes, and whispered, "Then return here the first sign of darkness. I'll be waiting, but not for long. Don't tell anyone!"

She stared up at her and shook her head, "I won't!"

Ms. Biddock hurriedly walked away and Ms. Winterton headed home.

CHAPTER THIRTEEN

THE WICKED RETURNS

D evilea arrived in front of her cottage, dreading a confrontation with Clemedeth. Clemedeth waited inside as she sensed her presence nearby and immediately recited, *"When she enters through that door, don't let her move one step more."*

Devilea opened the front door only to find her sitting where she had left her, at the kitchen table; only her eyes were open, staring straight across the room, with no expression on her face.

"Hi, Clemedeth, I see you woke up," she entered casually and then smoothed her soaked strands of hair away from her eyes.

Clemedeth slowly stood with a distant stare and then unexpectedly shouted, "How could you?"

The sound of her voice was one in which Devilea never heard from her before.

"What are you talking about?" she asked unaffected by her reaction.

"You know what I'm talking about. You tricked me!"

Devilea tried to walk away.

"Why… can't I… move?" She looked down at her legs. "I can't… move!" She raised her head quickly and saw Clemedeth with a devilish grin on her face. "What did you do?"

Soon after, Devilea's head went back unexpectedly and her mouth forced open. She saw above her a filled glass that eventually poured directly down her throat. Her eyes showed her, unsuccessfully, fighting the power used against her. Right after, she fell to the floor just as Clemedeth's head had fallen onto the table hours before. Clemedeth gave her the same potion she had given her.

"What goes around comes around," Clemedeth murmured under her breath.

As she levitated her onto the couch, she felt no remorse by what she had done. It was an unfamiliar feeling surfaced inside her, the same Devilea lived with, and she found it to be quite satisfying. She took a wand from the end table and waved over Devilea's slumbering body.

"Your hands and ankles are unable to move and your mouth is shut tight, until I question you."

She walked away knowing what she had done was not right; however the feeling of betrayal made it necessary.

Meanwhile, Clemedeth remained in the cottage, waiting for when Devilea would finally wake. To pass the time away, she went to Devilea's room, probing through her things, something she should have done a long time ago, but thought no reason to. That had certainly changed. Curious to find any hidden secrets, she looked under her bed and found a small silver box, empty with only its black velvet lining. She rubbed her finger against it, to feel if it was as soft as it looked, but instead felt something rough underneath! When she pulled the lining over, she saw paper, folded several times into a small square. Slowly, she unfolded what turned out to be, a letter.

* * *

Dear Devilea,

I want you to know that I love you very much, but I cannot look after you anymore. Although it pains my heart, I know this is for the best. Please do not feel any hatred towards me. I know this won't make any sense to you now, but I'm doing this for you. Follow this trail, and accept any help a stranger may offer.

Love,

Mom

* * *

Clemedeth stood up from the floor and sat on Devilea's bed, holding a letter she never knew existed. Her angry heart quickly changed into one with sadness when she began reminiscing about the day she and Devilea first crossed paths on Tarot's trail.

"Hello," she greeted the seemingly lost little girl with nothing in her possession, except for the clothes she wore and a small purple pouch, hung over her shoulder.

The little girl looked up at her with eyes so sad, stripped of any happiness, and replied, "Hello."

"Are you lost?" Clemedeth asked.

"Yes," she answered as a teardrop fell from her eye.

At that time, Clemedeth lived by herself. One day her mother disappeared and every day for the past three years, she waited for her return. The little girl reminded her of how she felt at that time.

"My name is Clemedeth. What's your name?" she asked with a smile.

The little girl answered, "Devilea."

Clemedeth wondered why anyone would give his or her child a name with the devil inside. There had to be a reason, a reason she had to put aside. It was getting dark and she was not about to leave her alone with nowhere to go.

"Were you with anyone?" she asked.

She answered, seemingly broken, "I'm by myself."

Clemedeth had no other option but to invite her to the cottage.

"Would you like to come to my home? It's right up the trail."

"Yes," she said in a soft voice. She remembered what her mother wrote in the letter, about accepting a strangers help.

"Come on, let's go," Clemedeth smiled.

They walked to the cottage, which at that time painted in bright white, had colorful plants growing in the front. When Devilea walked in, the first thing she noticed were the books on the shelves. Since then they had become a big part of her life, as she read every one of them.

*   *   *

Clemedeth began to regret what she had done to
Devilea. Before she went back to check on her, she folded
the letter just as it was when she found it and placed it
back underneath the lining of the box, as if never found.
Then, she walked down the stairs into the room where she
was still asleep. There she sat in the chair next to her,
wondering what she would say. Was it too late to help her
from the abandonment she had been carrying with her
silently all those years?

*   *   *

Oula had awakened from a disturbing dream, about
Micah not returning home. After he left, she slept straight
through to the next day. Only a couple of hours remained
until night would fall once again onto Wanderamid.
Quickly, she rose from her chair and shouted, "Micah!"
then moved back slowly, pulling the blanket all the way
up under her chin, her eyes staring aimlessly around her
still surroundings. Although she had promised not to
search if he was late, she was unable to keep her word; she
knew he was in trouble.

When she thought about what she should do, she
remembered a long time ago when she and her mother had
taken a walk, at the beginning of a trail behind their home.
They went to meet an old woman at a gloomy and
mystical place.

She recollected her thoughts of that day to have been
very tense. She had been scared for her mother's safety
and her own. The reason for that meeting was unclear to
Oula; she was just a little girl at the time, however,
afterwards her mother seemed somewhat relieved.

"Maybe she can help me. I must go and find her. I wonder if she's still alive," she muttered under her breath. "If she is, she must be up in her age. She might even be dead!"

With less than two hours of daylight left, Oula got out of the chair and walked to her bedroom to change her clothes, planning for a haunting hunt of a woman she was not sure was still alive. "What if Micah comes back and I'm not here?" she thought aloud.

After she changed her clothes, she wrote him a brief note.

*　　*　　*

Dear Micah,

I stepped out for a little walk. No, I am not looking for you. Please stay home and wait for me if you should come back before I return. I shouldn't be long.

Love,

Grandmother

*　　*　　*

She placed the note outside the front door so he would see it when he returned home, if he returned, and closed it, but kept it unlocked in case he lost his key. When she went to the back door, she took a deep breath, thinking about the place she was about to revisit and it made her nervous. She stepped off the back porch carefully and walked on the trail, eventually stopping where the woods began. With only a childhood memory, she continued the rest of the way. The trees were apart from each other, allowing her to walk freely, until debris of broken branches prevented her desired speed.

Another memory from that day came clearly to mind. She remembered her mother's hand grabbed hers tightly, as they entered further into the woods, away from their home.

*   *   *

"Mom, where are we going?" Oula whined.

"I have to take care of something, dear, and through these woods is the only way to do that," her mother replied.

*   *   *

Oula realized after just how much she had missed her mother.

Twenty minutes had since passed. She had become tired and it was hard to see as darkness grew all around her. She took out a candle from the shoulder bag she brought with her and lit it with a match. It gave her enough light to see through the eerie woods, as she neared the old woman's cottage. Suddenly, a brief wind swiftly brushed by her, blowing her candle out! It startled her and with shaking hands, hurriedly struck another match. As soon as she was able to see a little bit clearer, she walked faster, cupping her hand around the flame. After a while, her brisk travel took the breath out from her and she stood still to rest.

A sly voice of a woman echoed. Oula kept still, frightened by whom she could not see, yet brave enough to listen.

"Don't walk any further if you're unsure, you might be startled by what you endure. There is a cost for what you seek, even if you choose only to peek."

Oula ignored the warning and looked past the candle flame she held out in front of her, showing the cottage she had been to only once before, seemingly untouched. "I can't believe it," she whispered under her breath. It was just as she remembered.

She walked out of the woods onto the stone walkway leading up to the door, not even once hesitant with the words used by the voice on the eerie path in the woods. She looked up at the black cat door knocker, which was a little over her eye's height. A brush of dampness in the air touched her face as she raised her hand to lift it. An eye viewer in one of the eye's glowed, causing her to release it and back away while her heart pounded rapidly. Although she wanted to leave, she knew whatever or whoever on the other side, would disregard any further attempts to answer her again.

"Hello! Hello!" she leaned closer to the door.

A squeaking noise caused her to look down and see the knob slowly turning. Her heart stopped beating completely as she watched it open before her, gradually, and then a calming voice spoke to her from behind the arched door.

"You have heard the warnings and still you choose to remain? *What you seek must be dear to you in heart and the cost will also be dear to you to part."*

The door opened completely. Oula held her candle up high to see and then stood in disbelief.

"How can this be?"

*   *   *

Back in Whilom, Ms. Winterton walked on Whisper Lane from the park, staring down at the wide red brick sidewalk. Still a ways from her home, she had begun to wonder about what Ms. Biddock knew about her daughter. As she stepped onto the corner near her home, she raised her head and saw Officer Morley and Wodderspoon driving up, then parking in front of her cottage.

"Ms. Winterton!" Officer Morley shouted out from his window.

She completely forgot about them and kept walking towards her cottage as they exited the cruiser, wondering what to say.

"Hello, Officers," she finally replied with a nervous grin.

Officer Morley noticed immediately something different about her that made him feel awkward.

"Did you go to the park?" he asked.

"Yes, yes, I went, but… they found nothing."

"We're headed down that way. Would you like to come with us?"

"No, no, thank you. I'm very tired and want to get some rest. Please be sure to keep me informed though. Will you?" she asked and then her eyes strayed from his.

"Sure. Is there anything we can do for you?" he asked, concerned with her odd behavior.

"No. Thank you," she answered politely and walked away, heading towards her front door.

Both officers looked at each other and realized something was not right.

Officer Morley went on to say, "We'll stop by tomorrow so you can ride down with us."

She slowly turned and said aloud, "I would appreciate that. See you tomorrow." She gave them a soft grin before entering her home.

"Yeah—good-bye," he muttered under his breath.

Hesitantly, they sat back in their police cruiser and then drove away slowly. Ms. Winterton went straight into the kitchen to make a pot of coffee, to help keep her from falling asleep.

After a little while, there was a knock at the door, followed by another.

"Ms. Winterton, it's us, Officer Morley and Wodderspoon!" shouted Officer Morley.

"What are they doing here?" she murmured, irritated by their unexpected visit. "Yes… I'm coming." She acted sleepy and cracked the door only enough to look out with eyes halfway closed and rubbed them tiredly, "Yes, Officers. What can… I do for you?"

They both gave each other an odd expression and then Officer Wodderspoon answered, "We were wondering what we can do for you. Can we come in?"

"I'm really… tired," she gave a huge yawn. "I'll see you both tomorrow."

Before she could shut the door, he spoke again.

"We'd like to come in and keep you company. It's not good to be alone when you're feeling this way, ma'am."

She knew they were not about to leave so easily, so she opened the door and allowed them to enter. Suddenly, she remembered, the coffee! It was too late; they were already in the kitchen, sitting at the table.

"The coffee smells real good, Ms. Winterton," Officer Wodderspoon hinted for some.

"Yes, it sure does. But, I—thought you wanted to sleep," Officer Morley added suspiciously.

"It's a... habit I guess. You know. It's... something I do every day," she giggled nervously.

The officers felt she was hiding something or— maybe it was the stress from her daughter's disappearance.

"Would you mind if we had some of that coffee, Ms. Winterton?" asked Officer Wodderspoon. "It would be a shame for it to go to waste."

"I'll pour you both a cup you can take with you," she said anxious for them to leave. "I'm really tired. If you don't mind, I'd like to get some rest."

"We understand," he nodded and looked at Officer Morley.

"We understand completely," agreed Officer Morley.

She reached for the cups in the cabinet and then poured them some, relieved they would finally be leaving. They rose up from their seats and walked towards the door. As they turned to thank her, she reached in between them and turned the doorknob. They moved back with their cups held up high and away from her when she did.

"Thanks again for checking on me, but I'm fine—only—tired."

"No problem, Ms. Winterton," said Officer Wodderspoon, "If you change your mind, come on down. We'll be there for a while. Right, Trent?"

"Yep, we'll be there for a while."

"Like I said, I'm terribly exhausted—but thanks," she said appreciatively.

They tipped their big round hats to her as they left and she closed the door close behind them, and then leaned against it the same time she took a deep breath. Soon after, she proceeded to fix herself a cup of coffee, planning a way to get to the park, without anyone seeing her.

Meanwhile, the officers reached the park entrance. They had planned to stop by the tent, but then suddenly took a different direction when Officer Morley gazed over towards the tunnel and saw Officer Derwintwater.

"Officer Derwintwater!" They began walking towards him. "Hey, I wanted to see how you're doing. You were shaken up the other night."

"Ms. Winterton said the same thing," he replied.

"Ms. Winterton?" he asked with a puzzled look on his face.

"Yeah, she was walking around here earlier. I was sorry to tell her we didn't find anything new."

"How did she seem?" he asked interested.

"Well, you know, like she lost her kid."

"Did she seem different from the last time you saw her?"

"Well, one time I thought she left and then I saw her standing on the side of the tunnel. I thought she was hiding. Only a little time went by before she left. She said she wasn't feeling well, which is understandable."

He kept from mentioning she stayed by the tunnel while he went for coffee.

"Thanks, and I'm glad you're feeling better. We'll be going now."

"Hey!" Officer Derwintwater said aloud, "Thanks for the other night, for allowing me to go home early."

"Yeah, it was no problem."

They walked away and came across another officer standing outside by the tent.

"Officer," they both tipped their hats as they walked over to him. "I'm Officer Morley and this is Officer Wodderspoon."

"Please to meet you both. I'm Officer Oxnard."

"Have you found anything new in your part of the search?" he asked interested.

"No, I haven't. Ms. Winterton asked me the same question and I couldn't give her an answer either."

"You spoke with her, too?" he asked surprised.

"Yes, I did. She wanted to know if I saw anyone suspicious. I told her about a lady who was walking around here yesterday."

"What lady and what did she look like?"

"She was just a regular, nosey lady—except for those eyes."

"What about her eyes?" Officer Wodderspoon asked curiously.

"Well, she had these green piercing eyes with a lot of red blood vessels showing in them, more than I've ever seen anyone have. Mystical eyes, that's how they were, mystical. Well, it will be getting dark soon. If you need me for anything, just give a holler."

"Thanks, we will," replied Officer Morley."

"Green piercing eyes? I never thought an investigation could be this strange," Officer Wodderspoon said, scratching his head under his hat.

"Something's strange all right. Let's go back to the tunnel and then head home."

"OK," he replied.

At the same time they walked to the tunnel, Ms. Winterton prepared for her meeting with Ms. Biddock.

CHAPTER FOURTEEN

HEART TO HEART

Micah and the girls woke up from their short sleep in Wishing Willow. Ms. Marsail was in the kitchen nervously waiting to hear what they knew about Jack.

"I'm getting ready to tell my mother about my brother," Avanna warned them.

"Avanna, I don't think she'll believe you. How will you tell her that her son is a pterodoc?" Rena asked.

"And what will she do to us after you tell her something like that?" Micah began to worry.

"Well, we'll soon see," she answered. "Come with me."

They all got up and walked towards Ms. Marsail.

"Hi. Did all of you get enough rest?" she asked anxiously.

"Yes, we did, Mom, thanks."

"Yes," Micah and Rena answered at the same time, smiling.

"Um—are you ready to hear what happened, Mom?"

"Yes, Avanna—I'm ready," she replied and then added, "I'll fix some hot chocolate, and you can begin anytime. I'm listening."

"Mom, I'm ready now."

"OK. I'm listening. I won't make hot chocolate." She nervously sat down.

"First I—we," she looked over at Rena and Micah, "want you to know that what I'm about to tell you, will sound incredible. You have to believe me, because it's the truth."

"I understand, dear, please, go on."

"Jack is a monstrous creature that flies," she blurted out.

She stood up immediately from her chair, "What! Is this some kind of a joke? Are you all right? I knew it! You hit your head! Come on, we're going to the hospital!"

"No!" shouted Avanna.

"Ms. Marsail, she's telling you the truth," Micah said sincerely.

Ms. Marsail quieted down and then gazed over to Rena. "She's telling you the truth," she added innocently.

There was an instant of silence. Everyone was speechless. It was not what Ms. Marsail expected to hear. It was the most ridiculous story she ever heard.

"This is not funny. I ache every second your brother is away, as I did for you. Do you have any idea what I've been through with the both of you gone?" she asked as she began to worry about her daughter's sanity.

"Mom, please," she pleaded while the others kept quiet, "Let me tell you. I'm not making this up."

Her mother gazed at all three of them, only to see their serious expressions. Two people were in her house, she never saw before, and for a moment she thought, 'Where did they come from?' Then, she looked into Avanna's eyes, knowing she had never lied to her. "All right," she said softly and gripped the edge of the table as she sat back down, "Go on, I'm listening."

"Remember the day I disappeared and there was a storm?"

Her mother nodded, "Yes. How could I forget?"

"Well, I went in a storm drain tunnel, the one you saw all of us come out of, and found a crystal ball, a real crystal ball."

"OK, Avanna, that's enough!" She had become increasingly irritated with her story.

"Ms. Marsail, please listen to her," Rena desperately urged.

Ms. Marsail took a deep breath and nodded, "Go on."

"I was scared, Mom. The storm was getting worse, and when I moved further back in the tunnel with the crystal ball in my hands, a bright light shined out from it. I couldn't believe it! All of the sudden I was in another world. That's where I've been all this time. I went through so many tunnels trying to find my way back. Every time I went through them, I noticed I was getting older. I was old when I ended up in Rena's world. The same thing happened to her when she entered Wanderamid, that's what the other world is called."

Ms. Marsail's head went back and her eyes stared at the ceiling. Avanna knew her words were not enough.

"Look!" she pointed at Rena, "Look at Rena's hair!"

Rena bowed her head to show her gray hair. Ms. Marsail was speechless and confused. A young girl, the same age as her daughter, had gray in her hair.

"To make a long story short, we heard you calling for me and Jack. That's how we knew we were in the right tunnel. He called out my name just as we were in the middle of two worlds. When I turned around, I saw that the pterodoc was really Jack. Someone in Wanderamid turned him into a monstrous creature and we have a good idea who might have done it, too. We think it was a witch! We have to go back. I have to help Jack, and Rena has to get back home, so does Micah. I could tell you more, but we don't have much time."

Ms. Marsail almost believed her, but she could not accept her son was a monstrous creature. It was too unbelievable. 'That's impossible!' she thought.

"Do you believe me?" Avanna looked at her with hope in her eyes.

"I believe that you think you saw your brother as a creature, but I still say you hit your head and you're thinking all kinds of crazy things."

"I didn't hit my head! They saw and heard him, too! Do you think they hit their heads?" she shouted.

Right after she said that, she thought about the time Rena hit her head, but did not think it was the right time to mention that. She looked over at Rena and noticed the smirk on her face and her one raised eyebrow, and then she looked back at her mother.

"We have to go, but I'll be back, and with Jack."

She left from the table and went up to her room to get the crystal ball, only to find it gone.

"Where's the crystal ball?" she shouted.

Rena and Micah ran up to her.

"I left it on the bed," Rena said with certainty.

"I know you did. She took it," Avanna replied devastated.

"How will we get back now?" Micah asked.

"I'll talk to her, and don't worry, we'll get it back. It has to be around here somewhere."

They all went back to talk Ms. Marsail once more. There was only one-way Avanna could make her believe, and that was to show her, the power of the crystal ball.

"Mom, did you take it?"

"I have it in a safe place," she assured them.

"It's getting dark. Please, get the crystal ball and come with us to the tunnel, so I can prove to you I'm not lying."

Ms. Marsail thought it could not hurt to do that; after all, she wanted to believe her.

"I'll get the crystal ball, Avanna, but I will hold on to it," she insisted.

"OK, Mom. Thanks. I'll get Rena's clothes out of the dryer now." Avanna looked at Rena then Micah and smiled. "Let's go, Rena."

Ms. Marsail went up to her safe while Micah waited for their return.

They all returned at the same time and sat back down around the kitchen table. Micah and the girls grew nervous, knowing they would be leaving soon. The crystal ball in Ms. Marsail's hands made it clear to them they would surely be entering back into their next adventure, a daring one, and Avanna's mother would be alone—again.

"When we get to the tunnel, Mom, you'll have to give me the crystal ball and stay in Wishing Willow."

"I'm not letting you leave again!" she responded loudly.

Although their story was incredible, she was beginning to believe it.

Avanna looked at Rena and Micah and then back at her mother.

"You're not letting me go. Let me help Jack, so that he can come home with me, for good. It's the only way."

"I'll come with you. We'll find the tunnel back, together."

"That will be too dangerous, for all us."

"This sounds too impossible," she shook her head as the others nodded, agreeing with Avanna.

"But it's true," said Rena.

"It sure is," Micah agreed.

"Come with us, Mom, only to the tunnel, and remember, whatever happens, do not interrupt in any way. We'll be all right. If there's any interference at all, we could end up lost in different worlds. I promise, Jack and I will be back, and we'll all be together again."

"That part is worth believing," she smiled softly. "Let's go see what this crystal ball can do."

"Ms. Marsail, you'll need to bring a flashlight in case it's dark when you walk back home," advised Rena.

Ms. Marsail looked at Rena, who seemed very confident she would be walking home alone and quickly replied, "I'll be right back."

After she returned, they all gave a simple smile to one another and then hurriedly left. Ms. Marsail held on tightly to the crystal ball and Avanna's arm. Her greatest fear was that everything said to her was true.

When they arrived at the tunnel, they walked halfway inside and then made a sudden stop.

"Remember what we talked about, Mom. OK?" she reminded her in a soft voice.

Ms. Marsail tried to keep from crying. She would either find out her daughter completely lost her mind or lose her once again. Avanna held out her hands for her mother to hand over the crystal ball.

"I don't know what to believe, but just in case something does happen," she looked at Rena and Micah, "I want to say, it has been a pleasure meeting you both.

I—also—want to ask you to—take care of my daughter and—please, help her—help my son."

Rena and Micah smiled and nodded.

"We'll stay together until everything's right," Micah assured her. "It was a pleasure meeting you, too."

"Avanna saved my life in my home town and I'll make sure she and Jack return to you," Rena smiled.

"Avanna has found two great friends." She then took hold of Avanna's hand. "I will call for you and Jack every night. I love you both—with all of my heart. Always remember, I will never miss a night calling for you. If for any reason, you're not back, I will find you, with or without a crystal ball."

"I know." She tried to keep her tears from falling as they gave one last hug

"We should go now," said Micah.

They pulled Avanna away gently from her mother's hold.

"Stay near the entrance, Mom. I love you."

"I love you, too...."

A bright light came from the crystal ball, filling the once dark tunnel as she watched them walk further inside. It was an amazing sight. They all turned to take one last look at Ms. Marsail and smiled. She remembered not to go after them and only stood in silence, watching helplessly as her daughter walked into another world. The light remained bright even after they had gone through until gradually it too disappeared. She aimed her flashlight into an empty, dark tunnel. They told her the truth, just as she thought moments before their departure. The feeling was much different from the last time Avanna disappeared; she knew where she was going and knew the whereabouts of her son.

With a new memory and prayer, she walked home… alone.

CHAPTER FIFTEEN

A CHANGE OF HEART

*C*lemedeth was not sure whether to reverse the

spell that kept Devilea from making any unexpected attempts against her.

Devilea yawned, slowly opened her eyes, unable to move her body, and gazed at Clemedeth.

"Do you want to tell me something, like the truth? Why did you trick me?" Clemedeth asked, knowing she could only speak in return to her questions.

Although they had the same powers, the only way they could use them against each other, was when they felt unthreatened by the other.

"I didn't mean to!" Devilea blurted out, seemingly sincere.

"I've taken care of you, and been there for you. When you were alone and lost, I brought you to my home. I thought you would at least respect me enough not to use my own potion against me!"

"I'm sorry. I don't know what I was thinking, really."

"How do I know you won't do it again? Why did you do it anyway?" she asked, disappointed.

"I knew you would get in my way! I wanted the crystal ball!" she responded quickly, and truthfully.

Clemedeth's heart softened yet again when she felt she finally spoke the truth. However, before taking the spell off, she continued to question her more.

"What do you want with the crystal ball? What can the crystal ball do that you want so badly?"

"Those two crystal balls on the shelf in the next room with the empty stand in the middle, is for that crystal ball. We could have more power if we have it. It would make a complete set and give us complete power. I read it, in the books!" she answered excitedly.

Clemedeth saw in front of her a child of greed, a dangerous sign she overlooked. What could she do? If she brought up the letter she found, it could soften Devilea's heart, like it had hers, or it could build the bitterness hidden inside all these years, even more. She decided it was best not to tell her.

"Hmm, more power. What would that extra power do for you, Devilea? The power we have is a curse not a gift! Don't you remember? It changed our appearance and not for the better. Emera can come back and take it away anytime, and I hope that she does! Isn't that what you want?"

"No!" she shouted. "I want this power and more! It makes me feel important! Emera won't come back. And, if she does, I hope I have found the crystal ball by then, so she won't be able to change anything."

Clemedeth saw the emptiness in her eyes. She knew she was referring to her mother leaving her in the woods all alone, with only a barely filled bag and a goodbye note.

"You're important without power. Don't let what someone did to you in the past, that hurt you, affect how you feel about yourself."

"What do you mean by that?" she asked, seemingly bewildered and scrunched up her expression.

"Huh?" Clemedeth responded, realizing she brought suspicions about.

"What do you mean about what other people have done? I didn't tell you anything when I met you. Why did you say that?" she asked.

She wondered if Clemedeth found the note, her mother left her that she kept hidden under her bed.

Clemedeth quickly changed the subject, "What did you mean about Emera and the crystal ball? Is it her crystal ball?"

"I don't know. If it is, she doesn't have it. Rena, Avanna, and their friend have it," she replied.

"What friend?" Clemedeth asked puzzled.

"Some boy was with them when they went through the tunnel," she answered and then quickly after, thought she had said too much.

"Hmm, the boy has to be from here," Clemedeth thought aloud. "Why were they going through the tunnel with Avanna? It was her tunnel, right?"

"I guess. I don't know," she pretended to be clueless.

"Well, I'm glad if she found her way home," she smiled. "I'll take off the spell, if you promise not to use your powers on me."

"I won't use any powers on you," she replied to appease her.

"And, you won't be searching for the crystal ball," she added.

"I won't search for it."

"One more question. Did you ever do anything to anyone else with your powers?" Clemedeth looked directly into her eyes, looking for a sign.

"No. I haven't done anything to anyone," she answered convincingly.

Although Clemedeth had doubts, deep within, she removed the spell. *"Remove those blind restraints from her limbs and let no regrets emerge from sudden whims. There, you can move now."*

"Thanks," Devilea said under her breath as she sat up like a spoiled child. Although the spell had finally lifted, she still felt as if she was unable to move or speak and then hesitantly asked, "Do you... want me to leave?"

Clemedeth was unsure about how to respond. She believed there was a chance for Devilea to change her heartless ways. Were her actions brought about by her mother, or were her mother's actions brought about by her? Nevertheless, she was unable to send her out alone in the middle of nowhere, even with powers. There was hope Emera would return and reverse the curse she gave them; therefore, she needed to keep her close by, until that day came.

"You can stay and we'll take it day by day. OK?"

"Sure," Devilea replied briefly.

"If you're hungry, I can heat up some of that crow stew," Clemedeth offered.

"Sure, I'll have some," she replied.

Her desire for the magical sphere remained in her thoughts. The feeling was too strong to let go, in fact, it had become her passion. She knew she would see Avanna and the others again, but she was not sure when.

CHAPTER SIXTEEN

MEETING AT NIGHTFALL

Ms. Biddock prepared for her meeting with Ms. Winterton. In her black dress and big black hat, she floated down the side of the small mountain. When she reached the lake and glided across to the other side, she noticed the lights in the park with officers and forensic workers searching continuously for a girl, she knew they would never find. Sneakily, she went towards the back of the tunnel, and waited patiently for Ms. Winterton's return.

Ms. Winterton arrived at the park entrance, trying to keep herself hidden from all who were searching for her daughter, she knew they would never find. She continued the rest of the way, peeking from behind every tree, until she reached sight of the tunnel and then quietly walked all the way to the back.

"Sheesh, you scared me to death!"

Ms. Biddock stood with her finger placed up to her lips. Her eyes glowing in the early night convinced Ms. Winterton that there would be a magical awakening! Suddenly, they heard voices coming from inside the tunnel. Ms. Winterton recognized them to be Officer Morley's and Wodderspoon. She stared up into her unusual eyes, horrified they would find her.

"We have to go—now!" she whispered strongly.

"Follow me, quickly!" she responded.

They both scrambled through the woods, towards the edge of the lake.

The officers were already standing outside the tunnel entrance when Officer Wodderspoon heard noises in the back and quickly alerted his partner.

"Trent, did you hear that?" he asked suspiciously.

"Hear what?" he replied.

"It sounded like someone running through the woods," he responded with eyes widened.

"Why are you whispering? It's probably kids snooping around," he looked at him seemingly unconcerned.

"Look, over there. There's something green, glowing through the trees." He began walking briskly through the woods in the same direction they were heading, leaving Officer Morley behind, but then he followed.

Ms. Winterton stopped and whispered, "Did you hear that?"

"Hurry, they'll catch up with us. You must listen carefully to me and you must believe!" she urged.

Ms. Winterton nodded with a look of deep concern and then Ms. Biddock quickly recited, *"Darkness has come and the time is fading away. Lead us back to the place where I stay. Make the ones who follow, stop in their tracks, unable to distinguish all the facts."*

Both glided across the lake and the officers stopped in their tracks, however, Officer Wodderspoon had a clear view and could not believe what his eyes perceived.

"They're floating!" he shouted out in amazement.

"What did you just say?" asked Officer Morley with a bewildered expression.

"They're floating! Two people are floating over the lake!"

"It's probably the searchers in the boat. Will you keep your voice down?"

"There's no boat, only two people floating I said!"

"You mean swimming, floating, without a boat?"

"No, nobody is swimming or floating or using the boat in the water. No one is getting wet. They are f-l-o-a-ting o-v-e-r the water. Look!" he pointed in their direction.

"I… don't… believe it," he responded, dumbfounded while he watched two people floating over the lake, just as he described.

"One of them looks like Ms. Winterton."

"It can't be, she's sleeping, remember?" Then, Officer Morley shook his head and added, "Something's not right. Hurry, let's get in a boat, and go to the other side. Don't mention anything to the others. They'll think we're hallucinating!"

"OK. Come on. Let's go," Officer Wodderspoon replied anxiously.

They ran towards the boats, stepped inside one of them, and quietly rowed to the other side, without anyone noticing. The green glowing light continued traveling up the small mountain, through the storm-damaged trees.

"Keep an eye on that light!" Officer Morley ordered.

"I am, I am," he replied nervously. "It's gone!"

The light disappeared as they stepped out of the boat. Slowly and quietly, they began to climb up where the light ended, near a huge cottage. They walked all around it, listening for anything suspicious, and then heard Ms. Winterton's voice.

"I told you it was her," he whispered.

Officer Morley was surprised to hear that it was.

"Tell me what you know about my daughter?" she demanded.

They listened with their ears pressed against the front of the cottage, under a wide window.

"She found out who I really am and I couldn't let her tell anyone. I thought maybe she could help me get home, and that's when everything wrong," she regretfully replied.

"You expected a young girl to help you get home? What are you talking about?" She shook her head, confused.

"I didn't know the crystal ball was here all along. That's the only thing that can bring me back. If I had known I wouldn't have put—." She quickly stopped and tried to find another way to tell her.

Ms. Winterton stood waiting impatiently for her to finish.

"Go on. You wouldn't have what?"

"I wouldn't have put a spell on her," she admitted in a quiet voice.

"You put a spell, on my daughter?" She raised her arms straight out and was about to push her, however, Ms. Biddock shouted back in an alarming tone of voice!

"Wait!"

Her terrifying outburst startled Ms. Winterton. She immediately dropped her arms to her sides. Ms. Biddock hoped she would control her anger; otherwise, she would have had to use witchcraft on her.

The officers looked at each other, dumbfounded.

Officer Morley whispered with his face scrunched up, "A spell?"

"Where is she? Where's Rena?"

"That's why I brought you here. I found a way that will show you."

"Did you hear her?" Officer Wodderspoon asked loudly.

He was loud enough that they both heard him through the opened window, a few feet above their heads.

"Keep it down!" Officer Morley whispered strongly with furrowed eyebrows.

The felines were purring loudly, pacing back and forth on the windowsill. When they tilted their heads back slowly, they saw Ms. Winterton and Ms. Biddock, along with the felines, looking straight down at them.

"What do we do now?" Officer Wodderspoon asked nervously.

"Walk away, slowly—then run!"

He agreed, and they did just that, or tried to anyway. Their first few steps were as far as they went. Ms. Biddock immediately aimed at them and prevented them from moving any further. Their heads slowly turned and gazed back at the window they were staring out.

Officer Morley did not take the situation lightly.

"You are under arrest... for your involvement... in the disappearance... of Rena Winterton!"

Ms. Biddock tightened his loose lips. Officer Wodderspoon did not move an inch.

"Mm, Mm, Mm, Mm." Officer Morley struggled to speak and his face had become pure red trying.

"What are you doing?" Ms. Winterton yelled appalled by what she had done.

"They'll get in the way. You want me to show you where Rena is, don't you?"

"Yes, but leave them alone. I know them. Let them in. They won't say anything if you show us where she is!" She shouted out to them, "Isn't that right, Officers?"

"Yeah... right!" Officer Wodderspoon would have agreed to anything to get out of their current situation.

"Mm-Mm-Mm," mumbled Officer Morley, shaking his head.

"All right, but they better not make me mad." She finally opened the front door and shouted, "I'll let you move again, but if you try to escape, I'll turn you both to stone!"

After she removed the spell, the officers looked at each other with their wide-eyes and then walked hesitantly inside her cottage.

"Why were you following us?" Ms. Winterton curiously asked.

"Well," Officer Morley began to answer, seemingly annoyed, "You told us you were going to sleep, and then we saw you f-l-o-a-t-ing across the lake, IN THE AIR! I thought that was a good enough reason."

"Are you all right, Ms. Winterton?" Officer Wodderspoon asked genuinely concerned.

"Yes, Officer, thank you for asking," she turned and then smirked at Officer Morley, before introducing them to Ms. Biddock. "This is Officer Morley and Officer Wodderspoon. They started the search for Rena."

"Am I under arrest, Officer Morley?" Ms. Biddock asked, mockingly.

Officer Wodderspoon did not give him a chance to respond or surely, she would have silenced him again. He looked up at her, instantly captured by her unusual eyes, staring into his. "You have magnificent eyes." He felt the warmth of her heart through those eyes, a feeling he suddenly attached to emotionally, and did not want to part away from.

Ms. Biddock's eyes glued to his, speechless, for that was the first time ever anyone said that to her, besides her mother.

"Um, don't you need to show us something, Ms. Biddock, like where my daughter is?" Ms. Winterton reminded her sarcastically.

"Oh, yes… yes," she replied, mesmerized by the officer's kind words. "Wait here. I have to get my grimoire." She walked briskly to her office.

"She's a witch. She's getting her grimoire. That's… a book of spells. We're getting out of here, now!" Officer Morley ordered his partner. "We have to get her outside and to the boat!"

"Wait! I'm not going anywhere. She knows where my daughter is!"

"Ms. Winterton, she's a crazy—witch person. She doesn't know where your daughter is. I told you, we will find her, and we will."

"Did you see what she did to you? She stopped you from moving… and talking. I'm beginning to think maybe she should have kept you that way."

"Trent, she's right, you know… not about keeping you that way… we wouldn't get far. She definitely has magic powers."

"OK, I'm back. Follow me." She walked ahead of them carrying her book of spells, leading them down into the cellar. "Be careful, the steps are very steep." She turned the lights on and pulled the curtains closed. "Did you tell anyone you were coming here?"

"No, we didn't let anyone know. But, I'm sure they'll wonder why the boat is on the other side of the lake," Officer Morley replied nodding his head, smiling.

"Then I must hurry," she responded sarcastically, and then laid her magic book down on the round wooden table, lined with chairs evenly, side by side. "Everyone sit, please."

All were speechless and amazed; as they witnessed the book grow before their eyes after she had opened it.

"If you hear any disturbances outside, you must ignore them, for the peephole is all you should pay attention to."

Ms. Winterton looked at Officer Morley. "I will do whatever I have to do, to get my daughter back. Don't try to stop me."

No one said a word. They waited to see what she would bring about. Her arms swiftly stretched out in front of her and a powerful voice shouted out from within. *"Create a cavity for us to see, the world where I so long to be! Rena arrived not long ago; her whereabouts has to show! So open wide, let us look inside, for an image you surely can provide!"*

The cellar began to rumble and the chairs began to shake, as they held tightly to the edge of the table, so not to tip over. Nevertheless, a strong gust of wind swept across their faces and they quickly stood. Their chairs flew back as they kept holding on, watching Ms. Biddock with her arms stretched out wide. As the wind calmed, a sparkling hole suddenly appeared before them. They stared amazed with its zigzagging edges, opening more as each second passed. They were witnessing, a window into another world, forming before their eyes. Then, a bright light burst through unexpectedly and caused their eyes to close, and then slowly they opened to a view of three figures.

"It's Rena!" Ms. Winterton whispered loudly. "But, who is she with?"

Ms. Biddock announced in a faint voice, "It's my son—Micah." Her arms fell loosely and she collapsed in the chair behind her.

Ms. Winterton yelled, "You've got to get up!"

However, Ms. Biddock's concentration broke and once again, the peephole closed with a razor sharp sound, ending the view into Wanderamid.

"No, No!" she cried out and then she too slumped back down in her chair.

CHAPTER SEVENTEEN

AN UNKNOWN SACRIFICE

Oula could barely keep from falling as she stared into the old woman's familiar eyes.

"Mother, is it really you?" Her eyes filled with tears.

"Yes, my dear Oula, it's me."

They stood many years older than when they saw each other last. Memories from years before flashed in her mother's mind. Her heart became alive again with the love for her daughter. As they embraced and slowly walked inside, the door gradually shut behind them. They sat by the fireplace that revealed many lines on their faces, both sitting next to the special bond they thought had been lost forever.

"Mother, I thought you died. All these years I thought something terrible had happened to you. You've been here all this time?"

"Yes," She held back her tears, "Remember that day we came here, to this cottage?"

"Yes, I do. I thought about that day as I walked here," she replied with a mild grin, unable to fathom the moment.

"Well, I had worries then and needed help. In order to get the help I needed so desperately, I had to sacrifice what meant the most to me. The old woman that lived here granted me the time I needed before fulfilling my agreement. I asked if I could start when you were older. Those were heartbreaking years, knowing that I would have to leave, without telling you."

"What did you need help for mother? What was so terrible that you had to make such a sacrifice?" she stared, curious to hear her reason.

"I had a premonition once, that when you had a child, that child would have powers along with a different appearance, which would make her youthful years, suffering ones. I could not accept that." She shook her head and placed her aging, weak hands on Oula's, "Your father is a warlock. Any powers he has, passed to you, only they would carry through to your child. The old woman that lived here said she could help me prevent that from happening, as long as you weren't pregnant at the time I decided to leave."

"But, I was expecting Emera when you left. I didn't tell you because when I found out, you had already gone. I had her seven months later. You've been here all this time for no reason."

Oula was devastated and the thought made her mother feel faint.

"Mother, are you all right?" She grabbed a pillow and quickly placed it under her head.

"How is my granddaughter? Did you both suffer?"

"Yes, mother, we did," she answered regretfully. "All throughout her school years and I tried my best to help her. Her eyes were piercing green and she was taller than the other children were. They gave her a hard time."

"What do you mean by, her eyes were, Oula? What has happened to her?" she asked, concerned.

"I don't know." She lowered her head. Her face filled with sadness as she stared down at the floor. "One day she just… didn't come home." She lifted her head and said with tear-filled eyes, "You have a great-grandson too. His name is Micah, a brave young boy, fifteen years old. You don't have to stay here anymore. You have to come with me!"

"I'm unable to walk anywhere far, Oula, sometimes I can barely stand. I don't know what would happen if I walked away from the agreement. I have one year left to complete it. I didn't think I would live this long. If it's the last thing I do, I will help you and Micah find Emera. That's why you came, right?"

Oula began to cry. Although she had found her mother, her daughter, and grandson were still missing.

"I've lost Emera, and now Micah! He left to help these two young girls from that awful little witch over the hill. He's not back yet. I can't just sit and wait, knowing he could be in trouble."

"Walk with me into the next room, Oula, and I will help find them. I will not allow you to sacrifice time as I did. You must promise me that after they have been found, you leave quickly through the woods and never look back."

"I'm not leaving you here, Mother," she responded firmly, wiping away her tears.

"You must," she spoke in her weak voice. "Don't give precious time, if you don't have to. I don't have much left anyway. What's done is done."

Oula sadly walked her mother into the next room and helped her to sit down.

"Close the door, Oula."

She closed the door and sat down beside her, looking around at the seemingly normal surroundings. There had been no indication of anything magical, until her mother aimed to press an oval, ruby stone, attached to the table's edge, as big as the palm of her hand. The room began to transform as candlesticks appeared all around on the walls and lit up by themselves. In the center of the table, a huge, sheer ruby glass ball rose to the top, giving a shimmering light that filled the room. Then, she turned to look at her mother, amazed she was as young as the last time she saw her, forty-two years before, dressed in a red colored gown with cream-colored trim, sparkling with tiny ruby stones, flickering from the luminous lights.

"Remember me always as you see me now. Only those who saw me last can see me as I was in the past, and only in this room. Give me your hand."

Oula placed her hand into her mothers who then gripped tightly to hers.

"Keep still and concentrate deeply into the ruby crystal ball. Don't get distracted," she said.

Although Oula looked much older, she felt at that moment, the little girl she once was, as she waited patiently for her to recite.

"Micah has been away from his home, he's with two others who are unknown. His mother Emera also unseen, please bring them to us on your mystic screen!"

The candles blew out and an echoing voice stretched loud and then low in a strong whispering way. They could not identify whose it was, but then gradually, it had become clearer, one of a young girl. They stared deeply into the ruby crystal ball when a vision appeared, showing two girls, and a boy.

"It's Micah!" Oula shouted amazed.

"We must watch and listen," her mother whispered strongly.

"Rena, we're back! Look, we're not too far from where the other one was," she pointed further down the trail.

"Keep it down, Avanna. We have to watch out for Devilea," Micah warned.

"Micah's right," Rena agreed. "We have to watch out for her."

"I'm sorry. I just need to find my brother."

"We'll find him. Let's go to my cottage first. I have to make sure my grandmother's all right."

"Micah, you can go. It's a long way there and past the witch's cottage. I have to let Jack know that I came back for him."

Oula and her mother both looked at each other. "Jack?" they questioned, confused, at the same time.

Oula knew right away Micah would help the girls look for Jack, and she was extremely concerned.

"I'll go with you. You can't go alone. The only place Jack could be hiding is in a cave." He pointed through the trees. "The caves are in that mountain, through those woods."

Para turned and asked, "Why would Jack be hiding in a cave?"

"Ask the ruby crystal ball to show us this person, Jack." Oula was also curious as to why he would be hiding in a cave.

Her mother agreed and without hesitation called out, *"Show us—this Jack—who hides in a cave—on a mountain side. We need to see he is safe and hopefully still alive. Fill this ball with his features to show whom they need to save. Give us confirmation their path will lead his way!"*

The ruby crystal ball instantly turned dark gray, swirling within its mystic lens. A huge eye showed, blinking slowly and instantly they felt a strong sense of sadness. Then, the view became clearer, showing all of Jack.

"Aaaaah!" they screamed, as they saw a monstrous creature lying in a dark cave.

"He's ten times their size! He'll kill them all!" Oula shouted.

"Oula, please, calm down… oh no," her mother placed her hand over her heart.

"Mother, are you all right?" she waited for her to respond.

"Yes, yes… I'll be… fine. Stay still… let me catch my… breath. That creature gave me quite… a scare. If that's what, or who they're looking for, and it must be, the ruby crystal ball has never given any false answers, he must be harmless to them. He has to be the young girl's brother. Someone evil turned him into that—monstrous creature."

"I know who did it. It was that cruel, awful little witch, Devilea. I have a feeling she did something to Emera, too!"

"You must beware of someone with such powers. There is no telling what else she's capable of doing. The poor soul inside the body of that creature must be turned back to who he once was, or he will be cursed forever."

They both looked back slowly into the ruby crystal ball and watched him lay, lonely in a dull, dark cave. Just like Micah, they wanted to help him.

"We must find Emera's whereabouts," her mother urged.

She longed to see the grandchild she thought she saved from a cruel childhood.

"But," she went on to say, "I have to do it myself. You have to go and find Micah. There is not much time and there is no telling when this Devilea will find them. I won't let either of you down."

Oula was torn. Her heart ached at the thought of leaving her mother, who she had just found after forty-two years, and at the same time, did not want to lose the chance of helping Micah.

"All right, Mother, but I assure you, I will return."

Her mother pressed the ruby button and the ruby crystal ball lowered back inside the table. The room appeared as it was when they first entered. Oula gazed over at her mother, old and frail, like she was when she answered the cottage door. She smiled, and they nodded their heads sorrowfully, as they began walking back to the entrance that brought them together.

"I'll watch over you and remember always, no one will ever love you more."

"Oula hugged her, "And no one will love you more than I."

She turned and walked away slowly, not knowing if it would be the last time, she would ever see her again.

"Wait! Take this!" she shouted out to Oula as she pulled out an amulet from around her neck, a ruby octagon that fit in the palm of her hand and handed it to her. "This will protect you when you need it the most. Your thoughts of desperate need will bring out its power. With the touch of your hand, press it against your heart. Go, you must hurry!"

She handed it back to her, "But, you may need it."

"The only thing I need is for all of you to be safe," she responded with worried eyes.

Oula nodded and gave her a mild grin. "I will be back for you and then we'll all be together." She hoped she would live long enough to see that day and for her mother as well.

As she hesitantly turned away and walked briskly towards the woods, she suddenly stopped before entering to look back, only to see the cottage door closing. She continued, never to look back again, confident her mother would find Emera and she would find Micah and the girls.

CHAPTER EIGHTEEN

A WITCH'S CURSE

Micah and the girls began their search for
Jack. Neither knew he had a certain amount of time to
change back to who he once was. They on Tarot's trail,
and found a new path they never noticed before, Caven's
Way. It began like the other trails, only when they entered,
the trees closed behind them, hiding the entryway.

"Everybody, stay close," he whispered strongly.

"We will," Rena quickly responded, looking
nervously side to side, "Avanna?"

"Yes?" she tapped her back, "I'm right behind you."

She let out a heavy sigh, "I thought you were lost in
the fog."

Micah walked in front of them on the tight path. The
fog had become thicker, causing them to slow their pace.

"It's hard to see." He looked back briefly with his
eyes squinted, "Hold on to my backpack."

Rena and Avanna grabbed hold of his backpack and
walked behind him through the heavy fog. They saw the
tip of the mountain Micah spoke about, through an
opening of the trees and then suddenly, over their heads

heard the sound of branches moving, when there was no wind. They looked up to the sight of leaves falling.

"Can we walk a little faster?" Rena asked anxiously. "This fog is making me nervous!"

"I'll try." Micah continued to walk cautiously in front of them. "Don't let go of the straps."

Avanna peeked around his shoulder, "Are you sure Jack's in that mountain cave?"

"If you were a pterodoc, where else would you be able to go and hide away from Devilea?"

"I suppose you're right."

"Avanna, we'll find him. He has to be there," Rena believed.

Even through the heavy fog, Avanna noticed Rena's change in appearance; she aged more since Wishing Willow. So far, Rena had gone through three tunnels and she, one. Rena noticed Avanna's hair turned a little gray again too. It reminded them both of what happens when going through tunnels, searching for their way home.

The fog had lifted and finally they were able to see a little clearer. All of the sudden Micah stopped, along with the girls.

"Did you hear that?" he asked in a frightened tone of voice.

The girls stood still, without making a sound and listened again to branches moving above them. They all looked at each other and then slowly, tilted their heads back. A creature with green piercing eyes, like Ms.

Biddock's, looked down at them. In an instant, there were more of them, as they stood in fear, unmoving.

"What do we do now?" Rena asked, barely moving her lips, afraid even to blink an eye.

"I don't know! I'm thinking!" Micah whispered nervously.

"They're all around us." Avanna worried they would all jump down.

One jumped down directly in front of Micah while the girls hid closer behind him.

"What does it want?" Rena whispered, holding the strap with a tight grip.

"Let us through!" Micah shouted bravely.

She gazed down at them and asked, "Where—do—you—wish—to go?"

Micah stared up at the familiar sight in front of him that stood at least seven feet tall and asked daringly, "Who wants to know?"

"Micah, there are three of us and many of them." Rena nervously shook his arm, "Just answer the question!"

"All right," he pulled his arm away and then finally responded to the meddling creature, "We're on our way to the mountain."

The others, who remained sitting up in the tree, began whispering and then after quickly stopped.

"Why—do you—need to—travel to the—mountain?"

"Who are you and why do you want to know?" he demanded.

She moved closer to them, staring down with eyes glowing brightly. "My name is Fleur and we're—the aftermath—of a witches curse, when one chooses to reject another because of their appearance," she spoke in a regrettable tone of voice. "Once we were as you are, but now we're trypalls. For many years, we bullied a young girl in school, while unknowingly, created a bitter witch. She disappeared from Wanderamid for a long time now." She leaned down slowly, and then asked firmly, "Does that answer your—question?"

Her strong breath odor silenced them. They covered their noses and then quickly turned their heads away. When she gradually straightened up, the air cleared, only enough to tolerate and then hesitantly turned back to her.

"Which witch? What is her name?" Micah looked up with one eye squinted.

Furiously, she raised her fists straight up in the air, "Emera—Emera is her name!"

Micah remained unmoved when she mentioned his mother's name. Although their eyes were like hers, his mother was not a witch, he would have known.

In an instant, she calmed and curiously asked, "Do you know about the monster in the cave? Is that why you wish to travel there?"

Micah turned to look at Avanna, who had no expression on her face and then back at Fleur. "Yes, we know, he's her brother."

Avanna stood close at his side.

"He was cursed as a pterodoc. We've come back to help him."

"Help him?" she chuckled tiredly, wondering how they would do that.

"Yes. We have an idea who did it and plan to talk her into changing him back."

"Maybe she can help us!" another trypall shouted excitedly above them.

"Keep silent!" Fleur yelled nervously. "Only Emera can change us back to who we once were!" She leaned down to Micah and whispered, "Was it, Emera?"

"No. I'm—sure it wasn't," he hesitantly answered, covering his nose.

The girls scrunched up their faces and held their breath.

"Hmm," she sounded unsure and then slowly straightened up.

Fleur straightened up just when the girls could not hold their breath any longer.

"But, if we see her, we'll ask her to change you back," he attempted to appease her.

"We'll hold you to that. In exchange, we will show you a quicker passage inside Rawky Mountain, which will take any delays away from your search."

"That's nice of you, Ms. Trypall," Avanna responded, pleased no harm would come to them.

"My name is not, Ms. Trypall, child! My name is Fleur!" she shouted angrily.

They took a step back.

"I'm… sorry," she quickly calmed, "I've been this way… for a long time. It's very depressing, you see, our curse is feeling exactly what we had inflicted on Emera all those years. We all know now what we've done." She looked away sorrowfully and then swiftly looked back, "Follow me, and I will show you the passage." Right after, she shouted at the others, "I will return soon!

They all sat quietly and watched her lead them, fading into a hidden path they never would have found if it were not for her. It pained her to walk. Her long arms ached along with her eyes. Emera made sure all their past remarks would remind them every day, the suffering they caused her growing up.

Avanna felt a little sorry for her.

"Fleur, you don't have to show us where the passage is, just point in its direction."

"No! I must lead you to it," she insisted, "to guarantee your help in return."

Micah listened, but felt no sympathy for the trypalls. He thought they got what they deserved.

"We would help you anyway, right?" Rena looked at them both.

"Yeah—sure," Avanna hesitated and then nudged Micah's arm. "Right, Micah?"

Micah ignored the question and asked, "Are we almost there?"

"Yes," she answered unsurprised by his attitude.

The rest of their travel to the mountain, through the dark and misty path, was silent. At times, she stopped and turned around just to make sure they were still behind her. For the first time, she felt uncomfortable in a place she had lived since becoming a trypall.

"We're here," she finally announced.

They stood directly in the front of nature's wall, with trees of Roewkall Woods growing against it, as if trying to hide its' view. When they looked towards the sky, the leaves blocked any further visions of the mountain along with the darkness that filled the home of the trypalls. All of them began to wonder how they would enter with no opening in sight.

"Here is where you will enter." She stood before them with her body slumped over and her eyes glowing strongly.

"What do you mean? We need to go inside a cave. There's not a cave here. What are we supposed to do, carve one?" Micah complained. He thought they had wasted their time, believing in her.

"That way will lead you to the cave," she pointed away from where they were standing. "Then, the cave will lead you to the monster."

"Will you stop calling my brother a monster?" Avanna shouted.

"I'm sorry," she apologized. "I shouldn't have said that."

"Let's just go inside," Avanna urged the others.

"She's right, let's just go," Rena agreed.

"Go where?" he shouted.

Fleur angrily pointed at the mountain, "Stare at the mountain walls and you will see!"

Startled by her response, they walked stiffly behind her as she led them in front of an open space between the only two trees attached to the mountain. The veins of their leaves began to sparkle lightly, continuously, with a crisping sound. They stood staring only inches away without so much as a blink when a mirrored-like appearance magnified and caused them to become suddenly sick.

Rena, quickly lowered her head."I feel sick."

"So do I," Avanna, uttered faintly.

Micah's brows furrowed and his head hung low as he whispered, "We shouldn't have come here."

"What is that you hold in your arms?" Fleur curiously asked Avanna.

"It's a... crystal ball."

"A crystal ball... for what?" her interest grew.

"To get back home after we use it to help my brother."

"Hmm, can I see it?" She held out her long arm.

"No! We… have to go now." Avanna began to feel unsafe in her presence.

"Oh, all right, another time then, when we see each other again, right?"

"Yeah… right. Now how do we get inside?" Micah asked again, impatiently.

"You must keep your eyes closed and hold on to each other when walking through," she instructed. "If you want to help her brother, you must go this way. You'll only waste time going another."

Avanna shook her head in agreement. "We're not turning back now."

Micah looked at Fleur with weary eyes and asked, "What do we do once… we're inside?"

"There'll be great dampness all around. It will seem too cold and just when you think you can't bear the great chill anymore, you would have reached a corner. Place your hands against the right side, all three of you, and push hard! It is then you'll see an enormous space known as the core. Don't be afraid of the bats! Just as long as you ignore them, they won't bother you. As soon as one is attracted, the others will be, too. That's when you must run as fast as you can. The path you see will be the path leading to the m-o-n… I mean, your brother. I'll wait here, until your presence is no more. Remember, we will hold you to your word."

She stood silent, for she said all she had to say. It was up to them to follow her directions, bringing them to Jack. As they held on to each other, preparing to enter through the mirror-like image, Fleur unexpectedly yelled, "Run!"

She startled them and within the second before they jumped in completely, she reached swiftly with her long arm and snatched the crystal ball away from Avanna's hold! She ran back through the woods as fast as she could. It was her way of making sure, they would return.

Inside the mountain, Micah and the girls slowly opened their eyes when Avanna blurted out, "She took the crystal ball! Now we can't help Jack!"

"Don't worry," Micah responded in a soothing manner. "She only took it to make sure we return to them, and we will, to get it back."

"It's freezing in here," Rena quivered uncontrollably.

"It's just... how... she said... it would be," Avanna began to tremble. "Hurry, get to the corner before we freeze to death!"

"Wait! Look!" Micah pointed down at the ground and shook his head. "She forgot to mention that!"

CHAPTER NINETEEN

A SENSE OF CHANGE

While Clemedeth heated crow stew in the kitchen, Devilea sensed the crystal ball's change of hands. She knew at that moment, it was back in Wanderamid. Her stomach gurgled and it was not from hunger, but for the unstoppable desire to retrieve it!

"I'll be outside for a minute!" She hurriedly walked out of the cottage.

"OK! It will be ready in about five!" Clemedeth kept stirring the pot of crow stew.

Devilea closed the door and sneakily walked past the open window and onto Tarot's trail, as her senses led her towards its new possessor.

Clemedeth set the table with two bowls filled with her homemade crow stew. She was expecting Devilea to be walking inside at that moment, but she did not. As she walked over to the door and opened it to look out, Devilea was nowhere in sight, she was gone and Clemedeth knew where, to find the magical sphere. She grabbed her cloak off the rack next to the door and then took a wand from the end table where she noticed two already missing.

Meanwhile, Devilea stopped where the tunnel used to be. As she stood wondering what area they had arrived back in, she noticed the mountain view over the trees in Roewkall Woods, vaguely through the darkness.

"That's where Jack must be and I bet that's where they're going," she murmured.

Fuller made it back to the others, who then gathered around her. "What are you holding?" one asked curiously.

"It's a crystal ball." She excitedly held it up for them to see.

"Where did you get that?" another asked seemingly alarmed.

"I took it from the monsters sister," she smiled and then quickly noticed after their angry faces. "I had to! It's the only way I could make them come back to help us!"

"You started something Fleur! Now they will never trust us or help us! Don't you see?" he yelled furiously. "I believed they would have come back! We all believed it!" His anger instantly turned back to pure devastation. "It was safer with them than with us. Something terrible will happen. I can feel it."

"But I did it for all of us, to guarantee the help we need to become who we once were."

He filled with disgust and along with the others, climbed back up into the trees, knowing only evil would come from what she had done. Fleur climbed up the opposite side from where they were and waited. Within a few moments, she heard loud rustling of leaves.

"Close your eyes and keep them closed," she whispered strongly to them.

"Why? What's the matter?" they anxiously whispered back.

"Just do as I say and stay quiet," she demanded.

Their whispers stopped instantly.

It was Devilea and her senses became stronger with every step she took. Their whispers from above fell to her ears and she slowed down to a complete stop.

"Show yourselves! I heard your whispers!" Then, she warned them, "I have a magic wand in my hand and I will use it if you don't come out!"

Fleur placed the crystal ball steady and securely onto a branch beside her and then jumped off, down into the thick patch of fog. Devilea heard her, but could not see who or what it was.

"Where are you?" she shouted, looking around aimlessly, everywhere but up.

"I'm right here," she stood calmly, looking down at her.

"Move closer to the sound of my voice," Devilea commanded.

Fleur moved closer and then stood still, gazing down at her through the fog that began to break apart.

"Who are you?" Devilea snickered when she stared up and saw the odd creature, tall and with long arms that hung past her knees, her dark, green glowing eyes clearly showed many red blood vessels, more than Emera's.

"Fleur," she replied in a disgusted tone.

"Fleur?" she chuckled. "You don't look like a flower."

Fleur lowered her head and asked firmly, "Who are you and what do you want?"

"I'm Devilea, and I sense my crystal ball is here. Do you have it?" she asked, waving her wand and then aimed at Fleur's face.

"I don't know what you're talking about."

"Oh, but I think you do. Who else is here?" she looked around, suspiciously.

"There is no one else, just myself."

"But I heard whispers from more than one."

Fleur straightened up. "Well, you must have heard wrong."

Devilea held her wand up high and warned again, "If the others don't appear before me soon, I will turn you into a six-legged raccoon!"

"No! No!" they shouted and then jumped to the ground beside Fleur with their open green glowing eyes.

"Look what we have here," she smiled wide-eyed. "Now tell me! Where is my crystal ball?" Devilea stared up at their still expressions, waiting impatiently for one of them to answer. "Tell me!" she threatened once again with her wand held up high. Lightning soared out from its tip and hit the branch Fleur rested the crystal ball on, knocking it to the ground and landing right by her feet.

All the trypalls let out a huge, heavy sigh.

Devilea bent down and waved her hand under the thick mist where she heard the heavy thump and then felt what she hoped to be the crystal ball. When she picked it up, she was excited to see it was.

"How did you get this?"

"Give it back!" Fleur demanded. "We need it to guarantee they'll help us change back to the way we once were!"

"Who did you get it from?" She ignored her reasons and twirled the wand in front of them.

"I took it from a young girl," she regrettably answered.

"Were there two others with her?"

"Y-Yes," she answered, powerless against the evil child that stood before her with a mind as crooked as the nose on her face. "They're inside the mountain, searching for a pterodoc."

The other trypalls lowered their heads. They thought she said too much. Soon after, so did Fleur.

With widened eyes Devilea curiously asked, "Are they coming back here?"

"We were hoping they would," she spoke with a blank stare that clearly showed her hopes fading.

"Oh, I'm sure they will. You stole the crystal ball from them," she laughed with raised eyebrows.

"Only to make sure they'd keep their word!" Fleur justified.

Her laugh decreased to a mere chuckle. "Keep their word to help you?"

"They said that if they see Emera, the witch who cursed us, they will bring her here."

"Emera—ha, she's not even in Wanderamid, so you see, holding on to this crystal ball is useless to you. Get used to living as you are, because you're not going back to the way you were."

Fleur could not accept being a trypall forever. She stared down at the magic stick used to threaten them and desperately asked, "Could you help us with that wand of yours? Could you change us back?"

"The only one, who can undo what was done to you, would be the one who did it! I have no power to do so, nor do I care to try. Ha-ha!" She walked away laughing, holding her wand and crystal ball.

Fleur could not believe how evil a young girl could be, and then remembered that's how she and the others were to Emera.

"Emera will return! She will! You'll see!"

In an instant, Devilea stopped and slowly turned around, gliding back across the misty ground until she stood in front of them once again, her face red with anger.

"She will never come back. If you even whisper to anyone that I was here I will know and then turn all of you into something worse than you already are."

She terrified them with her threatening words, and with a blank stare glided in reverse, eventually turning and continuing out of the woods, back to her cottage.

"What do we do now?" a trypall asked loudly. "What do we say when the others come back?"

"We don't say anything. You heard her! We say nothing," Fleur responded nervously.

"They know you took their crystal ball! They'll want answers!" yelled out another.

"I know that, but we can't say anything. Stay hidden. I'll think of something to tell them, without mentioning Devilea."

They climbed back up in the trees, waiting for Micah and the girls to return. While they waited, one thing came to mind Fleur forgot to warn them about.

*   *   *

At the witch's cottage, Clemedeth opened the front door and felt the brisk air against her face before pulling the hood over her head. She began walking the opposite direction from Amble Road, the way Devilea mentioned Avanna and the others entered a tunnel. Although she had powers, it was uncomfortable for her to walk alone in the dead of night.

In the distance, an opening through the trees seemingly invited the moonlight to shine ahead of her path. An echo from someone's voice traveled towards her, a familiar devilish laugh, which could only come from one.

She shouted out, "Devilea!"

There she was, a moonlight ray shining down on that devilish grin only she owned with a crystal ball in one hand and a wand in the other. Then, her laughter stopped.

"Clemedeth?" she murmured.

It was too late to hide the magical sphere, she was sure she had seen it.

"What are you doing out here all alone?" Devilea acted concerned.

"You're asking me that?" she replied, staring at the crystal ball in her hand as she approached her.

"I saw Rena. She told me to tell you good-bye. I went with her to the tunnel and she rolled the crystal ball back to me. Now, they're both where they belong. Well, now we can go eat that crow stew. Let's go!"

"Wait a minute. Do you expect me to believe that?"

Devilea was speechless, but not for too long.

"If you don't believe me, go through the woods, over there, where I came out from," she pointed towards the dark, foggy wooded area behind her.

Clemedeth stood for a moment, undecided.

"No, that's all right, let's go home." She thought to search in the morning and then remembered the friend Devilea mentioned earlier. "What happened to the new friend you saw them with?"

"What friend?" Devilea asked, dumbfounded.

"You said that there was a boy who went with them through the tunnel, remember?"

"Oh, that boy, yeah, well he wasn't with Rena when I saw her this time. I don't know… where he is. Maybe he stayed in Avanna's world. I didn't… ask her."

"Hmm, I wonder where he went. He had to have been from here."

"I really don't know. Like I said, he probably stayed with Avanna," she responded unconcerned.

When they saw their cottage nearby, Devilea began to run all the way to the front door. Clemedeth followed. She immediately headed for the shelf, where the other two crystal balls were, placing the one she had onto its empty butterfly stand and at the same time Clemedeth hung her cloak on the rack, all the candles went out.

"Devilea, where are you?" she shouted.

"I'm here… over by the shelf!"

Soon after, they were in awe as they watched thick, strong rays come out from all three crystal balls, shining brightly through the open windows of their cottage and seen throughout Hemlock Village.

"What did you do?" Clemedeth yelled from across the room.

"I only set the crystal ball on the stand," she said, pointing at the shelf.

"Get away from it, hurry!" she demanded.

Devilea ran to her side as the light gleamed brightly along with a sound that caused only Clemedeth to cover her ears. They stood watching, oblivious to what would happen next. The power from the three crystal balls had finally emerged, and then the light soon after, began to fade. With the wave of her hand, Clemedeth immediately lit all the candles before every room had a chance to turn pitch black. Then, she turned around and was surprised to see Devilea's eyes with a powerful glow to them.

"What happened to you?"

"I don't know… I feel different. What happened to you?" Devilea noticed her eyes glowing.

"What have you done, Devilea?" she asked in a worried tone of voice.

"I told you before that we'll have more power!"

"But you couldn't handle the powers we had! Please, go and sit down on the couch."

Clemedeth was overly concerned about how Devilea would use those added powers.

Devilea walked to the couch slowly. Clemedeth walked behind her with the lit candle. After Devilea hesitantly sat down, Clemedeth sat beside her and set the candle on the table. She thought about what to say, but at the same time, knew her words would be unheard. Maybe it was best not to say anything. She stood up and instead, suggested, "Let's just eat our meal."

"OK," Devilea responded calmly, silently overjoyed with her new added powers.

They both went into the kitchen. Devilea sat at the table and waited for Clemedeth to pour them something to drink.

"So, how are you feeling?" Clemedeth asked curiously.

"I feel great, like I can do anything," she smiled, content.

"We could do anything before, what's the difference?"

"I don't know yet!" she had become increasingly annoyed with all of her questions. "Let's just eat."

"We'll talk about this, later."

Clemedeth quickly became unconcerned, due to Devilea's attitude. The extra powers that entered Devilea, entered her, too, and she was ready to use them.

Before their eyes stopped glowing, Devilea placed her drink up to her lips and looked at Clemedeth.

Did she trust her enough to drink it?

CHAPTER TWENTY

HEMLOCK'S EVENING RAYS

Oula arrived at Amble Road, ready to walk the path her grandson traveled. Rays of light were shooting towards the starry sky of Hemlock Village. Within seconds, it was over. Exhausted from her walk back through the woods, she forced herself to continue towards the hill that would lead her to Micah and the girls. The streets were empty and silent all around her, as she was finally approaching the foot of the hill. She stopped to take a deep breath, wondering how she would make it to the top; however, her strength seemed to grow more and more with the determination she had in bringing her family together.

She put one foot in front of the other as she began to climb. Just when she thought she was unable go any further and with only two feet away from reaching the top; she managed to grab hold of a thick vine hanging from a low branch. She pulled as hard as she could, until finally her strength brought her to view the beginning of Tarot's trail, the witches' trail. Carefully, she walked down the short hill, staring at what seemed to be, a tight and rough path.

"Oh, my, this will be a task," she murmured before starting her quest onto the misty trail.

*   *   *

All those years after Emera finished school, she remained on her property. Everything she ever needed, she grew conveniently in her yard. When Micah turned five years old, Emera did his schooling at home. After she disappeared, he taught himself, with help from his grandmother.

*   *   *

Although the moonlight peeked through the trees, there still was not enough light for Oula. She pulled out her candle, lit it, and then walked through still air, until she would finally become tired. The candle went out as she let out a deep breath, staring at what she believed to be, the witch's cottage. Bats flew out from the trees and blocked the starry sky above, preventing her from taking another step.

"Go! Shoo!" She waved the unlit candle frantically in front of her to keep them away.

Clemedeth stood up from her chair. "Is that someone yelling outside?"

Devilea moved the glass away from her lips and set it down on the table. They both walked briskly to the front door, curious to see who was yelling in the darkness of night. When they opened it, they saw an old woman waving a candle at bats flying all around her.

"I'm going out to help her."

"I'm going, too," replied Devilea.

They both went out the door and Devilea swiftly put her hands up in the air, aimed at the bats, and in an instant, they hung lifeless above their heads.

"Phew!" Oula was exhausted and her hands fell to her sides. She stared amazed at the sight of bats, frozen in flight.

"Are you all right?" Clemedeth asked while Devilea stood quietly beside her.

Oula knew who they were and remembered Devilea being the one with the crooked nose.

"Yes, I'm fine," she grinned nervously.

"Why is an old woman like you, roaming on the trail at night?" Devilea asked suspiciously.

"Devilea, can't you see, she's tired. I'm sure the last thing she wants to do right now is answer your questions."

"Hmm, I guess you're right."

"Well, thank you for your kind assistance. I'll be on my way," she hesitantly walked around them.

"Wait, come in, and have something to eat," Clemedeth offered kindly.

"Here we go again," Devilea mumbled under her breath.

Clemedeth heard her and with raised eyebrows said, "It's the least we can do, since it's our bats that terrorized her."

"I really should be going," Oula nodded with a nervous grin. "Good-bye."

Devilea wondered why she was so nervous and then tried to persuade her to stay. "Come on, just for a little while.

She was hesitant, but finally accepted, "Only for a few minutes."

Clemedeth was happy that she did, "Oh, that's great!"

Before Devilea entered inside, she waved her hand and the bats moved once again. They flew towards her and as they sensed her evil stare, directed back over the cottage roof, from where they came. As she entered the cottage, she saw the old woman already sitting at the table while Clemedeth filled an extra bowl.

"I'm Clemedeth, and this is Devilea," she introduced as she placed the bowl filled with crow stew down in front of her.

Oula smiled nervously, "My name… is Oula."

"Are you from around here, Oula?" Devilea asked.

"Yes," she answered and then her stomach weakened as she stared down into the bowl. "Really, I must be going. It's late and I have to get home. Thank you so much though, for your kindness."

"Are you sure? You can stay here until daylight if you'd like," Clemedeth offered.

"Really, I should go now."

Devilea stood with her. "I'll watch the bats don't try to attack you again."

"Thank you," she replied gratefully and nodded. "Good night."

A feeling of relief came over her when she took the first step out the door. They stood watching her walk safely onto the trail. Devilea remembered not seeing any cottages in the direction she left, leading her to believe Oula was untruthful about heading home.

"She was a sweet old woman, wasn't she?" Clemedeth smiled, turning away from the door.

"Yes, she was. She seemed a little nervous though."

"No, she didn't, Devilea. She's an old woman. You always seem to find something suspicious with everyone."

Devilea gave a heavy sigh. "I'm really tired."

"Let's finish our meal," Clemedeth suggested and then walked away, towards the kitchen.

"No thanks, I've had enough. I'm going to bed."

Clemedeth stopped and turned to see her standing by the stairs. "Are you sure?"

"Yes, I'm sure. I'll see you in the morning." She began to walk up.

"OK, good night."

"Good night." She ran the rest of the way.

Devilea went to her bedroom and thought about how she could leave without Clemedeth noticing. Meanwhile, Clemedeth cleared the kitchen table and kept her ears open, knowing it was not the end of the night for Devilea. After, she rested on the couch and her eyes slowly closed, drifting into thoughts about her mother, who disappeared years before.

*　*　*

"Clemedeth!" her mother called out from the bottom of the stairs, "Come down for a minute!"

The vision showed Clemedeth walking down each step in slow motion as her mother stood waiting for her with a worried look on her face. At that time, she thought nothing of it.

"I'm going for a walk," her eyes gazed at the shelf then back at Clemedeth. "I'm proud of you and love you so much."

"Mom, I'll be here when you get back. You're only going for a walk, right?" she looked up at her with eyes so bright.

"Yes, dear," she put her arms around her, "I'll return. I'll return."

*　*　*

Clemedeth tossed and turned on the couch and then quickly rose up, covering her face with her hands, wiping away her tears. She had no idea how much time passed and ran to Devilea's room only to find she was not there.

"Devilea!" she yelled, searching in every room.

After, she ran down to the front door and grabbed her cloak off the rack. Her wand was still in the pocket as she walked out the door. Then, she stopped, wondering whether to search for her or wait until she returned.

CHAPTER TWENTY-ONE

A WELCOMING TWIST

Officer Morley attended to Ms. Winterton, slumped in her chair, passed out, after she had lost Rena once again. Officer Wodderspoon walked over to Ms. Biddock, who also passed out.

"Flynn, could you go to the kitchen and get two glasses of water?" he asked anxiously.

"Yeah, sure, I'll be right back," he quickly left Ms. Biddock's side.

"Ms. Winterton!" Officer Morley shouted in her ear, "Are you all right?"

His voice awakened Ms. Biddock instead. She moaned before opening her eyes to see him trying to get Ms. Winterton to answer and walked over to them.

"Ms. Winterton," she tried to help wake her, "Ms. Winterton."

Ms. Winterton slowly turned to her and asked in a faint voice, "Where did you send Rena? Bring her back to me."

Ms. Biddock saw the sadness in her eyes and felt the sorrow she had caused. "I'll bring her back," she said.

"I have the water!" Officer Wodderspoon ran down the stairs and jumped over the last two steep steps, water spilled out of the glasses when he did.

He handed them each a glass of water.

"Thank you," they both replied gratefully.

"Ms. Biddock, did you say the boy in the peephole was your son?" he asked, curious.

"Yes, his name is Micah." She turned to Ms. Winterton, "I know what you're thinking. If it makes you feel any better, Micah is a good boy, and I know he'll protect Rena."

"Oh, I shouldn't worry that the son of a witch, who caused my daughter to go into another dimension, is with her. Is that what you're saying?" she gradually sat up straight.

"He's not like me. He's better than I am. I know how worried you must be, but you don't have to worry about Micah."

"We need to open the peephole again," Officer Morley suggested. "This time we need to be stronger," he looked over at Ms. Biddock with raising eyebrows.

"Yes, he's right," she agreed. "Let's all stand. Again, you must all be quiet and do as I say."

They all stood, waiting for her to recite the words, opening the window to Wanderamid.

"Show us again what you presented before, three figures walking through all open doors. Clueless to

dangers approaching so close, bring us the answers we need the most!"

The swirling winds came like before slamming closed the cellar door.

"Emera, where are you, we're searching for you! If you can hear me, answer!"

Ms. Biddock heard a voice she could not recognize calling for her.

"Who's Emera?" Officer Wodderspoon asked with a confused look on his face.

Ms. Winterton and Officer Morley scrunched their shoulders and both replied, "I don't know."

They all looked at Ms. Biddock.

"I am," she admitted.

Officer Morley's eyes widened, "You're Emera?"

"Yes. However, I don't know who is calling for me. Concentrate hard for a vision," she ordered calmly, curious to see who it was.

They all concentrated and a vision finally appeared of an old woman looking directly at every one of them. She stared at Ms. Biddock's eyes and knew instantly it was her granddaughter.

"Emera!" she shouted, excited to have found her, "It's me, Grandmother!"

"You can't be my grandmother, she's dead."

"I didn't die. There's no time to explain right now." She hurriedly informed, "Your mother was here asking for help to find you and Micah."

With eyebrows furrowed, she asked, "What are you talking about?"

"Micah went to help two young girls, in case they needed help from Devilea, the rotten witch. Your mother wanted to know where he was, so she came here, and I found them through the ruby crystal ball. She's gone to search for them. I gave her my amulet for safety, but I'm still worried. I told her I would find you. You need to come back. Where are you?"

"I'm in a town called Whilom. Devilea is the reason I'm here. I have to find the crystal ball; that's the only thing that can bring me back. I'm not sure the girls still have it. Devilea must not get a hold of it. Without it, neither the girls nor I will be able to return home."

"Stay right there, Emera, I'll be back." She went for her grimoire to search for another way to bring her back, without the crystal ball.

"Grandmother!" she called out to her, "I'm losing you! Don't go!"

The vision was gone, but the peephole was still open.

"What's going on?" Ms. Winterton asked, watching as the vision disappeared.

"No one move. Keep still," Officer Morley whispered loudly.

"Do as he says," agreed Ms. Biddock.

Another vision appeared, although it was not clear enough to see, they could hear voices.

"Don't forget what Fleur told us," Rena reminded.

"That's Rena!" Ms. Winterton said, excitedly. "Rena!"

"Quiet, don't call her yet. We must hear where they are," Ms. Biddock advised firmly.

"I remember. Just watch out for those bats," warned Micah.

"And, walk slowly," added Avanna.

Ms. Winterton listened and watched with the others as the vision became clearer. She gasped. "Why are they in a cave?"

"Wait! Look!" shouted Micah.

"What's going on?" she watched helplessly with worried eyes.

No one knew how to answer. The vision disappeared and Ms. Biddock's grandmother came back into view.

"Emera, I'm back!"

Ms. Biddock anxiously told her, "While you were gone, we saw Micah and the girls. They were in a cave."

"They must be close to Jack," she assumed.

She scrunched up her face, "Jack? Who's Jack?"

He's a pterodoc, supposedly cursed by Devilea," she responded calmly.

"What's a pterodoc?" Ms. Winterton looked at her with a confused expression.

"A monstrous creature with wings, but don't worry, he's harmless. By the way, who are you?"

"She's the mother of one of the girls," Ms. Biddock replied briefly.

"This is getting me more confused." Her grandmother shook her head and then asked, "Did you see your mother at all in your vision?"

"No, I didn't. I'm starting to worry about her now."

"So am I," she sighed and then remembered, "I have my grimoire. I'll recite a spell that just might work. I will open a peephole here, but will keep the vision in my crystal ball. I need all of you to believe, which shouldn't be hard by now, right? Only you, Emera, can come through, not the others. It's best they stay where they are."

"Grandmother, do you mean to tell me that I could have gone through the peephole? All this time I've used them for visions and tried to communicate with them, but I had no idea I could go through them." She slowly shook her head as she looked down.

"Sometimes, Emera, we don't think of other ways because we're stuck with certain ways. Do you understand what I'm trying to say?"

She looked up with a worried grin. "I think so."

"All right, then. Maybe some day we can talk about it," she nodded. "Are you ready?"

"Wait!" she turned to Ms. Winterton. "I need you to care of my felines. I'll come back for them when we bring Rena back. You have to stay in Whilom, so we can hear you calling for her, when we find the tunnel to bring her home. You see, they change locations there. That's why it's difficult to return quickly."

"How will I know what is going on? I don't even know if I can trust you."

Officer Wodderspoon knew the time for Ms. Biddock to leave was about to arrive. At any given moment, his whole life would remain meaningless, if he chose to give up what he felt strongly to be his one and only chance at real happiness.

"I'll go with her," he said.

"What?" Ms. Biddock turned to him, surprised. Although she felt the same as him, it seemed so surreal.

Officer Morley shook his worried head, speechless.

"You can bring only one with you, Emera," her grandmother approved.

Ms. Biddock turned to Ms. Winterton once more and asked, "Will you take care of my felines, and will you make sure you call out for Rena every night, so we can find her tunnel home?"

She looked at everyone, curious to hear what her answer would be and then replied, "Yes. Please hurry and bring Rena back home."

Ms. Biddock looked at Officer Wodderspoon, "We will."

Both officers shook hands before their departure.

"Flynn, are you sure you want to do this?" he asked, stunned by his offer. Although he had more to say to his friend, there was not enough time.

I'm sure, Trent," he nodded with a calm grin. He then assured Ms. Winterton, "Don't worry; we'll do everything we can."

"I'm not sure this will work, Emera, and…. Flynn is it?" her grandmother warned.

"I have a feeling it will," Ms. Biddock smiled and then asked, "Are you ready Officer?"

"Please, call me, Flynn," he smiled in return. "And, yes, I'm ready."

"Good Luck—to the both of you. Be safe." Officer Morley stood still as he watched his partner about to enter another dimension.

Ms. Biddock and Officer Wodderspoon smiled as they held each other's hand tightly, waiting for her to bring them through.

"Hold on tight for there may be a fall, this travel you make without a crystal ball. The other side is seconds away, so bring forth determination to make your way. The winds grow stronger and the fear stays longer, as you pass through. The sickness you feel will seem so unreal, as the end results follow soon."

They went into the peephole hands first and a strong force slowly pulled them until they entered fully. Ms. Winterton and Officer Morley watched, as they faded into thin air. Their bodies only a bright white mist, swirling into the entrance of Wanderamid. It closed swiftly and then silence filled the cellar space as their thoughts, questioned reality. Suddenly, a circle of light moved on the cellars closed curtain!

Ms. Winterton panicked. "Shut the light!"

*   *   *

Back in Wanderamid's Rawky mountain cave, Micah and the girls stared down at the ground as they stood inches away from a hole filled with darkness, with only a tight ledge to walk around it. An opening at the top of the mountain gave them light, but it was not enough.

"Rena, take my hand and Avanna, hold on to Rena's. We're all going to walk along the ledge to get to that corner Fleur told us about."

"I'm scared," Avanna said with a frightful tone in her voice. "What if we slip?"

"Walk slowly, and don't look in the hole, only on the ledge, to see where you're going," he explained calmly to her.

"That doesn't answer my question, Micah. What happens if one of us slips? I don't think Rena's strong enough to hold on to me."

"OK. Rena, you get in front of me, that way I'll have your hand and hold Avanna's with my other."

"That's sounds better," she said, slightly relieved with the new plan.

"Well, what if you slip?" Rena thought of another possibility.

"I won't slip! Right now I'll jump in!" he became annoyed with all their questions. "Now can we do this or not?"

"OK, we can do this," she replied nervously.

"Remember," he reminded the girls, "Don't look in the hole."

"We won't," Avanna replied.

"Lean against the wall for support and take little steps at a time."

They held each other's hand tightly as they took each step, focusing only on the ledge they walked on. The corner seemed closer, but not enough, as the mist in the hole lifted, limiting their view even more.

"Stop!" he suddenly stood still. "Make sure your feet are touching the wall. Slide against it slowly and be careful not to trip."

"OK!" they both responded nervously.

The white mist gradually turned blue and it became colder. Their bodies were slowly freezing, making it harder for them to move.

"I don't think I can move anymore, I'm too cold," Rena shivered uncontrollably.

"So… am… I," Avanna replied with a shaky voice.

"I feel… it, too. Try to think… warm. We're… almost there."

"Something's pulling… me." Avanna screamed, "Aaaaah!"

Micah still had both Avanna and Rena's hands.

"Help me, Micah," she cried as she hung inside the hole.

Rena shouted as she looked down, "I can't see her!"

"I still have... her hand," Micah struggled to hold on to her. "Rena! Can you get to the corner —yourself?"

"Yes, but you need me to help you."

"I need my other hand to help Avanna. Slide against the wall and wait at the corner."

"I don't know where... the hole ends."

"Just... slide against the wall and stay still... when you reach it!"

"O...k," she hesitantly answered.

"Avanna, try and swing your other hand up to me. Try!"

"OK, but I'm still being pulled. Please help me!" she cried.

"Swing your arm!" he shouted.

Avanna swung her other arm the same time Micah waved his free hand under the blue, cold mist she was in. "I got... you."

With his feet gliding against the mountain wall, he pulled her along with him while she still hung inside, held by an unforeseen force. Whoever or whatever it was, did not want to let her go.

"Let… her… go!" he yelled from the top of his lungs and then pulled with all his might.

"Micah!" she looked up at him and he saw her terrified expression.

"Put one foot at a time on the ledge, hurry!"

"I can't, they're frozen!"

Rena made it to the corner. She stood frightened for Avanna and cried out, "Avanna, remember, anything's possible!"

"Something is hitting the bottom of my feet!"

"Hold on!"

Micah slowly pulled her up and then quickly let go of her one hand. He grabbed onto her waist and lifted her onto the ledge in front of him, then pushed her towards Rena, who was standing at the corner, relieved it was all over.

"Avanna, you scared me," she gave her a hug. "I thought you were going to… I'm just glad you're OK." She looked at Micah and smiled, "Thanks, Micah. I'm so glad you're with us."

"I said I'd protect you," he reminded them. "Are you ready to get out of here?"

"Ready," they both responded eagerly.

"Then let's push hard against the wall."

They all pushed against the damp cave wall with all their strength, grunting with every step, as it slowly and painfully engraved the palms of their hands, neither complained. When they could go no more, it finally opened, leading them into the open space, the core of the mountain. They entered inside with their heads hung low, so not to attract the bats Fleur had mentioned.

Avanna gasped when one flew over their heads.

Micah heard her and whispered loudly, "Keep your heads down!"

Rena was curious and lifted her head to see hundreds of bats hanging from the ceiling She immediately began to tremble and then screamed, "Run!"

All of them ran up the stone steps as fast as they could. The bats swarmed over them, and as they finally reached the top, they saw Jack lying on the damp cave floor.

"Jack!" Avanna screamed; the swarm of bats still behind them.

He opened his eyes and saw Avanna and her friends in need of his help. Slowly he stood his heavy body and then began roaring loudly! The bats flew into one another as the sound pierced through their heads, causing them to change direction. Avanna and the others covered their ears and crouched down on the cave floor as his loud roar echoed in the wide-open space. The sound of bats flying over them suddenly stopped. Finally, they were gone. Then, they stood back up before Jack, thankful for his help.

"Jack, it's me, Avanna. I don't know if you can understand me. I told you I would come back for you. Mom wanted me to tell you that she loves you, and that she's waiting for the both of us to come home."

His eyes turned glassy and he gave a heavy sigh. He knew he couldn't go home, not the way he was.

"He understands you, Avanna." Rena watched as tears formed in his eyes.

All who were there with him felt his sorrow.

"Well, we should be going now. Don't you think?" Micah blurted out.

"Jack won't be able to go down those steps," Rena responded as she wiped away a tear that fell from her eye.

"Look!" Micah pointed out towards the opening of the cave. "He can fly out!"

"But, how will we get out? I'm not leaving the same way we came," Avanna spoke out when she thought about the hole and the bats. She looked over at Jack, saddened by what he had become. He felt her fear and then lowered himself to the ground.

"He wants to fly us out," Micah said, amazed that he understood.

"He can't carry us all!" Avanna said. She thought that their weight would be too heavy for him.

"You and Rena can go together. He can come back for me," he suggested. "He'll have to leave you on Tarots trail, outside Caven's Way."

"But we have to find Fleur!" Avanna shouted. "She has the crystal ball!"

"We'll go back into the woods once we're all safe on the ground," he calmly assured her.

"Alright," she hesitantly nodded and looked back at her brother with a mild grin, "Do you understand what he said Jack?"

Jack roared loudly.

"OK!" Micah placed his hands tightly over his ears, "Good boy, Jack! After you set them down come back for me. I'll be waiting here."

Micah helped the girls onto Jacks back and they gripped his wrinkly skin tightly as he flew out the cave's entrance, over Caven's Way, approaching Tarot's trail. Micah sat on the ledge waiting for his return.

"Over there, Jack! Down there!" Avanna said aloud.

He dove through the opening and landed them softly in front of Caven's Way, lowering all the way to the ground, and then they jumped off.

"Jack, go get Micah and then come back here."

CHAPTER TWENTY-TWO

THE RUBY AMULET

Although Oula was searching for her grandson, she could never let him know that. She promised him.

When she approached the main entrance to Caven's Way, she heard faint voices and slowed down her pace. She slowed down and hid behind each tree she came to, one at a time, until she was able to them hear more clearly.

"You have a little gray, but not that much. What about me, do I have any?" Rena lowered her head for Avanna to see.

"It did the same to you. I guess whatever we enter in Wanderamid, will make us a little older, just like the tunnels," Avanna assumed.

All of the sudden Oula heard loud flapping of wings in the sky.

"Look!" Rena pointed out towards the sky. "They're here!"

It was Jack. He landed next to the girls with Micah on his back.

Oula remained quiet.

Micah noticed their hair turned grayer.

"What happened to you?"

"It must have happened when we went through the mountain's entrance. Just like the tunnels, it made us older," explained Avanna.

"There's nothing we can do about it now. We have to help Jack." Rena was ready to do all she could to help him. "Let's find the trypalls and get back the crystal ball."

"Should Jack wait here?" Avanna asked. She was not sure where the safest place would be for him.

"No. He should wait on Amble Road. He'll be safer there, away from Devilea's sight," he said confidently.

"Jack, go on the other side, to Amble Road and wait for us there. We have to go back onto Caven's Way, to get the crystal ball. It's our only way to get home."

Jack roared.

"Shh! Try to keep quiet. Go on. We'll meet you there. I don't know how long it will take us, but we'll be there. I promise, Jack."

Jack slowly lifted up and flew over the trees towards Amble Road.

"I know that was hard for you, Avanna," said Rena.

"Don't worry, we'll help you get your brother back to the way he was," Micah reassured her.

"Thanks."

"I'll go in first. You girls stay behind me."

"OK," they replied at the same time.

They walked onto Caven's Way trail, determined to get back what Fleur took away from them. Oula secretly followed and mimicked the girl's steps to remain unnoticed.

Devilea was still on Tarots trail when she heard Jack, flying over the trees.

"Hmm, it seems as though they found you," she murmured, as she looked at the sky. "I'll deal with you later. I have to check on the little creatures first, or should I say big creatures."

Micah and the girls arrived at the same spot they met the trypalls. They looked up in the trees and saw Fleur looking down at them.

Avanna immediately shouted, "Where is my crystal ball? Come down here, now! You tricked me! We told you we'd be back!"

Fleur jumped down and stood in front of them. "Yes, to get the crystal ball, not to help us!"

The others jumped down and stood by her side.

Micah took a step forward. "Hand it over, Fleur."

Rena looked up at her with her face scrunched up and her eyes squinted, "Why did you even take it from us?"

"It doesn't matter. We don't have it anymore."

"What do you mean?" Avanna asked with a bewildered look on her face. "You took it from me!"

"I lost it," she replied briefly. "It's somewhere… in the woods."

"You're lying," Micah expressed his disbelief.

"We need the crystal ball to get home!" Rena shouted.

Fleur stared at the girls and ignored everything they said. "You both look different from the last time I saw you. What happened inside the mountain?"

"Oh, yeah, the mountain, "Micah remembered, " You forgot to mention something or maybe you meant to."

"What is he talking about?" she asked the girls puzzled, and then soon after, it came to her mind. "Oh, you're talking about the hole! That was not intentional. I truly forgot about that."

He squinted his eyes angrily, "I don't know how I can believe someone… who stole from us!"

"Fleur, give us the crystal ball now," Avanna demanded. We have to go!"

Oula was listening as she stood behind a tree unnoticed when suddenly a sickening feeling came over her. She turned, surprised to see it was Devilea and a little taller than she remembered, floating above the misty ground.

Devilea leaned down slowly and mockingly whispered in her ear, "Hel-lo—Oula."

Oula immediately reached under her shawl for the amulet given to her by her mother and held it tightly in her hand, pressed it against her heart with closed eyes, and wished she; Micah, and the girls would disappear.

In a flash, they were all outside her mother's cottage.

"Grandmother?" he looked at her with a puzzled look on his face.

"Where are we?" Avanna looked around an unfamiliar place.

"And who lives there?" Rena added, pointing at the cottage.

Oula stood with the amulet still held tightly in her hand. "I'm so glad you're safe, Micah!" she pulled him close with one arm.

"Are you all right?" he asked concerned.

"I'm fine now that you're back." She wiped the tears of joy from her eyes.

"How did we get here and why are you here?" he asked, shaking his head, confused. "You should be home."

"Micah, is this your grandmother?" Rena interrupted. Oula was glad she did.

"Yes, it is."

"Hello. I'm Rena and this is Avanna."

They both smiled.

"It's nice to finally meet you girls."

"What's that you're wearing around your neck?" he asked. He had never seen her wear such a big chain before.

With all the excitement seeing her grandson again, she had completely forgotten about the ruby amulet still clenched in the palm of her hand. When she released her hold, they were amazed at what they saw.

"That's beautiful," Avanna said with a gleaming smile.

"Yes, it is," agreed Rena.

"I never saw you wear that before," Micah scrunched up his face and looked at it closer, "Where did you get it?"

"My mother, your great-grandmother, gave it to me," she smiled.

"You must have had it a long time," assumed Rena.

"No. She gave it to me today," she responded quickly.

"She couldn't have given it to you today," Micah chuckled. "I think you need to…." He suddenly stopped.

There was a loud, strange sound from up high, where they stood near the entrance to the woods, branches broke and fell by their feet.

"Move back!" he yelled to the girls, as he pulled his grandmother away.

"Aaaaah!" yelled Officer Wodderspoon as he and Ms. Biddock fell through from the top of the trees and thumped to the ground.

Ms. Biddock landed on top of him. Both moaned from their hard fall.

"What's that?" shouted Rena.

During all the commotion Oula's mother opened the front door of the cottage.

Oula turned her head and called out to her, "Mother!"

"Oula, you're back!" She was delightfully surprised. "I found Emera!"

Emera saw her standing with her back to her, "Mother!"

Oula heard the voice of her daughter, she had not seen in three years. She turned around slowly and stopped when she saw her. "Emera!"

"Mom, it's really you," Micah chuckled in disbelief.

Rena and Avanna could not believe that Emera was Ms. Biddock.

"What?" Rena muttered under her breath, then turned to Micah, then back to Avanna and yelled, "Run, Avanna!"

They both ran through the woods and away from Ms. Biddock.

"Rena, Avanna! Why are you running! Come back!" Micah yelled, and with a dumbfounded expression, looked over at his mother.

"Please, stop them!" Ms. Biddock urged Officer Wodderspoon.

His eyes widened before he advised her calmly, "Use your… magic."

"Huh?" Micah murmured. He began to realize that the trypalls were speaking of his mother.

Ms. Biddock saw the expression on Micah's face. She felt she had betrayed him by not telling him about her magic powers. It was something she had to explain later. First, she had to stop Rena and Avanna. Her eyes stared towards the woods and she raised her arms.

"Calm yourselves and slow down fast! Reverse your steps to where you stood last!"

Her arms fell swiftly and soon after, Avanna and Rena screamed, "No!" They both floated back towards them in reverse, landing where they stood moments before.

"Are you all right?" Micah asked, concerned with their behavior.

"Stay away from us!" Rena stepped away and Avanna stood close behind her.

His eyebrows rose. "Why? I didn't do anything."

She pointed at Ms. Biddock, "Is that your mother?"

"Yes. That's my mother." He stood firmly by her side.

"She's the reason I'm here," she said, angrily.

Micah turned to his mother and asked puzzled, "What's she talking about?"

"I can explain."

"It was a mistake," Officer Wodderspoon interrupted.

"Who are you?" Micah questioned the man he knew only as the one falling out of trees with his mother.

"I'm Officer Wodderspoon. I came here to help Rena get home. Ms. Winterton is worried about her, as she should be." He bent down and picked up his hat that soon after, covered his slightly turned gray hair.

"You know my mother?" Rena's voice suddenly calmed, but then quickly after, she looked at Ms. Biddock with an angry expression. "What did you do to my mother?"

"No, Rena. She didn't do anything to your mother. In fact, your mother's in Emera's, I mean, Ms. Biddock's cottage with my partner, Officer Morley, as we speak. She was helping your mother find you," he explained calmly.

Rena was confused and said, "We heard you try to stop the spell. I could have gone home, but you stopped me."

Ms. Biddock stood filled with regret. "I tried to tell you that I only wanted the crystal ball. Before that, I had no idea it was in Whilom. I needed you to get it from the witch, who tricked me into your hometown, but it was too late and I couldn't reverse the spell. You saw the tornado send me back to my cottage.

Rena looked at Avanna and then back at her. "We remember. But, how did you get here, without the crystal ball?" she asked in a suspicious tone.

"I created a magical peephole from my grimoire, and saw you and your friend in one of the visions. When I heard your mothers cry, echoing through my windows, I knew that I had to let her know you were all right. My grandmother helped us enter through an opening to Wanderamid."

"Why didn't my mother come with you instead of—him?" she pointed at Officer Wodderspoon.

"Because you will need to hear her calling for you, when you find the tunnel that will lead you home. Besides, it's too dangerous."

"We don't have the crystal ball anymore!" Avanna blurted out.

"Everyone, let's calm ourselves down," Officer Wodderspoon suggested.

"Yes," Oula's mother agreed. "Come inside."

Micah looked at the girls and nodded for them to walk ahead of him. Ms. Biddock and Officer Wodderspoon walked behind. When they all entered inside the cottage, they stood near the wood burning fireplace.

Emera hugged her son and then squeezed him tightly. "I've missed you so much."

"I've missed you, too," he replied with a smile, slightly embarrassed.

"Hello, Mother, it's good to be back," Emera hugged her along with Micah.

"I'm so glad the both of you are finally home. I have someone I want you to meet. Come here, Mother. This is your great-grandson, Micah, and your granddaughter, Emera."

"I never thought I would see this day," she smiled tearfully.

"If it wasn't for her, we wouldn't be here together right now."

"Thank you for your help, Grandmother," Emera said with watery, glowing eyes.

"And, thanks for bringing us all together," added Micah.

Rena walked up to their little reunion. "What do we call her?"

"Well, you'll call me by my name, Para." She smiled and then added, "We will all help you get back home."

"But, my brother, Jack." Avanna lowered her head and rubbed her tear-filled eyes. "We vanished from Caven's Way, before we could find out who had the crystal ball."

Oula quickly responded, "I was at the witch's cottage and saw a few on one of the shelves."

"They aren't the ones," said Rena, "I saw them, too. There were two of them."

"No," Oula was positive, "I'm sure I saw three. I'm not senile yet!"

Rena believed her. "Then that could only mean Devilea has it, along with more power."

"We have to get it back," Emera said with a worried expression.

"My brother is on Amble Road waiting for us. I have to make sure he's all right." Avanna ran towards the door.

Para shouted, "Wait, you must have something to eat first!"

Avanna stopped and turned around.

"I'll place a shield of protection around your brother until we reach him," Emera told Avanna.

"All of you go and sit at the table. I will make us something to eat." Para hurried towards the kitchen.

"I'll help you," Oula walked away briskly.

"We don't have time for that, Grandmother. I'll prepare us something," said Emera. "Everyone sit down and close your eyes. Think of something simple you crave and it will appear."

They all waited for Oula and Para to join them at the table before they all sat down. Then, they closed their eyes and thought about what they had been craving. When their eyes opened, they were amazed at what they saw.

"Much better than crow stew right, Avanna?" Rena asked, staring at her cheeseburger and fries.

"Yes, it sure is," she replied surprised.

Meanwhile, back at Caven's Way, Devilea floated back towards Tarot's trail, to the witch's cottage when suddenly; she stopped with an urge to find Jack. Wherever he was, the rest were sure to be.

CHAPTER TWENTY-THREE

DISHONEST DISTRACTION

Officer Morley shut the light in Ms. Biddock's cellar. They stood still as they listened to the footsteps outside the window.

"I know it's the other officers!" she whispered anxiously. "You have to go outside and pretend you were looking around. You can come back later. They can't know I'm here."

"What will you do when I'm gone?" he asked, concerned, worried she would try to enter the peephole.

"I won't lie. I will try to reopen the peephole, to see if they made it through safely and have found Rena."

"Just promise me you won't try to go through. It's too dangerous," he looked into her worried eyes.

"I won't. You heard Emera. I have to stay here in Whilom so Rena can hear my calls."

"All right," he believed her. "Let's go upstairs. Lock the door behind me when I leave. I'll return later. It will be light out soon."

"When you come back, knock on the door in three's and pause in between, so I know it's you."

"OK," he nodded seriously.

They went up the steps quietly and he left through the front door. As soon as he took his last step off the porch, the officers were walking around the side.

"Officer Morley!" they both shouted.

"Officer Oxnard. Officer Wysor. What are you doing here?" he acted surprised.

"We noticed that the other boat was on this side of the lake," Officer Wysor smiled, curious to hear his response.

"Oh, I was just expanding the search. I… should… have said something," he smiled nervously.

Officer Oxnard stood still and noticed Officer Wodderspoon was not in sight. He looked at him and asked, "Where's your partner?"

"Oh, well… he isn't with me. I… guess he's home, or out on the road. Well, I'll be seeing you. I'm going home to get some shut-eye. I'll see you guy's later." He walked away, seemingly tired and then began a faster pace.

"We're going to check this cottage. Maybe the people who live here saw something that can help with the investigation."

He stopped dead in his tracks and turned swiftly, "No!"

Both officers looked at each other, startled by his response.

"What?" Officer Oxnard shouted.

"Uh, there's no one living there." He quickly walked back towards them.

"Oh, well, we'll walk back with you then."

He was easily convinced.

"All right," Officer Morley was instantly relieved.

On the other side of the door, Ms. Winterton listened to their conversation and as she turned away, her elbow knocked the lamp off the end table. The unexpected noise startled the felines and they jumped off the windowsill. The two officers looked at the window at the same time and saw the curtains move.

"I heard something break in that cottage. Look, the curtains just moved." Officer Wysor nodded in the direction of the cottage.

"I saw it," his partner replied anxiously and pulled his gun out of his holster, shaking as he held it up, aiming at the window.

"Woe! Put that gun away!" Officer Morley shouted and then hurriedly explained, "The cats inside made them move. I saw them before through the window."

"Oh," he was quickly reassured and placed his gun back in his holster. "Let's go, Wysor."

"Yeah, yeah, I'm coming." He turned and walked away with them.

All three walked down the mountainside. When they saw the boats, they all quickly stepped in the ones they had arrived in and rowed back until they reached the park side, securing them on land.

"I'll see you both later," Officer Morley waved and walked away.

"We'll see you and Wodderspoon tomorrow," Officer Wysor waved back as he and Officer Oxnard walked towards the tent.

Officer Morley thought about how he could get back, without the use of a boat. He noticed further down, the lake grew tighter, making it an easy swim across when the time came to return to Ms. Biddock's cottage.

On his way home, he stopped by Ms. Winterton's home, to see if she left her door open. She did. It gave him the opportunity to enter. He went up to a room he thought to be hers and searched her dresser drawers for clothes she could change into. After, he locked the door and drove to his cottage, where he lived alone. He found his waterproof duffle bag in his closet. It was just what he needed to use, when the time came for him to swim across the lake. As he lay resting on his bed, trying to make sense of what happened, his eyes soon after closed.

Meanwhile, at Ms. Biddock's cottage, Ms. Winterton went inside the kitchen. The felines followed her, meowing constantly before she realized they were hungry.

"Are you kitties' hungry?" she smiled down at them.

She searched the cabinets until she found the cat food, and filled their bowls to the top. They ate all she had given them and then purred happily while they rubbed against her legs.

"Are you ready to come down to the cellar with me?"

They stared up at her with their glowing green eyes.

"Come on."

They followed her down into the cellar and she turned on the light, anxious to look inside the grimoire Ms. Biddock used earlier to create the vision of Wanderamid.

"I can open the peephole. Anything is possible. It must be possible!" she murmured anxiously to herself, desperate to see her daughter again.

For a moment, she thought to wait until Officer Morley returned, but she was just too impatient and wanted to try right at that moment. She practiced repeatedly until she was ready to recite. She stood firm and then hesitantly held her arms out wide.

"First as a peephole then growing in size, I wait patiently to follow undisguised. With a need to satisfy a reach-gone cold, I stand here wishing another world to unfold. A vision I want desperately to see! Let these powerful words use my heart as the key!"

The peephole appeared just like before; a tiny hole sparkling as it grew larger with its zigzagging edges. It startled her, but she did not move an inch. Impatiently waiting for what would appear or what she would hear, her heart started to beat faster as it grew with each second. Then, she began to hear voices, many of them, one resembling that of Rena's. The power she felt was indescribable. It was all from the love for her daughter, she was able to open the window to Wanderamid.

A puzzling vision came through, showing a table filled with food with people supposedly eating. Only their hands were in view.

"You must hurry and then go to Jack," advised Para. "There's no telling how long the protective shield will last."

"Grandmother, will you show me where you contacted us from?"

"Yes," Ms. Winterton whispered strongly as she stared and anxiously listened.

"Come this way, Emera."

Emera turned to the others, who were enjoying their meal, "I'll be right back."

As they walked away, Ms. Winterton finally saw her daughter and Officer Wodderspoon.

Meanwhile, Para and Emera went in the other room, to the ruby crystal ball.

"Ms. Oula?" Officer Wodderspoon noticed she was not eating. "Will you show me where they went, just in case they contact my partner?" he asked before taking another bite of his meal.

"Yes." She lifted slowly from her chair. "Follow me."

"Wait, I'm going, too." Rena quickly stood up from her chair. "I might see my mother."

"I'm right behind you," Avanna quickly followed. Sadly, she would not be able to see her mother.

They followed Oula and Officer Wodderspoon. As they entered inside the room, Para immediately warned them. "You must keep quiet and walk in slowly. Any noise could break our concentration.

They nodded and sat at the table, quietly watching the peephole opening more before their eyes.

Ms. Winterton's vision changed from the table view to a ruby crystal ball.

"Hello! Hello!" she shouted desperately. "Can you see me?"

"Yes, Ms. Winterton!" shouted Officer Wodderspoon.

Rena stood up with the brightest smile, her eyes glistening, "Mom!"

"Rena, are you all right?" she laughed nervously, relieved she was safe.

"Yes," she replied, as tears began to drip down her cheeks.

Emera looked at Rena and then at Ms. Winterton. "I know you want to talk more, but we don't know how much time we have. Ms. Winterton, we still have a lot to do here in Wanderamid. The crystal ball is missing, and we have to find it. They can't go through the tunnel without it. We also have to help Jack change back to his normal form. It might take some time before we are able to contact you again."

"I understand. Please take care of my daughter." Oddly enough, she believed she would.

"Don't worry, Ms. Winterton, we will," assured Officer Wodderspoon. "Where's Trent?"

"He'll be back later. I'll let him know you made it there safe."

"I'll try to contact you again, Ms. Winterton, another time," said Para.

"Thank you," she responded gratefully. "Rena, be careful and I—Rena?"

The vision was lost and left only a swirling mist in the ruby crystal ball.

"Mom!" she shouted. Her mother was gone.

"I'll contact her again later, my child, I promise," assured Para.

"Mom, we have to go to Jack," said Micah.

"Yes, you must all hurry!" Para agreed. "I sense trouble will be finding him soon."

Avanna trembled when she heard those words. She had to get to Jack before anything else happened to him.

"Please, let's go now!"

"Mother," Emera looked at Oula. "Stay here with Grandmother. The five of us will go."

"I planned to go with you," she said, tiredly.

"It will be too much for you to handle, especially if Devilea's there."

"Then take this amulet." She removed it from around her neck.

"Mother, I have powers you know."

"I don't care. This will add to them." She held it out in the palm of her hand, "Take it, please!"

"I'll tell you what. I'll give it to Micah." She took it out of her hand and gave it to him.

"I'll take good care of it, Grandmother." He placed it around his neck and then inside his shirt.

"Let it take care of you," she replied with a worried grin.

"We'll be back, Mother," Emera said with great confidence, then turned to her grandmother smiling.

"Let's go. Please!" Avanna pleaded.

They all walked out of the room, one by one and then out the front door. Everyone looked back, smiling and waving at Oula and Para. Silently they walked on, following Emera, who was leading the way.

Suddenly, a whipping, crackling sound echoed all around them.

"What was that?" Rena whispered strongly.

"I don't know," Avanna said while she looked all around.

Micah turned to his mother and Officer Wodderspoon with one raised eyebrow. "Are you thinking what I'm thinking?"

Emera shook her head. "We must get to where Jack is, quickly. I will have to meet you there. Just follow the trail. Micah you lead them."

"You're not going by yourself. I'm going with you," he demanded.

She looked at Officer Wodderspoon and sighed, knowing Micah would not give in. "Could you watch over the girls?"

"Sure," he said.

"No," Avanna spoke firmly. "We will all go with you."

Emera knew they were as determined as her son was, although each had their own reasons. Without any argument, she allowed them to. There was no time to scold anyone, especially those who were there due to her mistakes.

They heard the terrible sound, again. Emera worded strongly, "Close your eyes, and don't open them until I tell you."

At the witch's cottage, Clemedeth sensed Devilea's presence. She heard the same cracking sound towards Amble Road. It was so loud, that she felt strong vibrations underneath her feet. Something was happening over there and she was positive Devilea was involved. The added powers made Clemedeth stronger and before she realized, she was flying above Tarot's trail and landed on the small hill above Amble Road. She looked down and without surprise, saw Devilea standing in front of a pterodoc.

"Who placed this shield around you?" Devilea demanded him to answer.

Jack only roared and shook his head.

Each time she whipped the shield, she had become angry, not knowing who created it.

"Devilea! Stop! What are you doing?" Clemedeth screamed furiously from the top of the hill as she watched her torturing the helpless creature.

Devilea stood still, turned slowly, and looked up. She had enough of her constant interruptions and immediately aimed her wand towards her. With an overpowering force, she sent her back to their cottage, where she lay still on the ground from Devilea's swift reaction.

"Tell me who placed this shield around you!" she demanded once again.

Jack roared, unable to make her understand, he had no idea.

"Was it, Emera? Is she back? Hmm, it must have been the little old woman, Oula. She must know more than just disappearing tricks."

Emera and the others arrived and hid behind the trees, unnoticed by Devilea.

"Stay here," Emera, mouthed voiceless.

"I'll come with you," whispered Officer Wodderspoon.

"No," she whispered firmly. "You must stay with them. I'll be fine."

He took his gun out of his holster, preparing to scare Devilea into turning Jack back to the way he was.

"What are you doing?" Emera shook her head, confused.

"I'm getting ready."

"For what?" she spoke calmly, not understanding his reason. "You do know that she can take that away in an instant. It doesn't mean anything to us witches."

He suddenly felt foolish. "I... suppose you're right."

The girls turned to Micah and giggled when he rolled his eyes.

"You meant well, Officer Wodderspoon." She turned to the others, "Right?"

They smiled and agreed.

"That idea would have worked in Whilom, but this world is much different."

"I would have done the same thing," Micah tried to ease some of his embarrassment.

Devilea cracked her whip again. They all peeked to see Jack quivering like a frightened child he truly was. He slowly lifted his head and saw behind Devilea, someone he hoped would soon relieve his fear.

"Devilea," Emera spoke her name in a tone to surprise her or better yet, to spoil her moment.

"Emera!" she snapped.

"Well, it seems as though you're still up to no good and you look a little different, too."

"I don't only look different, I am different. A lot has changed since you left," she said.

"Since I left? You mean since you tricked me!" Emera became instantly annoyed with her.

"I didn't trick you, Emera. I used what you gave me to my advantage."

"What advantage? From what I see, you've become a pathetic, miserable witch, who's not even an adult yet. You've become evil, more than you have ever been."

Micah and the others listened and Jack stood firmly watching. He had no idea his sister was only a few feet away.

"Where is your, friend?"

"My friend—oh—you mean, Clemedeth. I guess she's resting somewhere. It's not my time to watch her! She's been waiting for you—for her own reasons."

"I'll find her later," Emera said with confidence. "Right now everything I had given to you will be taken away."

"Oh, well, I don't think so," she responded, unaffected by her warning.

"Why is that, Devilea?"

"There must be a reason a shield was placed around this—creature," she spoke in a tone of disgust. "If you try to take away my powers, he will be destined to be just as he is—forever. Only I can change him!"

"No!" Avanna came out from behind the tree and pleaded. "Please, change him back now."

Devilea turned her eyes back to Emera; Avanna's burst did not surprise her. "Who's pathetic now, Emera?" she laughed.

"You are!" Rena ran out and stood beside Avanna. Micah and Officer Wodderspoon followed.

"Well, who have we here? I see you brought some more friends with you. You've become soft while you were away," she smirked.

Emera held her hand up high and began to recite. *"Lift the curse..."*

"Good-bye!" Devilea disappeared in an instant.

"Where did she go?" Avanna turned full circle. The only hope returning her brother back to himself disappeared before her eyes.

Rena panicked. "We have to go to the witch's cottage!"

"Wait. I will remove the shield from Jack and then you must all go back to the cottage from where we came. I need to go after her alone."

"I'll go along with you," Micah offered bravely.

"No, Micah, Officer Wodderspoon will. I need you to watch over the girls. Bring them back to your grandmothers' and feed Jack once you're there."

"Do you think you'll find her?" Rena hoped for a positive answer.

"I'll find her and I will clear up any mistakes I've made—if I can remember them all."

Even though she caused the mess they were all in, Rena gave a quick grin. She believed she would correct all her wrong doings.

"Be careful, Mom, and you, too, Officer Wod-der-spoon."

They both lifted up over the hill to Tarot's trail. Although he wanted to go with her, he knew he had to keep his promise to the girls.

"Jack, you need to fly over there," he pointed in the direction of the cottage. "When you see the second cottage, wait for us. Do you understand?"

Jack roared weakly, slowly flapped his wings, and then lifted over the trees.

"We'll meet you there, Jack!" Avanna watched as he flew over them and away.

"He'll be all right, Avanna," Rena smiled.

"Hurry, we must run quickly," Micah urged.

They ran towards the beginning of the trail that led to Micah's home. With the amulet around his neck and his backpack over his shoulders, he truly felt like a warrior.

"Look, there's a cottage!" Rena pointed out.

"It doesn't look like anyone's home," Avanna noticed.

"It's mine," said Micah.

"That's where Ms. Biddock lives?" Rena asked, surprised.

She pictured her cottage would be ten times the size of Clemedeth and Devilea's. It was an ordinary home.

Was it… an ordinary home?

"And, my grandmother," he added. "Come on, let's keep going. Go around the back."

They all ran to the back of his home and towards Para's cottage.

"I hope Jack is there," Avanna started to run faster.

"I know he is, Avanna," Rena tried to keep up with her.

They heard a loud thump ahead of them that caused Avanna to stop in her tracks. The others stopped behind her just in time.

"Did you hear that?" Her eyes froze wide open.

CHAPTER TWENTY-FOUR

A SECRET ADMIRER

Officer Morley had awakened from his nap. He had no idea how long he had been sleeping, squinting at the watch on his wrist, until the time came into focus. Only an hour had passed since he had closed his eyes. He grabbed the duffle bag and went to his room to pack an extra uniform to change into once he returned to Emera's cottage. After he secured his home, he left in his cruiser and raced back down to the park.

'I have to hide in the woods, away from the entrance,' he thought.

When he finally reached the park, he found an open space, wide enough to drive through, branches snapped all around his cruiser as he did. He went as far away as he could from the road and then stepped out of his cruiser, quietly walking the rest of the way to the lake. Before he went in the water, he placed his gun and flashlight inside the duffle bag and then closed it tightly to prevent water from entering. Soon after, he heard a rustle of leaves from behind.

"Hey," Jodon caught sight of the officer. "What are you doing?"

Officer Morley turned gradually and suddenly became nervous when he saw a young man standing, staring at him and then at his bag, with a confused expression.

"I'm—searching," his answer followed by a sudden loss of words.

"Searching for Rena?"

"Yes, now go on home," he proceeded to face the lake, hoping he would walk away before he went in.

"Wait!" Jodon shouted.

Officer Morley turned and reacted with a firm and strong whisper, "Keep it down."

"Why are you going in the lake, with your clothes? There are two boats a little ways down," he said, pointing to where they were.

"Don't you think I know that already?" he became quickly agitated.

"Well, it doesn't make sense. You are a police officer right?" He thought not an intelligent one.

"Listen, I'm here on official business. Now—run along," he shooed him away.

Jodon stayed right where he was and he was not about to leave.

"Well, if you won't tell me, maybe the police officers by the tent…."

"Woe, woe!" He tilted his head and his face scrunched up, "What's your name?"

"Jodon," he answered and then asked suspiciously, "You know where she is, don't you? You know, I saw her before that storm," he calmly recalled. "Something happened the day before. My friends and I saw her running away from the school. Something scared her in there. The windows broke on the second floor. I saw it happen! The next day it was as though they were never broken. When I saw Rena by the lake, I didn't want to bring it up in front of my friends. I thought I would see her again, to find out what happened, but after that big storm we had, I didn't see her around anymore."

"You said you and your friends saw her running from the school. Did you or your friends tell anyone about it?"

"No way, I told them not to say anything. Nobody would believe us anyway. They were real scared," he chuckled. "I was, too, but I didn't shake like they did."

"Thanks for the information, son. I have to go now."

He attempted again to go into the lake.

"Wait a minute!" he shouted.

Officer Morley let out a huge sigh and turned around with a grim expression.

"Are you for real? Do you know who I am? I am the police and you're interfering with an investigation!" He had become increasingly annoyed with his constant interruptions.

"You didn't answer when I asked if you knew where she was."

He whispered firmly, "If I knew where she was I wouldn't be attempting to swim across the lake."

"No. If you didn't know where she was, you would be using one of those boats over there," he waved his arm towards the boats.

"I will give you to the count of three to go home. One, two…."

"And, if I don't, what will happen?" he interrupted bravely. "You'll call all the other police officers you're trying to hide from? I wasn't born yesterday—sir," he spoke in a seemingly smart, but respectful way. "Let me go across with you."

"What!" his face furrowed in disbelief.

"If I don't go with you, I'll tell the other officers what I saw that day and that I saw you swimming across the lake with a duffle bag; sounds suspicious to me."

"I'll be gone for a while, son. I'm sure your mother will be looking for you. If that happens, it will take half the search off from finding Rena. Is that what you want?"

"Officer, my mother is too busy, drinking. She wouldn't notice how long I've been gone because she can't even see straight half the time. My father isn't even around. Will you let me go with you or not?" He stood waiting patiently for his answer.

The officer was speechless. He had no choice other than to allow him to go with him.

"Come on," he replied regrettably.

"I can't swim," Jodon muttered under his breath.

"I'm sorry. Did you just say what I think you said?" he twitched his head to one side.

"I—can't—swim," he spoke slowly and clearly.

"Why did you ask to swim across with me if you can't swim?" he stood baffled.

"I can hang on to the duffle bag!" he answered as it was the only obvious way.

Officer Morley shook his head; too much time was already wasted. "Grab onto the bag, keep your head up and your mouth closed!"

Jodon responded eagerly, "Yes, sir!"

"And another thing, once we get to the other side you had better listen to my orders or I will bring you to the tent myself and you can tell them all that you told me!" he added firmly.

"Yes, sir!" he gave a quick salute. "Take off your shoes and hold them up high, so they don't get wet."

Officer Morley rolled his eyes and they stepped into the lake quietly, after they took off their shoes. Jodon held on to the duffle bag and the officer pulled him across. When they reached the other side, he helped Jodon climbed up out of the water first and then he climbed out after he threw the bag over.

Both were soaked from the neck down.

"Put on your shoes and follow me," he whispered.

Jodon nodded and then after, they climbed halfway up the slope until they aligned with Emera's home. They walked cautiously to the side of the cottage.

He turned to Jodon, who had a serious expression on his face and said, "Wait—here."

Jodon squatted behind the bushes.

"When I call for you run up to the front door."

Jodon looked up at him with a straight face and gave his thumbs up, "Got it."

Officer Morley peeked around to make sure no one was watching. He ran quickly up the steps to the front door and knocked in three's, paused and then knocked again. Ms. Winterton was in the cellar when she heard his signal and rushed up the stairs. Even though she felt confident that it was Officer Morley, she still took the precaution, checking out the window first. Anxiously, she unchained the lock and opened the door.

"Hurry, get inside."

Officer Morley turned and called out in a low voice, "Jodon!"

Jodon stuck his head up and then stood slowly before swiftly running up the porch steps and through the open door.

"Who's this?" she asked, surprised by the unexpected visitor.

The officer let out a huge sigh, "This is Jodon, an acquaintance of your daughter. He's determined to help find her."

"But, he's just a teenager. They'll be searching for him. What were you thinking?"

"If I didn't bring him, he would have gone to the other officers. He has information we can't afford to be leaked out right now."

"Oh," Ms. Winterton replied and looked over at Jodon, the young man who had the guts to blackmail an officer, for her daughter.

"Hi, I'm Jodon," he introduced and held his hand out to her.

Ms. Winterton shook his hand and smiled, "Hi—I'm Ms. Winterton."

"Did you open the peephole?" Officer Morley was curious to hear if she could.

"Yes. I did. I'll tell you about it after I get... Jodon, something to drink, and dry his clothes," she pinched the wet shirt off from his shoulders. "Let's dry them first, shall we?"

"Sure, Ms. Winterton," he nodded and smiled.

"We'll be right back," she said.

They both walked through the hallway and Ms. Winterton gave him a pair of old shorts she found to change into before drying his clothes. After he changed, he went into the kitchen where she was waiting for him.

"Here are my wet clothes, Ms. Winterton."

She smiled as he handed them over to her.

"Wait here, I'll be right back." She walked away to place them in the dryer and then went back into the kitchen where she saw him sitting at the table. "Let's have something to drink while they dry," she suggested. "It shouldn't take more than 20 minutes."

She searched inside the refrigerator for a cold drink and found black iced tea. She poured him a glass and sat down at the table with him.

"So... you know my daughter?"

"Well, I spoke to her a couple of times. I don't mean to sound disrespectful, ma'am, but you don't seem worried. I mean, I'm sure you are but...."

"No need to explain yourself, Jodon. I am worried," she looked deep into his eyes, "I'm very worried. You'll understand why very soon."

They both sat and talked as they waited for the dryer buzzer to go off.

Officer Morley was in the cellar waiting with Emera's felines.

"Ms. Winterton, are you coming down here?" he shouted impatiently.

"We're almost done up here. We'll be down in a few minutes!"

The dryer buzzer went off the same time Jodon finished his drink.

"What's in the cellar, Ms. Winterton?" he curiously asked.

"Oh, I can't explain it. You'll have to see it to believe it. Even after you see it, it might take some time to believe it."

He was puzzled by her reply.

"Let's go," she walked over to the cellar door and shouted, "Officer Morley, are you ready?"

"Yeah, I'm waiting on you two!"

After Jodon changed back into his dry clothes, they went down the steep steps that were wet from Officer Morley's drenched clothes and walked toward the table.

"Sit next to Officer Morley, Jodon. Whatever you see or hear, try and keep quiet," she patted his back.

"Did you see Flynn?" Officer Morley asked.

"Yes. He asked where you were. I told him you would be back."

He looked at her, raising his dark eyebrows. "Then he's all right. They're both fine?"

"Yes, they're all fine," she confirmed.

Jodon listened as they spoke and then curiously asked, "Who's Flynn?"

"He's my partner."

Jodon looked at Ms. Winterton, "Is Rena with him? He found her?"

"Yes, and Emera, the woman who lives in this cottage is with him, too."

"Then why are you still looking for Rena if she's been found?" he asked, confused.

"They went where Rena is, to help her get back."

"Well, where is she? Why don't we go and help?"

"She's far away, Jodon. I can't go where she is."

"Well, how did his partner and that lady get to where she is?"

"They went through a peephole, which shows visions of another world. Officer Wodderspoon and Emera were brave enough to go through it. It's very dangerous. They are very lucky they made it. I wouldn't want Rena to return the way they left. I don't want her to take that chance, no matter how desperate I am to have her back home."

He shrugged his shoulders, "Then how will she get back?"

She knew that any answer given would only confuse him more. She looked at Officer Morley and he began to answer his questions for her.

"When everything goes well in Wanderamid, Rena will return through the tunnel, down at the park."

Jodon thought they were both crazy. He wanted to escape and at the same time, wanted to find Rena. He felt helpless and trapped with two people who obviously lost their minds. The story they told him seemed unbelievable. He had no other choice, only to sit in the cellar and wait for them to create what he believed to be an imaginary peephole. He did not fully understand what that was.

"How dangerous was it for them to go through the peephole?" He was interested to hear how he would describe it.

The officer, surprised by his interest, didn't think twice about it.

"There is no telling when it will close. It's very dangerous because it swiftly closes with a frightening razor sharp sound. So, just think, use your imagination as to what could happen if someone doesn't make it all the way through, before it closes."

Jodon cringed at the thought and then turned to see Ms. Winterton ready to begin.

"Remember, concentrate with me, and believe in what seems to be, the impossible." They both nodded and then she recited, *The hole within an empty space, show us light in the darkest night. Lead these visions on a path to ease our worried minds at last!"*

A brisk wind touched their faces and then again even stronger than before, as they watched a peephole form in front of them. Jodon was surprised to see such an incredible sight. It opened wider and then even more until a vision appeared showing Para. He sat speechless with his mouth open, amazed at what he witnessed.

"Hello!" she shouted.

"Hello?" Para was not sure who it was.

"It's Rena's mother!" Ms. Winterton announced.

"Oh, yes. Rena is with the others. I can't stay on long. My daughter and I heard a loud thump outside. She's going to check and I must go with her."

"Wait!" Ms. Winterton cried out. "Where did Rena go?"

"She went with the others to get Jack." Para's expression turned puzzled, "What is he doing?"

"What is who doing?" she asked, stumped with her question.

"Get down, Jodon!"

Officer Morley realized too late what he was about to do.

As quickly as Ms. Winterton thought to yell out his name, he had already jumped into the peephole!

"I'll bring her back, Ms. Winter... ton, I'll...." His voice faded.

"Jodon!" She looked at Officer Morley shocked by what Jodon had done. "He's gone."

The officer stood speechless and helpless. There was nothing he could have done, only pray that he made it through to Wanderamid safely.

Ms. Winterton stared back at Para, "He went through! Please, find him!"

"We will, we...."

Their connection ended.

Ms. Winterton's devastation turned to anger. "Why did you bring him here? What will we do now? His mother will be looking for him and then the police! I'll never get Rena home."

"We don't have to worry about his mother, she drinks a lot."

Ms. Winterton open and closed her eyes slowly. "She does—what a lot?"

"She drinks–a lot. That will buy us some time."

"How do you know that?"

"Jodon told me."

"And you believed him?" she rolled her eyes. "He's a teenager! He would have told you anything to ease your worry."

"Hmm—well—it worked."

Ms. Winterton shook her head, distressed.

"It will be fine," he said with confidence.

"A young man just went through to another world. Now there are two teenagers lost."

CHAPTER TWENTY-FIVE

DEVILEA'S SURPRISE

Devilea saw Clemedeth lying on the ground, in front of their cottage. She was moaning before opening her eyes to see Devilea staring down at her with an expression far from any she had ever seen before on her face.

"Devilea?" she mumbled with furrowed brows.

Devilea stood over her without lending her a hand. Her only concern was to hurry inside to the crystal balls, all three of them. She turned away with a blank expression, unsympathetic to her needs and glided across the ground, over the porch. The dome-shaped door slowly opened as she entered straight through towards the hanging shelf and then lowered herself to the floor. She unhooked her cloak and opened it wide, placing each crystal ball one by one in its pockets and then turned away in slow motion, walking back outside.

Clemedeth stood waiting for her.

When their eyes met, they stared at each other coldly, knowing they could never be the friends they once were.

"I can't let you leave with them, Devilea. They're my mother's, not yours."

"But, Clemedeth, if it wasn't for me finding the missing one, you wouldn't have the powers you have now."

"I don't want these powers and I don't want you to have these powers. Can't you see how you've become?"

Devilea was unmoved by her words.

"What I've become? I've always been this way; you were too caught up in making everything perfect, you couldn't even see who I really am."

Clemedeth stood strong before her, ready for any confrontation that would surely happen. In the distance, Emera and Officer Wodderspoon began to hear them and their voices had become clearer with every step they took closer. Devilea's eyes turned away when she heard noises coming from behind Clemedeth.

"Oww," Officer Wodderspoon's forehead smacked straight into a branch that hung low in front of him.

Emera quickly turned and placed her finger against her lips, "Shhh! Be quiet!" She watched as his head wobbled. "Why didn't you go around it?"

"Who's there?" Devilea's eyes searched aimlessly, but saw nothing.

Emera whispered, "Wait… here."

He nodded in pain and stayed hidden behind the trees… recovering, as she slowly revealed herself.

"Devilea, you left so suddenly. Where are your manners? Oh, yes, it slipped my mind, you have none."

"Emera," Devilea uttered under her breath.

"Emera," Clemedeth was surprised to see her and immediately pleaded, "Please release the curse!"

Devilea looked at Clemedeth with stone cold eyes and laughed as loud as she could, "Ha, ha, ha, she won't release the curse. Tell her, Emera! Tell her about the— creature."

Emera had forgotten about Jack again and from the expression on her face, Devilea knew she had. She waited to hear her explain, but was not quick enough. She turned to Clemedeth and gladly explained all herself.

"The pterodoc that Avanna and Rena told us about before—is Avanna's brother. He can never turn back the way he was, unless I reverse the spell. If Emera even tries to release the curse, Avanna's brother, better known as Jack, will never be the boy he was born to be."

"When they asked us about the pterodoc, you said you knew nothing about it. You lied?" Clemedeth stared at her with a look of disappointment that grew rapidly into anger, visible to all who were around.

Officer Wodderspoon came out from behind the trees. Emera turned and shouted, "Go back!"

Devilea laughed, "Who's that, Emera, your boyfriend?"

Clemedeth had enough and raised her hand in the air, *"Those you had deceived every day, will now control your powers and you will..."*

Before she had a chance to finish, Devilea quickly raised her hands and in an instant, she was gone.

"Where did she go?" Clemedeth looked around with a defeated expression. "What will happen to Avanna's brother now?"

"She's not too far," Emera was confident. "I have a feeling she'll want to experiment with her new powers. You share the power with her. If I take yours away, she will still have half of what she has now. As for Jack, well, we will have to find her before it becomes too late to even attempt to save him."

"We should go back to your grandmothers," Officer Wodderspoon suggested. "She could be there for all we know."

"He's right," she agreed. "Clemedeth, maybe you should come with us."

"No. I'll stay here. I have reason to believe she just might return."

What could that reason be?

"If she does, and you need our help, give us a sign."

"If or when she returns, you will know, no matter how far you are," she assured them.

"I have to inform the others what happened," said Emera.

"Emera," Clemedeth began to ask, "Could you please let Avanna know that I'm sorry what happened to her brother, and I will try my best to help him turn back to who he once was?"

"I have to take some of the blame," she admitted. "I gave no thought as to who would be affected by the curse

I placed upon you both. I knew who she was and wanted to teach her a lesson, but in some odd way, it taught me one. I won't release the powers I gave you now; you will need them to protect yourself, from her."

"Thank you, Emera," she smiled appreciatively.

"Remember now, Ms. Clemedeth, give us a sign if you need any help." He turned and walked away.

Emera was actually getting used to his presence. He certainly could not protect her because she had all the powers, but it was comforting to know that he truly wanted to be there with her as she did with him.

As they walked away on Tarot's trail, Clemedeth entered back into her cottage. As she sat at her kitchen table, she suddenly felt a familiar closeness. A lavender scent surrounded her and brought her comfort. She laid her head down over her folded arms and then it quickly disappeared before her mind drifted off into a deep sleep.

Officer Wodderspoon and Emera arrived at the trail, leading them through the woods towards Para's cottage, watching out for anything suspicious.

Meanwhile, Oula was about to open the front door of her mother's cottage, when all of the sudden, she heard someone yelling outside.

"Woe! Aaaaah!" Jodon fell through the trees, just like Emera and Officer Wodderspoon had, landing with his face inches from the ground, and then gradually stood sluggishly, moaning until he realized he was facing a huge creature with wings. "What the…!"

He started to walk backwards further into the woods, the same time Oula opened the door with her mother close behind.

"Jack!" Oula whispered strongly and then looked to her left, startled by a young stranger. "Who are you?"

"That's Jodon," said Para.

Jodon stopped when he recognized Para and shouted, "Hey, You're the old woman from the peephole! Be careful, it's a monster! Get back inside!"

Oula looked at her mother bewildered. "You know him?"

Before Para could answer her, Micah and the girls were walking towards the cottage. Jodon began slowly walking backwards in front of them. Micah caught sight of the stranger and began running towards him.

Jodon heard him from behind and turned around quickly. "Hey!"

Micah jumped and then dove right on top of him, turning his face down into the ground. Rena and Avanna ran to help.

"Hold... his... feet down!"

Jodon struggled to lift his head, "Mm—Mm!"

"No, Micah!" Para shouted.

He raised his head and with a confused expression asked, "What?"

She frantically waved her arms in the air and yelled, "Get off of him!"

Rena and Avanna released their hold from his feet and Micah quickly backed away.

Jodon started gasping for air and spitting out the dirt from inside his mouth. He looked up at Micah while he wiped his lips and then around his blinking eyes. "Are you crazy?" he shouted. "There's a monster with wings right there, and you attack me?"

"Hey, he's my brother!" Avanna ran over to Jack and stood by him.

"OK, now I know you're all crazy!"

"Who are you?" Micah slowly stood back up.

Jodon slowly stood up after him.

"Everyone, calm down," urged Oula.

Rena heard a familiar voice and hesitantly walked in front of him to see who was underneath all that dirt.

"Jodon?" she asked with surprising widened eyes. "Is it really you?

"Rena," his heart softened instantly as he looked into her big brown eyes.

"You know him?" Micah and Avanna asked at the same time.

She chuckled; amazed it was really him, "Yes."

"Are you all right?" Jodon asked, concerned.

"Yes," she smiled. "Why are you here?"

Suddenly, Jack's presence did not alarm him. It seemed as though no one else was around, only he and Rena, nothing else seemed to matter.

Micah began to feel a little jealous and it showed in his expression. Avanna noticed and pretended to feel sick, so he would feel needed again. She pressed her hand against her forehead.

"I don't feel well."

Micah quickly attended to her. "I'll walk you inside so you can lie down."

"But I have to make sure Jack gets something to eat."

"I'll take care of Jack, too," he assured her.

"Thanks, Micah," she smiled and winked at Jack as he walked her towards the door.

Para and Oula watched, shaking their heads, accompanied with their discreet chuckles.

Before Jodon answered Rena's question, there was a sound of rustling coming from the woods. Shaken by all that happened since his arrival in Wanderamid, he hesitantly turned his head and saw two figures running towards them, one with glowing eyes.

"What the…! Run!" He pulled Rena by the arm and ran the other direction.

"Wait, Jodon!" she pulled back and he stopped dead in his tracks. "It's only Ms. Biddock and Officer Wodderspoon."

"Who?" he asked wide eyed and embarrassed.

Micah scratched under his nose, hiding his smile, trying not to laugh, but let out a noticeable chuckle.

"Stop it," Avanna whispered strongly, nudging his arm. "He didn't know."

"Sorry, bro," he immediately apologized.

"Yeah, right, and I'm not your bro," Jodon replied annoyed.

Emera stared at the unfamiliar young man.

"Who's this?"

"He's from Whilom," Rena smiled.

Officer Wodderspoon seemed dumbfounded. "How did you get here?"

"You must be Officer Morley's partner," Jodon remembered.

"He must have gone through the peephole." Emera had come to realize that was the only way; and she was right.

"Why did you go and do that for!" Officer Wodderspoon immediately became angry.

Jodon stood speechless. All he wanted to do was help Rena get home. Micah knew how he felt, and thought of a way to cover his embarrassment.

"Didn't you say that the peephole was dangerous to go through?" Micah asked Officer Wodderspoon as he stood before the cottage door with Avanna.

"Yes, it's very dangerous!" He remained irritated and then scolded Jodon, "You're lucky you didn't get hurt! This isn't a game!"

"To his defense," Micah went on to say, "he's proved himself to be brave enough to help us against Devilea."

Emera was proud her son stood up for Jodon.

"You know, he's right," she looked at Officer Wodderspoon and then winked her glowing eye at him. In an instant, he was calm.

"All right," he said calmly. "The rules are that you young men listen to our rules and make sure the girls are protected."

Emera gave him a soft smile.

"Yes, sir!" they both replied.

The girls smiled and Para stood watching along with Oula.

"Let's go inside," Para suggested. "Micah and Jodon, come with me to get food for Jack."

Oula grinned at her mother as they all went inside. The officer closed the door behind them.

Emera prepared to explain briefly, what had happened in Hemlock Village. She had no idea how Avanna would react to the news.

"How do you feel, Avanna," Rena noticed she stopped pressing her hand against her forehead.

"Oh, I feel much better," she smiled and nodded.

Outside the cottage, Devilea landed smack down in front of Jack. He tried to let out his roaring voice, but she swiped her fist in the air at the same instant and was unable to make a sound.

"I don't think so, Jackie boy."

He lifted his foot, about to slam the top of her head, but she stopped him immediately, changing him back to who he once was. Right after, she snatched him up and flew swiftly over the trees where they both disappeared.

"We'll be right back," said Micah. He and Jodon headed outside to feed Jack.

"Wait!" Avanna shouted anxiously. "We're going with you."

She and Rena followed and as Micah opened the door wide, Avanna immediately noticed the front yard empty. Jack was nowhere in sight.

"He's gone!"

CHAPTER TWENTY-SIX

WHITE LIES

J odon's mother awakened from her nap. An eerie silence surrounded her.

"Jodon!" she shouted.

When there was no answer, she slowly rose up and began searching every room, beginning with his. She started to panic, as he was nowhere in sight.

"Something's not right. He's always here for dinner," she whispered under her breath, as she looked up at the clock, hung up on the wall in the hallway.

She walked briskly down the stairs, to the front door and quickly opened it, staring out into the empty street, the night air seeping through the screen onto her face. Gradually, she closed the door and without hesitation, went directly into the kitchen, reached for the phone that hung on the wall, and dialed 911.

"This is Whilom Police. Is this an emergency?" the dispatcher asked calmly.

"Hello, this is Ellyn Kennings. My son hasn't come home. Please, I need help."

"How old is your son, ma'am?"

"He's fifteen years old. Please send someone fast," she pleaded while at the same time tried to remain calm. "This just isn't like him." Her worst fears began to grow with each second passing.

"What is your address?"

"21947 Cocoon Circle. Please hurry!"

"A police cruiser is on their way, ma'am. They should be there shortly."

"Thank you. I'll be waiting."

Officer Wysor and Oxnard took the call of the missing young man and drove towards Ms. Kenning's cottage.

In the meantime, she opened her front door once more, waiting for the police to arrive while the darkness fell before her, and then suddenly, there were bright lights! A police cruiser silently pulled up in front of her home, their flashing lights caused her to squint. Her heart raced and she became extremely nervous, watching the two officers approaching the front door.

"Are you, Ms. Kennings?" Officer Wysor spoke through the screen door.

"Yes, I am." She opened the door.

Both officers tipped their hats to her, entered inside, and then stopped next to the kitchen entrance.

"I'm Officer Wysor and this is my partner, Officer Oxnard."

"Thank you for your quick response," she responded gratefully. "My son is always here at dinner time and if he makes other plans, he always tells me ahead of time. I know something's wrong."

"We're talking about a teenager, who is also a boy," he spoke seemingly unconcerned.

"What? What does that mean?" She asked offended by his remark.

"Let's give him another hour or so, he'll come around. What's his name anyway?"

"Anyway?" she repeated mockingly, "Anyway, his name is Jodon Kennings. He always goes to Fountain Lake Park."

"What's with that park?" Officer Wysor asked his partner with a bewildered look on his face.

"I don't know, but it's already dark outside," he replied concerned. She had mentioned the same area Rena Winterton disappeared. He pressed the button on the radio, attached to his shirt, over his shoulder, and spoke to the dispatcher. "This is Officer Oxnard. Please get me Officer Liam."

"Officer Oxnard, please hold," the dispatcher paused and then announced, "Officer Liam on with Officer Oxnard."

"Officer Liam, this is Officer Oxnard. We have another missing teenager. This one is a fifteen-year-old boy. His name is Jodon Kennings. His mother seems to think he went to Fountain Lake Park."

"What the heck is going on in that park?"

"That's what we said. It seems very strange. Officer Wysor and I will be there soon, 10-4."

We'll be expecting you, 10-4."

"Ms. Kennings, what was your son wearing?" He clicked his pen, preparing to write down her answer.

"When I saw him last, he was wearing blue jeans and a black shirt."

"Thanks, Ms. Kennings. We'll keep in touch," he nodded with a grin and quickly let himself out.

Officer Wysor turned to her, "We'll let you know if we find anything."

She stood in awe as she watched him turn around, about to leave, and then in a calm and confident tone said, "If I don't go with the two of you, I will take my own car and go down there myself."

"Ladies first," he extended his arm out for her to go ahead of him.

She left the porch light on, walked out, and then immediately looked back. "Leave the door unlocked please."

Officer Wysor smiled and then muttered under his breath, "This will be a long night."

As they reached the park, Officer Oxnard parked a few feet from the yellow crime scene ribbon that blocked off the main entrance. Soon after they exited the cruiser, an eerie stillness surrounded them.

"I'll be right back, wait here."

Officer Wysor had a confused look on his face, "Where are you going?"

"I don't know. I'll be right back. Stay here with Ms. Kennings."

He walked down further away from the entrance following tire tracks he noticed, leading him into an open space in the woods. As soon as he took a few steps inside, he observed a police cruiser and immediately pulled out his flashlight to see whose it was.

"Wysor!" he called out to him as he stood wondering why the officer parked there.

"Yeah!" he responded, walking the direction he heard his voice. Ms. Kennings was close behind.

They were not at all surprised when they saw a police cruiser, after all, there was an investigation going on. Nevertheless, why was it in the woods when there was plenty of space by the entrance?

"Whose is it?" Officer Wysor looked at him curious to hear whose it was.

"It's Officer Morley's," he quickly responded after checking out the number that was on the cruiser.

"I thought he said he was going home," he wondered aloud.

"That's what he told us," he replied in a suspicious tone of voice.

"Let's go further inside," Officer Wysor pointed in the direction of the lake.

They walked deeper into the woods, towards the lake. All of them looked down in the water and then the officers shined their flashlights along the edge.

"Look!" Officer Oxnard noticed something on the ground.

Officer Wysor shined the flashlight in his partner's eyes. "What?"

He scrunched up his face and then turned his head, "Take that light away from me, and aim it near the edge– over there. There are footprints in different sizes. One's bigger than the other."

Officer Wysor looked down. "Yeah, you're right," he agreed and showed Ms. Kennings.

"Shouldn't we call the other officers?" she asked as her heart beat faster.

"I think Officer Oxnard and I should look into this a little more before we do that. Maybe Officer Morley knows something and maybe he's on the other side of the lake."

"How would he get to the other side?" Officer Oxnard asked and then pointed, "Look, the boats are still there. They haven't been moved since we pulled them on land."

"Maybe he swam over," Ms. Kennings quickly assumed.

'Why would he swim there?' thought Officer Wysor. "Let's go on over to the other side."

"You think he's over there, don't you, Wysor?"

"I might be thinking something like that, yeah," he responded, rolling his eyes.

They all began walking towards the boats and heard voices in the distance as they did, becoming louder as they neared them. Police and forensic workers were taking a break in the tent. They tried not to make a sound when they stepped into one of the boats one by one, quietly rowing across to the other side and then secured it, tying the rope around a nearby tree. They helped Ms. Kennings step out and then walked silently along the edge until they were exactly across from where they found the footprints. Without uttering a word they continued to walk up the mountainside, Officer Wysor led the way. Soon after, they had come across a huge cottage, the same one they stood in front of hours before.

"Stay here," he ordered in a strong whisper.

"Will do," nodded Officer Oxnard.

Ms. Kennings stayed nervously quiet, hoping he would find her son. He walked to the front of the cottage and saw there were no lights on, then continued discreetly around the back. Lights shined through the curtains from the cellar window where he heard Officer Morley's voice.

Ms. Winterton cried out, "What will we do?"

"Calm down. I'll think of something," he assured her.

"But his mother must be looking for him," she paced back and forth nervously.

"He mentioned his mother was a drunk and his father isn't around."

"I know and you believed him. How could you?" she replied, frustrated he believed such a story.

"You could have told him to go home," he argued.

"You said he knew too much!"

He held both hands up to a stop, "OK, so we both messed up."

"Now what do we do?" she shook her head in despair.

"We open the peephole again to make sure he's all right," he suggested.

Officer Wysor listened on bended knees by the window and muttered strongly, "What the heck is a peephole? WOE!" He lost his balance and fell against the window, nearly breaking it.

"What was that?" Her heart dropped from her chest down to her stomach.

"Who's there?" Officer Morley shouted through the window. "I have a gun!"

"It's... Officer Wysor!" he announced loudly. "I know you have a gun, so do I!"

"What should we do?" she whispered anxiously. "They're already looking for Jodon!"

"Don't be so paranoid," he was seemingly unconcerned. "They probably don't even know him."

"Open the front door!" Officer Wysor yelled as he tried to get up. "WOE!" He fell back down.

Both looked at each other with wide eyes, and then Officer Morley suggested, "Let's go and open the door. Follow with whatever I say."

They went up to the front door and waited for the officer. When he finally entered inside, his eyes roamed aimlessly, searching for anything suspicious.

"What are you looking for?" Officer Morley noticed his roaming eyes.

"There's a young man missing. A fifteen year old named, Jodon Kennings."

Ms. Winterton folded her arms and looked at Officer Morley with relaxed eyes and a partial grin. He gave a partial grin in return.

Officer Wysor continued, "His mother's looking for him. She said he hadn't been home for dinner."

Ms. Winterton saw Officer Morley rolling his eyes, speechless.

"She's outside with Officer Oxnard." He walked back to the front door and called out, "Oxnard, come in, bring Ms. Kennings!"

They stood up from behind the bushes and hurried up the front porch steps. Ms. Kennings instantly recognized Ms. Winterton as she walked briskly through the open door. She knew she was the mother of the missing girl, Rena.

"Your Rena's mother, aren't you?"

"Y-yes," she hesitantly answered her.

"I'm terribly sorry. I know she'll be found soon," she said.

"Thank you and I'm sorry about your... son."

Ms. Winterton felt terrible knowing what happened to him and even though not intentionally, she felt slightly responsible for his disappearance.

"We found footprints on the other side of the lake," Officer Oxnard informed them.

He noticed Officer Morley's clothes wet, which would explain that he had to have swum across the lake.

"There were two sets, one larger than the other."

Ms. Winterton put her head down slowly. She had become tense and it was noticeable to all who were around.

"What are you doing in here?" Officer Wysor looked at him with suspicious eyes. "Who lives here? I know you don't, Ms. Winterton."

"This is her friend's cottage. I'm keeping her informed with all that's going on with the search for her daughter."

"Why are you wet?" he asked bluntly, curious what his answer would be. He knew he didn't use a boat to get to the other side.

"I fell in the lake," he chuckled nervously. "Sometimes I can be very clumsy."

Officer Wysor sensed he was keeping something from them.

"Hmm, what's down in the cellar? Do you mind if we take a look?"

"Down in the cellar?" He became seemingly annoyed with all his questions.

"Yes, down in the cellar. That's where you both were. Is there someone down there?" he asked firmly with raised eyebrows.

"What do you think; we have her son down there? What are you insinuating, Wysor?"

"Now, now, calm down, the both of you," Officer Oxnard tried to keep the peace, as it became uncomfortable watching his two fellow officers arguing.

"I'll be back," Officer Morley grabbed his duffle bag to change out of his wet clothes.

"Wait a minute!" Officer Wysor raised his voice. "What have you got in that bag?"

"I have a change of clothes." He held it out to him. "Would you like to open it and see for yourself?"

Officer Wysor saw a tag hanging from the bag that read, "waterproof".

"Isn't that a coincidence, it's waterproof," he said with wide eyes, pointing at the tag.

"Yeah, yeah," Officer Morley nodded and walked away.

"Shall we, Ms. Winterton?" he offered her to lead them down the cellar.

"I prefer to wait for Officer Morley, if you don't mind," she answered with her arms folded tightly in front of her.

"Sure, why not!" he raised his voice the same time as his arms, before they quickly fell back down to his sides.

Officer Oxnard looked at Ms. Kennings, shaking his head, embarrassed by their behavior.

"Ms. Winterton," Ms. Kennings began to ask, "from one mother of a missing child to another. Did you see my son?"

"Uh…."

"OK, I'm ready," Officer Morley, returned just in time.

"Let's go down to the cellar," Ms. Winterton quickly suggested avoiding lying to Ms. Kennings.

Both led the way while the others followed. When they walked down the steps, they immediately saw nothing out of the ordinary, except for an old, green leather bound grimoire left on the table. Beside it were footprints left when Jodon stood to enter into Wanderamid and Officer Wysor noticed.

"What do we have here?" he said, pointing at the table.

"Those… are my… footprints," Officer Morley responded nervously.

They both looked down at his shoes, at the same time, and then back at the table. It was obvious his were, without any doubt, larger.

"Where's the boy, Morley… Ms. Winterton?" Officer Wysor questioned strongly.

Ms. Kennings, startled by his question, waited quietly for them to answer him.

"They're mine!" Officer Morley shouted. "I was looking out the window!"

Ms. Kennings was unable to keep silent.

"The table is at least eight feet from the window and the curtains are closed. Where is my son? Jodon!"

Ms. Winterton worried her screams would attract other unwanted visitors.

"Wait! Keep it down. He's not here." She turned to the two officers, "He's not here. We're telling the truth."

"You have the right to remain silent. Anything…."

"Wait. What are you doing?" Officer Morley interrupted.

Officer Wysor continued, "Anything you say or do can and will be held…."

"Wait, Wysor! This is crazy! What are you doing?" shouted Officer Oxnard.

"I'm going to arrest them! What does it sound like?"

"Wait," Ms. Winterton said calmly. She looked over at Officer Morley. "Tell them everything."

He leaned towards her with his head down and whispered, "Do you know what you're saying?"

Ms. Kennings and the officers tried listening to his whispers.

"They'll have to believe us when they see the peephole." She was sure it was the only way.

He responded with doubt. "If they let us get that far."

"Everyone, please, sit down," she asked calmly as they both faced them.

"Why? If you know something, tell us!" Ms. Kennings shouted impatiently.

"We have to show you, but you have to believe."

"Maybe you should arrest them officers. Something's not right with them," Ms. Kennings suggested angrily, due to their odd behavior.

"Ms. Kennings," Ms. Winterton placed her hand lightly on her shoulder and looked into her eyes, "Please–sit–down."

Ms. Kennings nodded and sat in the chair closest to her and the others sat down right after. Ms. Winterton opened the grimoire and it grew before their eyes, causing them to scoot back in their chairs.

"She's a witch!" she shouted and then abruptly pushed the chair away from under her with the back of her knees and immediately stood.

Both officers stood along with her, aiming their guns at them.

CHAPTER TWENTY-SEVEN

THE UNBELIEVABLE TRUTH

Ms. Winterton gasped when the officers pointed their firearms, straight at them. Her mouth froze open, surprised by their reaction.

"No," Officer Morley began to explain calmly. "She is not a witch. Please put the guns down. We just want to show you, what you've been asking us."

"That book just grew, Morley! We saw it! Only a witch could do that!" Officer Wysor shouted, pointing his gun away from them and onto the grimoire.

Officer Oxnard remained speechless and wide-eyed.

"She's trying to find her daughter, just like Ms. Kennings is trying to find her son. Now if you want to see what is going on, you can't get excited like this or we won't be able to show you. Do you understand that?" He tried to convince them as firmly and calmly as possible.

Officer Oxnard nodded, signaling him to lower his gun as he did, still keeping it in hand. They were not fully convinced to put them away completely.

"Look at their eyes!" Ms. Kennings shouted, pointing at the three felines that came out from the corner, with glowing green eyes.

She startled the officers and they quickly aimed their guns at the felines.

Officer Morley rolled his eyes. "Will you all sit? They're only cats!"

"I never saw cats with eyes like those," she responded stiffly.

"They're not normal... I mean... they're normal, but... well... I don't know what I mean. All I know is that they won't harm you. Please, sit so we can get on with this," he tiredly shook his head.

The officers and Ms. Kennings sat down slowly while they kept a close watch on the felines. Ms. Winterton took a deep breath as she thought about where to begin her story, and how to make it believable as possible, as her eyes made contact with those she had to convince.

"Ms. Kennings," she spoke softly,"... Rena and Jodon are together, in another world."

"They killed them!" Her eyes widened with fear. "They killed...."

"No! No!" Officer Morley immediately stood.

The other officers stood right after and aimed their guns at them again.

"What are you doing?"

"You heard her! You both killed them!" Officer Wysor yelled. "I'm placing you both under arrest! Anything…."

"Stop, Wysor!" he demanded, and then calmly added, "We didn't kill them. They're alive."

"What?" Ms. Kennings asked stunned. "Then where are they?"

"Ms. Winterton told you. They're in another world."

"They did kill them! Bring me to my son!"

In an instant, she flew across the table with her arms straight out in front of her and grabbed Officer Morley's gun, pulling it out from his holster. As she fell to the floor, she immediately stood up and pointed the gun at the both of them with shaking hands.

"Put the gun down, Ms. Kennings. You don't know what you're doing." Ms. Winterton tried to calm her. "I didn't believe it myself when I first heard it. Please, let us explain."

Ms. Kennings remained holding the gun.

"A little… help… officers," Officer Morley said in a calm voice, trying not to upset her more than she had already been.

He waited impatiently for them to respond.

"Oh–yeah," Officer Oxnard finally responded. "Put— the gun–down Ms. Kennings, so we can get to the bottom of this. We have everything under control. Put–the gun– down, so they can tell us where your son is, ma'am."

Officer Wysor moved not an inch, his eyes glued to the gun she held in her hands, unsteady. He hoped she would give in soon, before forced to use his own.

Ms. Kennings looked at him with tears running down her face. She had come to realize only Ms. Winterton and Officer Morley could give her such information. Steadily, she slowly handed the gun over to him and he quickly took it away from her.

Ms. Winterton walked with her back to the table.

"Let's all sit down again, shall we?" she suggested calmly, while she thought about how she would tell her story once more with a different choice of words, that would only continue to sound unbelievable.

Before she started, she made sure Ms. Kennings would have all her attention, keeping strong eye contact with her only.

"I will make this as brief as possible. The only true way you will believe all I'm about to tell you, is to show you." She took a deep breath, "Whatever I say and then ask you to do, please just go along with it, without voicing out any opinions or disbeliefs, for it is critical that we all believe and keep an open mind. You'll be very surprised, as so was I and Officer Morley."

She seemed to have had all their attention.

"When I was told my daughter was not in the same world as the one we're in, I was in total disbelief. However, I had no other direction to follow, to show me where she might be, so I listened to a story too crazy to come up with on your own. The story told to me, was indeed true. I found myself standing in front of a peephole, created to have contact with my daughter, but only in view and with words. I have since spoken to her again. Your son, Jodon, was here when I opened the peephole to see how Rena was. He saw how devastated I was, and I think he was too. Anyway, before we could even stop him, he had already jumped from this table, inside the peephole and in Wanderamid. As he went through, he said he would bring her back home."

She stopped and took another deep breath. Although, her words seemed genuine, Ms. Kennings was not easily convinced. Ms. Winterton turned to the grimoire on the table and placed her hands on top of it. Her eyes stared at the walls in front of her, as she recited with quivering lips, to create yet again, the vision to Wanderamid.

"Open the world where our children exist! Lead us to see those whom we miss! Too many hours led into the night to see what's before us in your luminous light! We stand here waiting, sorrowful. Deliver this world of the crystal ball!"

The cellars damp, still air, became noticeably colder. A soft wind formed around them as they sat still with eyes glued in the direction Ms. Winterton gazed. The feline's furs flew back as they too faced the wind that had become stronger. Then, the wind lessened and a spark appeared suddenly in front of them with an apparent opening, forming in the thin air. It increased with zigzagging edges and began to show a view inside Wanderamid, with Para on the other side.

"I see Ms. Winterton!"

Rena heard Para, rushed into the room with Jodon behind her, and saw her mother, "Mom!"

"Rena! How are you?" she cried.

"I'm fine, Mom, don't cry," she replied, wiping her own tears.

"Jodon is fine," said Para.

"Can we see him, too? His mother... is here."

Ms. Kennings could not believe what her eyes perceived, her son in another world, just as they told her.

She shouted out, "Jodon!"

"I'm sorry, Mom, but I had to get here, to help Rena get home."

Ms. Kennings held back her tears and nodded with worried eyes. "It's time to come back. You can't stay there."

"I know, but it's not that simple."

"I apologize for interrupting, but we have to find Jack. He's missing again and we need the peephole to find out where he is," Para explained.

"We'll contact you again, later," Ms. Winterton assured her. "I love you, Rena."

"Love you, too," she smiled softly and nodded. "We're OK."

"I love you, Jodon," Ms. Kennings stared with tear-filled eyes into his.

"Love you, too, and don't worry, we'll get home, I promise." He waved and smiled as he tried to keep a tear from falling, but was unable to stop it from dripping down his face. His mother noticed and waved back with a soft smile.

Ms. Winterton closed the grimoire and all contact between them, stopped. She turned to Officer Morley and they both smiled.

"I'm—sorry," Ms. Kennings apologized softly. "I don't know what else to say."

"That's all right," Officer Morley replied.

"Yes, it's all right," accepted Ms. Winterton.

"I… a… want to… apologize, too," Officer Wysor added.

"No need to, Officer," he shook his head.

"But I almost arrested you–three times," he responded regretfully.

"You didn't know."

"No I didn't, but I should have given you time to explain and I didn't give you that chance."

"Yes… you should have," he agreed. "But, I forgive you and now we need to figure out what to do with the investigation that's going on out there," he pointed in the direction of the park.

"How do we stop it?" Officer Oxnard asked and then added, "Oh, and by the way, please accept my apology as well. I'm sorry I aimed my gun at you.

"All is forgotten," he assured.

Ms. Winterton nodded with a soft smile.

"Who's Jack?" Ms. Kennings asked with a puzzled look on her face.

"Oh—he's a monstrous creature, with wings," Ms. Winterton responded in a relaxed manner.

"Ahhhh," she sighed before almost making her way to the floor. Officer Oxnard rushed around the table, just in time to catch her.

"Maybe—you shouldn't have mentioned that part," Officer Morley gave his belated advice.

"You're right, I… wasn't thinking." She looked at Officer Oxnard and asked politely, "Could you carry her up to the couch in the living room? I'll make us some coffee."

"Sure." He carried her up the steps and they all followed with the felines close behind them.

Ms. Winterton found a blanket to cover her with and then before she walked away to brew some coffee, she asked, "Officer Morley, why don't you come with me?"

"Sure." He turned to the officers and said, "I'll be right back guys."

As they entered the kitchen, she searched the cabinets for coffee. "Here's something—black tea. I'll make this," she said satisfied and then added, "I think they'll need some help."

"No, they're fine, she's sleeping," he responded calmly.

"No," she shook her head and explained, "I don't mean them—everyone in Wanderamid."

"Wait a minute,' he looked at her with widened eyes, "You're not thinking of going there."

"My daughter needs me and there's no telling how long they'll be gone."

"You've got to give them time, Ms. Winterton."

"Will you just call me, Rylia, please?"

"If you call me, Trent," he responded with a smile.

"OK, Trent. I'll give them just a little more time."

"I hope you mean that, Rylia."

CHAPTER TWENTY-EIGHT

DEVILEA'S COVENANT

Devilea finally landed, with Jack, on Tarots trail. She stood in front of him, staring as if it was the first time she had ever seen him.

"It's been a long time, Jack."

He looked at her, frightened as could be. His transformation was unexpectedly quick and left him shocked. Only moments before, he was a pterodoc and a part of him still felt like one.

She held his wrist tightly at the beginning of Caven's Way.

"Does it feel good to be—you again, Jack?"

He remained confused, unable to answer.

"You'll be staying with some—creatures," she explained with a grin. "You will listen to them, or something terrible will happen to those you care about!" She held the crystal ball for him to see. "Your sister, Avanna, wants this beautiful clear stone—and so do the others, but I'll make sure they never get it."

He continued to remain speechless. He knew what she was capable of and willingly went with her as they entered into a very damp and dull place. His knowledge about her powers weakened any attempts to escape.

In the midst of Roewkall Woods, she had begun to call out as Jack stood beside her, imprisoned in her clutch. "Fleur!" she shouted, turning full circle, pulling him along with her.

The branches above them began to sway. The trypalls jumped, one at a time, down to the ground. Jack lowered his head, scrunched his shoulders, and then gradually focused with squinting eyes on the creatures that stood tall before him.

"Why have you come?" Fleur asked and then glanced at the boy beside her. It was obvious, by the expression on his face; he did not want to be there.

She held Jack's arm up, over his head. "I brought collateral."

"Collateral?" she asked with a puzzled look on her face.

She and the others were disappointed it was not Emera who had arrived instead, to change them back. They were clearly devastated and had no interest in being a part of Devilea's scheme.

"Yes. This is Avanna's brother, you know, the pterodoc," she chuckled excitedly.

Fleur walked up to him and his eyes widened as a foul odor caused his head to turn and sneeze. He turned back with his hand covering his nose, blocking the indescribable smell.

"What do we need from him?" she asked with an obvious, broken spirit.

"Have they brought Emera to you yet, to change you back?"

"No, they didn't." She lifted her long arms in front of Devilea as the others looked on and then lowered herself until they were face to face. "Does it look–like they did?"

"Well, maybe hiding Avanna's brother will give you some power."

Jack sensed his situation about to become worse. He pulled away from Devilea's hold and began flapping his arms.

She quickly grabbed one of his flapping arms and began laughing aloud, "You're not a bird anymore! You can't fly away from me anymore! Ha! Ha! Ha! You'll have to keep a good eye on this one," she urged Fleur and then swiftly gazed directly into his sad eyes, "Or, maybe I should just change him into a one-eyed snake."

"No!" he pleaded. "I won't try to leave!"

"Oh, you can talk now, huh?" she chuckled. "I don't know why I changed you into a pterodoc when I'm having such a good time with you just the way you are."

Jack did not say a word.

"You don't think they'll be able to save him?" Fleur spoke with doubt in her voice. "They found him when he was twenty times his size. What makes you think they won't find a simple boy?"

Fleur's questions insulted Devilea's intelligence. Even though Devilea needed her to keep an eye on Jack, she could no longer hide the anger she felt.

"I will make a mirrored hideaway. Keep him in it so all visions reflect away from him."

Her sudden fierce response caused Fleur, along with the other trypalls, to step back. After only a few moments, she bravely asked another question.

"How can we be sure he won't try and escape when you leave? He'll be no good to us, gone."

"The—mirrored—hideaway—will—be three sided. There will be an opening in the front. Have the other trypalls take turns guarding him, so he won't escape!" She had enough of her foolish questions and shouted, "Do you want this gift of blackmail I'm handing over to you or not?"

"Yes," she answered and the others nodded excited in agreement.

"Walk in between those trees," Devilea pointed to her left, "until you see the mirrored hide-out and place him in it. Guard him with your life," she advised and then pulled Jack over to her, lifting his arm for her to take him.

He felt Fleur's slimy hands and although they made him squirm, he could not wait until she took him there, away from Devilea.

"Wait! How will we keep him from escaping? We're not as fast as we use to be," a trypall yelled.

"Anyone who guards the entrance at the time of his escape will have the power to stop him. It will not be permanent, only used for the capture. His punishment will be up to you." She turned to Jack, "Bye!" Her laughter echoed as she floated away, out from the dark, dreary atmosphere.

Soon after she left, two of the trypalls, Onfroi and Leanon, brought Jack to the mirrored hideaway Devilea created especially for him. They guarded him while their hopes of becoming human again became closer to reality.

"We'll get you something to eat," Onfroi said as he sat down and leaned against the hideaway entrance. "You should use what time you have left to pray your sister and her friends keep their word, asking Emera to change us back the way we were, if she ever returns to Wanderamid." He turned to Leanon and ordered, "Get him something to eat! He's no good to us dead you know!"

Leanon nodded and then left immediately to get them food, while Onfroi sat back and thought about how he had almost given up hope. Jack lay down on the ground, looking at the only view he had, the creature guarding his exit.

In the meantime, Devilea kept herself distant from Clemedeth, walking the opposite way on Tarot's trail, away from what was once her home. She knew everyone found Jack missing, and would begin searching for him. The night had fallen and she was content with her three crystal balls inside her cloak pockets. While she walked in all her glory, she noticed a tunnel ahead and a voice heard, calling for Avanna and Jack.

"It's their mother. What a surprise," she murmured with widened eyes. "It's time for some more fun."

She had never been through a tunnel with the crystal ball, and was curious to see what was on the other side.

* * *

In Wishing Willow, Ms. Marsail thought of the worst. A full day had passed since she accompanied her daughter and friends to the entrance of Wanderamid. The children playing in the distance made her miss her own even more.

One little girl nearby, away from her mother, noticed her standing inside the tunnel, calling for Avanna and Jack and then placing her hands over her face, sobbing. Then, all of the sudden, there was a blaring light and it frightened the little girl enough that she began to tremble and quickly hid behind the nearest tree.

Ms. Marsail lowered her hands after she felt a warm feeling in between her fingers and on her face.

"Avanna, Jack!" she held her hands out in front of her, trying to see who was walking through.

Hesitantly, she backed away when she saw someone she had never seen before. It was, Devilea. The little girl gasped the same time as Ms. Marsail when she saw her walk towards her with a hood over her head that could not even hide that crooked nose. She stood frozen behind the tree, too scared to make another sound and had no choice but to listen.

"Who are you?" she asked suspiciously, disappointed it was not her children.

"My name is Devilea. Are you Avanna's mother?" Devilea asked, seemingly anxious.

"Yes. Do you know her?" She became hopeful and then a sudden distrusting feeling quickly came about.

"Avanna's in trouble!" she blurted out.

Ms. Marsail noticed the crystal ball in her arms, the same one Rena held when she left. Something was not right.

"Where did you get that?"

"What?" Devilea's face scrunched up.

She pointed out, "That crystal ball, Avanna had it when she left. How did you get it? Where's Avanna?"

"Now, Ms. Avanna and Jack's mother, you should calm down." Her demeanor became as crooked as her nose.

"What? You bring my children back to me, now!"

The little girl heard her mother calling for her.

"Kolly, Kolly!"

"Give me that crystal ball," she demanded as she reached for it and then grabbed it, both pulled back and forth, neither would let go.

Kolly watched them fighting over it. "Oh, no!" she cried out and then quickly covered her mouth.

Devilea turned her head, and that Ms. Marsail the opportunity to run with it towards the back of the tunnel.

Devilea ran after her, but tripped over her long cloak. When she lifted her head up, she saw that she was gone. "Nooo!"

Would she ever return to Wanderamid or bound forever in Wishing Willow?

Kolly saw all that had happened and ran as fast as she could towards her mother's call, running up to her from behind, just as Devilea stood at the tunnel's entrance. Her mother heard someone running up from behind and turned.

"Kolly, where were you?"

"Can we go home, Mom? I don't feel so good."

Her mother placed her hand on her forehead and felt no sign of a fever. "Sure," she held her chin up gently, "Let's go and I'll fix you some chicken soup."

Kolly walked close beside her and then slowly turned to look back. Her eyes met with Devilea's, as she stared with a vengeful grin. Kolly held her mother's arm tightly with trembling hands, tightening her eyes closed with fear.

Devilea saw the face of yet another annoyance, causing her to once again, lose the crystal ball. Then, oddly enough, she felt the light still powerful against her back.

Was the entrance to Wanderamid still open?

Ms. Marsail entered Wanderamid with a sick feeling in her stomach, bringing her to crouch down on the tunnel floor. She raised her head and noticed many trees outside.

"Am I in the middle of the forest?" she murmured.

The sick feeling slowly disappeared and she was able to bring herself to a stand. Although she was anxious to find her children, she walked cautiously towards the unfamiliar exit. Her body shivered more, as she finally reached the end. Hesitantly, she peeked; a cool chill touched her face and she quickly stepped back. Her heart began beating rapidly, so she took a deep breath to calm herself and then peeked out again, in the still of the night.

"What do I do now?" she whispered nervously under her breath. "Where do I go?"

She thought it best to remain where she felt safe, just until sunrise, but, before she was about to sit, the tunnel began to sparkle and the walls around her seemed to be fading. She got out quickly and stood in the middle of a trail, watching the tunnel slowly dissipate. The thought of not running out at the right time horrified her, and not knowing what to do next. A sudden strong gust of wind ran through her, and she felt her heart stop as it did. Then, the tunnel was gone. She tried to catch her breath and for a second, thought it to be her last, as her arms reached for a nearby tree to lean on. The path she was on would either direct her near Caven's Way, further down towards the witch's cottage or out of Hemlock Village. Fortunately and unknowingly, she had chosen the correct path. She pulled out the flashlight, used every night in Wishing Willow, to help guide her in the beginning of an unexpected journey. Then, a faded hissing-squeak sound caused her to wait. She stood still and aimed the flashlight all around, but saw nothing and then heard it again. She turned to her left, and then to her right where there was an empty bag on the ground, surrounded with crackers and cubes of cheese near a huge bush that stood at least twelve feet tall. As she walked closer to it, a one-eyed snake with a head of a rat startled her and showed its sharp fangs.

"Aaaaah!" she screamed and ran lifting her feet high off the ground as she did, and her body shook in disgust, trying to avoid any others that might have been around!

Clemedeth awakened by the frightening cry that traveled through her open kitchen window. She rose up and quickly walked to her front door for some fresh night air, reliving what had happened hours before. Seconds after, she heard the faded cry again, confirming it was not from her dream. The sound made her cringe once more and she grabbed her cloak off from the hook beside her. She went outside and slowly walked towards the corner of the cottage, onto Tarots trail as she draped the cloak around her shoulders. It was then she heard someone running closer to her direction with light swaying in the same rhythm of the sound. She stopped and squinted to see who it was.

Ms. Marsail ran out of breath again and focused only at the cottage with lights on.

"Eeeek!" Clemedeth startled her. She wore a cloak, similar to Devilea's. She shined the flashlight in Clemedeth's face, but she turned away.

"What's the matter?" Clemedeth asked, as she turned with her hands held up in front of her face. "Do you need help?"

Ms. Marsail realized that it was not Devilea, from the tone of her voice.

"I'm terribly sorry," she apologized and turned off the flashlight. "I—thought you were someone else." Her screams used all her energy and left her exhausted.

Clemedeth lowered her hands and saw her worried expression. "Can I help you with anything?"

"I'm trying to find my daughter… and… my son." Soon after she spoke, she began to cry.

"Come to my cottage," she welcomed her. "We'll talk there."

"No," she shook her head, "I… couldn't impose."

"It's dark outside and you don't know where you're going. Or do you?"

Ms. Marsail cried uncontrollably, "Nooo-ho-ho!"

It will be easier for you to travel in the daylight," Clemedeth advised.

Ms. Marsail took a moment to think as she wiped her eyes. "All-right… thank… you-hoo-hoo," she cried, grateful for her help.

They both walked around the corner and went inside. Clemedeth immediately placed a pot of water on the stove.

"What's your name?"

"Where are my manners? My name… is… Lystra… Lystra Marsail," she gave a mild grin, wiping the last of her tears. "It's very… kind of you to invite me into your… home."

Clemedeth handed her a tissue and she blew her nose. She stared at her surroundings and noticed all the old books on the shelves and the kitchen jars filled only with things witches were to have. Her heart began beating fast and in an instant, felt overwhelmed with fear. She was frightened and thought about running out the door.

'Is she related to that, Devilea?' she thought.

"You can take off your jacket," Clemedeth smiled.

"No thank you. I'm still a little chilly," she replied while making sure the crystal ball was securely in her pocket. "Do you live here—alone?"

"No, I mean, yes, now I do. It was a friend that I helped, but she turned out to be—ungrateful."

"What does she look like? Maybe I've seen her."

"Well, she's short with a crooked nose, is the best way to describe her."

That was enough description for Ms. Marsail.

"Well, you know, I really should be going."

Her quick reaction caught Clemedeth's attention.

"Wait! You've seen her, haven't you? You've seen Devilea!" her eyes widened in surprise.

Lystra was halfway to the door.

"No, no. Thank you for your hospitality." She rushed the rest of the way.

"I'm nothing like her! Please don't be afraid of me! I need to know where she is. She has something I have to get back. It will help my friends who are trying to get home," she explained desperately.

Ms. Marsail turned around and curiously asked, "What would that be? What do you need to get back?"

She quickly responded, "Three crystal balls. They belong to my mother."

"If I can rest here until the morning, I will tell you what I know. I'm not feeling so good." She placed her hand over her heart.

"You can sleep on the couch. I'll wake you when the sun rises. I'll even bring you to where you need to go," she offered.

"Thank you," she nodded gratefully.

Clemedeth led her to the living room and fixed the couch extra comfortable for her to rest on. Ms. Marsail lay down with her jacket on and drifted into a much-needed sleep, guarding the crystal ball under her arms. Clemedeth left two lit candles on the table beside her, turned off the stove, and began to walk up the stairs, when there was a knock on the door. She stopped halfway and hurried back down before the noise woke Lystra. When she opened it, she saw that it was Emera.

"Jack's gone, again!" she said aloud.

Clemedeth quickly placed her finger up to her lips and whispered, "Shhhh!" She hoped Emera had not awakened her guest, then waved her hand for her to enter, "Be quiet."

"Is Devilea here?" she whispered excitedly.

"No, but, someone who's seen her is," she replied calmly and then added, "She'll tell me where she is in the morning."

"No, by then it might be too late," she said, anxiously. "We must wake her now. Avanna is…."

"Avanna, where's Avanna?" Lystra heard her daughter's name and rose up from the couch.

Clemedeth rushed into the living room, Emera followed. "Lystra," she stood in front of her with Emera beside her. "We were going to wake you. We need to know where Devilea is— now."

Lystra looked up at Emera with tired eyes, "Who are you?"

She wore the same cloak as Clemedeth and Devilea, witches' clothing. In an instant, she sat up and moved to the other end of the couch, then quickly stood and walked backwards, cautiously keeping them in her sight.

"You mentioned my daughter's name," she kept moving away and then stopped as she leaned forward, her eyes glued on the both of them. "Do you know my daughter?"

Clemedeth and Emera looked at one another with wide eyes, not knowing how they should answer and then turned to face her again.

"Umm…." Clemedeth responded with a confused expression.

Emera let out a huge sigh.

CHAPTER TWENTY-NINE

A CHANGE OF PRINTS

Back at Para's cottage, everyone called out to Jack. Avanna found six footprints on the ground near where Jack was; two were that of his pterodoc feet, the other four were two different sizes. She wondered whose they were and then figured it out quickly after.

"She changed him back!"

"If she did, it's only because she would be able to control him better and hide him easily," explained Officer Wodderspoon.

Rena looked up at him with troubled eyes. "When will Emera be back? When will she tell us where Devilea is?"

Para placed her hand on Rena's shoulders, "Come, lets' all go inside. We'll wait for her return. There isn't anything we can do right now."

"But what about Jack?" Avanna asked.

"Emera will bring us the answers," Para assured her. "She will have a plan on what is to be done next."

Avanna hesitantly followed them back inside. Each sat silently as Oula and Para fixed hot chocolate in the kitchen, all were hoping for Emera's quick arrival.

Meanwhile, Jack sat in his mirrored hideaway off Caven's Way in Roewkall woods while Fleur thought about the day Emera would change them back to who they once were. Nevertheless, even with Jack to use as blackmail, each one of their disappointments and devastation continued to grow.

Leanon dragged his sore feet until he finally reached Fleur.

"We need to give the boy some food!"

She was very angry to see him. "What are you doing? You have to guard him!"

"He's not good to us dead, you know! Besides, Onfroi is guarding him as we speak."

"How do you know he'll even be good to us alive?" she asked and at the same time, thought he was probably right. "Go… get him something. Whatever we eat, he'll eat! We'll keep him barely alive." She walked away with disgust, and then turned back quickly. "Wait! Weorth, go with Leanon and help him find food for all of us!"

Her dominant attitude did not seem to take any effect with the other trypalls; they dealt with it for many years. In fact, before the curse, she was the same way.

Weorth and Leanon started their search for food. They collected berries and nuts, only found in Roewkall woods, placing them in their creature made baskets, made from thin twigs. When they were finished, they headed back.

Leanon kept one basket.

"I'll bring this to Onfroi and Jack." He held the basket up for them to see. "I'll come back when the sun begins to rise."

They all nodded with tired eyes and depressed expressions, grunting, as they had already begun to eat. Leanon turned away with his own heartfelt agony and walked back through the woods.

He knew he had reached the mirrored hideaway when he saw Onfroi's feet down in front of him and then lifted his head glumly. "Onfroi, I'm back!" he announced in his low, hoarse voice, holding the basket out in front of him. "Take some."

He lifted his head slowly, "Thanks, Leanon."

Onfroi peeked inside where Jack was resting on the ground. "Jack, hold your hands out for berries and nuts."

"Berries and Nuts?" he scrunched up his face.

"Yes, I said berries and nuts! Did you eat any better as a pterodoc?"

"Yes… I did," he hesitantly moved closer to the opening.

"Well, you're a boy now! If you're not thankful for this, then, be thankful that you're not a pterodoc anymore!"

"OK, OK—I'm thankful. Thanks… a lot."

He noticed Onfroi's face changed for the worse when he became angry and backed away to the side, quietly eating his trypall meal.

"Leanon, sit, and eat," Onfroi pointed at the ground. "After you finish, get some sleep. I'll stay awake and make sure he doesn't escape." He glanced over to Jack and nodded.

When he finished his meal, he looked closely into Onfroi's eyes, "You'll be awake while I nap, right?"

"Yes," he nodded. "I'll be awake."

"Don't let him out of your sight. If your eyes close one time, they might not open!"

He raised his eyebrows and said firmly, "I'll be awake, don't worry."

"This is the closest we've ever been, to becoming who we once were. I'll be very angry if something goes wrong." He looked seriously into his weak eyes, halfway shut from his heavy eyelids.

"Nothing will go wrong! Now go to sleep!"

He gazed back at Jack and noticed him listening. He saw a frightened young boy in a desperate situation, just like them.

Shortly after, Leanon fell asleep.

Jack whispered, "Who… were you?"

Onfroi turned his head and stared back inside Jack's new prison, remembering what little he could, and answered sullenly, "We were like you—normal."

"How did you become who you are now?"

"It's a long story. But, I can tell you this, the only one who can change us back, is Emera."

"She didn't seem too bad. You must have done something bad, for her to turn you into...."

"To turn us into what...creatures?" he asked offended.

"No... I... well... I guess that's what I was going to say," he responded honestly.

"Akkeeeee," his huge, rotten teeth showed and his eyes glowed through the darkness.

Jack's whole body tensed and quickly backed away. Onfroi realized, by his reaction, how much of a creature he truly was. Any human feeling hid deep inside him.

"We were very mean to her growing up, thirteen years to be exact. We've suffered for thirty!"

Jack kept his distance. "Does she know you're even here, in the woods?"

"We haven't seen her once. I don't even know if she will ever forgive us for what we've done. Just as her bitterness grew, so has ours. That's our curse, to suffer as she did." His head dropped down and his scrawny shoulders covered his ears.

"Let me go, please. I'll find her and talk to her," he pleaded.

He lifted his head, "Akkeeeee!" Saliva passed through his teeth, dripping down his cracked lips. "Don't you dare, test me! Akkeeeee, you'll be s-s-sorry."

Jack quickly placed his hand over his mouth and gagged from the horrifying sight. He stared with disgust, afraid to move. "I didn't... mean... to..." he mumbled, slowly releasing his hand from over his mouth, "I think I'll... go to sleep... now."

"Yes-s-s-, maybe you s-s-should. Hey! You said before that Emera didn't seem bad." He looked at him with desperate eyes, "Is she here?"

"I... don't remember saying that. You must have heard wrong," he lied.

"Hmm," Onfroi wondered grimly as he leaned back slowly against the corner of the entrance, opposite from Leanon, who slept through their whole conversation.

Jack curled up on the floor, but kept his eyes open, wondering what the coming day would bring, and then eventually surrendered into his dreams. Onfroi remained awake, listening to the sound of silence in the home he lived in for thirty years. A long night was ahead of him and he grew more tired with each second. He thought to wake Leanon, but changed his mind, since it was still too early. He would hold off for as long as he could—if he could.

Back at the witch's cottage, only one person knew Devilea's whereabouts.

Emera revealed her doubts. "If you're Avanna's mother, how did you get here? Devilea has the crystal ball needed to travel through the tunnels."

"I know," Lystra reached into her jacket pocket and pulled out the crystal ball.

Clemedeth and Emera stood in awe with their eyes filled only with its view. They began laughing excitedly in amazement.

"I can't believe it!" Emera placed her hand over her heart. "Where did you get it—from Devilea?"

"Where else, she's the only one who had it!" Clemedeth responded ecstatically.

"Now, can you bring me to my daughter?"

Lystra's calm voice caused them to settle down.

"Of course we will," Emera patted her shoulder.

Lystra looked up at her with sad eyes and asked, "My son, Jack, he's with her right? Avanna found him?"

Both were speechless. What could they say? Their strong postures slumped over in an instant, unable to find words of comfort.

"Jack isn't found yet, is he?" Their silence answered her question and she slowly closed her eyes.

"Did Devilea say anything about Jack?" Clemedeth asked.

Lystra gradually opened her eyes and replied, "She told me that Avanna was in trouble. I didn't believe her."

Clemedeth gazed over at Emera.

"I think it's time to go to my grandmother's," Emera suggested. "Maybe she can give us some answers and Lystra can see Avanna."

"Let's go," Clemedeth agreed.

All three walked to the front door and then Clemedeth stopped suddenly, waving her hand once in the air and brought about a light wind that blew all the candles out.

Lystra was amazed. "How did you do that?"

"Oh, it's nothing really," she smiled.

They walked out into the brisk Wanderamid air.

"We'll hold on to you, Lystra," Emera told her as they lifted off the ground, gliding over Tarot's trail.

"Watch out for those snakes that have the head of a rat!" Lystra warned them.

"No snakes will come near us," Emera said to ease her fears.

"If they know what's good for them," laughed Clemedeth.

Lystra kept quiet the rest of the way, anxious to see her daughter and at the same time, worried about what happened to Jack.

"We're almost there," said Clemedeth. "You know, I met Avanna here a long time ago. We've been friends ever since she arrived in Wanderamid."

Lystra nodded and smiled, then immediately after, her smile turned into a nervous grin when they approached an uninviting sight.

"Maybe we should walk the rest of the way."

Clemedeth noticed she was nervous. "We're almost there Lystra. There's no need to be scared."

Lystra's heart had begun to beat faster. "I want to walk instead... please, put me down!"

"OK," Clemedeth looked over at Emera and they lowered to the ground.

A brush from the wind went across Lystra's face and she began to tremble. "What was that?"

Clemedeth and Emera turned full circle when it happened again!

"Did you feel that?" A chill went up her spine and then she noticed a look of uncertainty on Clemedeth's face.

"We really shouldn't stay in here too long. Let's walk fast," she advised, since Lystra was not comfortable gliding. "We're in their territory."

"Wait!" Lystra whispered strongly as she looked around suspiciously. "Let me get out my flashlight." She took it out of her jacket pocket and searched for the light switch in the thick fog. "So, Clemedeth," she tried to keep her mind off the ghostly surroundings, "Whose territory are you talking about? I don't see anyone around. Who would live here anyway?" she chuckled nervously.

"They are spirits, who don't like anyone roaming through their home."

"That's true," Emera nodded and agreed.

"Spirits—you mean—like dead people?" She hoped that what not what she meant.

"Yes, spirits are dead people–that's what we mean," Clemedeth confirmed.

Lystra heard faint whispering through the ghost-like atmosphere. She stopped instantly and then gradually turned to Emera and Clemedeth.

"Please say that you said something."

Clemedeth shook her head, "I didn't say anything."

"I didn't say anything either," Emera added.

They stood motionless while her shaking hand failed to keep her flashlight steady. She slowly aimed between them and their eyes followed the beaming light leading to a ghostly figure floating high above the ground.

"GET OUT—OR FOREVER YOU SHALL REMAIN!"

"Aaaaah!" she screamed and ran in the direction opposite the mean-spirited ghost.

Emera and Clemedeth glided above ground, trying to catch up with her.

Clemedeth shouted, "Wait!"

Lystra kept running.

"Lystra," yelled Emera, "slow down!"

Meanwhile, at Para's cottage, Rena heard screams and they seemed to be getting closer.

"Someone's coming!" she ran quickly out the door.

They all followed her into the opened space, lighted fully by the clear sight of the moon, its craters visible to the human eye.

"Aaaaah!" she continued to scream as Emera and Clemedeth tagged behind her, floating above ground.

Rena and the others walked slowly towards the woods when they saw her hysterically running towards them, shining the flashlight right in Rena's eyes as they became face to face.

"Ms. Marsail!" her eyes widened in surprise and then quickly moved the light away.

Lystra gasped, "Rena."

Avanna ran up to her, "Mom!

"Avan…."

"She fainted… help me!" Avanna cried out to the others.

Jodon and Micah helped just before her strength ended.

"I'll carry her in, boys," Officer Wodderspoon walked over, ready to take charge of the situation.

Micah gazed at Jodon, rolled his eyes, and then looked up at Officer Wodderspoon. "We have her already."

Emera's head lowered slightly and her eyes focused on Micah.

He understood his mother's gesture and hesitantly added, "Thanks anyway—Officer Wodder—spud," he purposely mispronounced.

"Wod—der—spoon," corrected the officer.

Emera gazed at Micah, raising one eyebrow and he smiled back, shrugging his shoulders.

"Bring her inside," Para calmly directed so not to worry Avanna, "and lay her down easily on the couch."

"I'll get her something to drink," Before Oula walked away, she went over to Emera and with both hands, held hers. "I'm so happy your back."

"I am, too, Mother."

They both smiled and then Oula continued towards the kitchen.

"How did she get here?" Micah asked his mother while he and Jodon carried Ms. Marsail inside. One held her arms and the other, her lifeless legs.

"I'll tell all of you, but first we must make sure she's all right."

"Yes, let's make sure," agreed Clemedeth.

Both silently felt something was seriously wrong with Lystra.

When they laid her down, Rena grabbed a pillow and placed it under Ms. Marsail's head.

"Thanks, Rena," Avanna said gratefully.

"She'll be all right, Avanna, she's just tired."

All of the sudden, there was a loud thump. The crystal ball fell out of Ms. Marsail's pocket. Everyone stared in amazement. Clemedeth swiftly picked it up, while the others stood with their frozen faces.

"The crystal ball... is here!" Rena said aloud.

"Where's Jack... and Devilea?" Avanna asked aloud.

"Shhh!" urged Emera. "Your mother doesn't know everything yet."

"Jack," Ms. Marsail moaned, moving her head slowly from one side to the other. She let out a huge sigh and then suddenly, her head was still.

"Will she be able to handle the news?" Para questioned Lystra's health.

"Well, we told her Jack wasn't found yet. We didn't say anything else. It was best she saw Avanna first."

They all sighed and nodded.

"Here some juice." Oula walked into a room full of sad faces and leaned over to Para and whispered, "What's going on, Mother?"

"The crystal ball has been found... and Ms. Marsail is sleeping."

"Ohhh," she gazed at Avanna, understandably saddened by her mother's condition. "We'll just let her sleep, to get her strength back."

"You can set the drink down, Mother. Thanks for getting it," Emera nodded gratefully.

"Oh, it was no problem at all." She set the glass on the table and sat herself down to rest her tired feet.

"What's next on the agenda?" Officer Wodderspoon looked at Emera.

"Don't you know?" Micah asked mockingly.

"Why–no, I'm sort of new to investigations involving magical interferences."

"Huh? Micah turned to the others and silently mouthed, "Magical interferences?" He rolled his eyes.

Jodon chuckled, shook his head, and then looked at Rena. "Let's go outside."

Rena tapped Avanna's arm and she slowly gazed up at her with a blank stare.

"She'll be fine, Avanna. She needs to rest. Come outside with us."

"OK," she slowly lifted herself off the floor.

"Good," Jodon smiled. "Come on, Micah."

"We will eat within the hour," said Para.

Micah turned around, "Thanks, Grandmother."

Emera waited until they were all out the door.

"We must talk in the other room," she secretly urged. "Clemedeth, bring the crystal ball, please, and never leave it unattended."

They followed her into the other room.

CHAPTER THIRTY

THE HEART GROWS WEAKER

All, except Clemedeth, had raised eyebrows.

Their eyes glued to Emera's, as they impatiently waited for her to speak.

"There's... something else wrong with Ms. Marsail. I didn't want Avanna to hear this, but Clemedeth and I sensed it in the woods. We think she's keeping something from us, about her health. We must look after her closely." She took a deep breath and looked at her grandmother, "We have to open the peephole. It's time to find out where Jack is."

Para, without hesitation, held out her hands and spoke out loud, *"Open wide, and show us Jack, time is moving fast and we need him back! Once a pterodoc and now, hopefully a boy, show where he is before he's destroyed!"*

A sudden breeze came about and grew stronger with each passing second. The peephole opened, instantly showing a vision of Roewkall woods, where the trypalls lived. All were silent as they listened to unfamiliar voices along with only a view of tall thin trees.

"For ___ ... ___ ... know," said a trypall, "Jack is dead…"

"Noooo!" Ms. Marsail clutched onto the doorway as the weight of her body leaned hard against it, slowly sliding down to the floor.

Everyone ran to her side and helped her back to the couch. The peephole closed instantly as they did.

Para walked behind them. "Ms. Marsail, you should have stayed on the couch to rest."

"Rest?" she shook her head as she walked limped in their hold and then stopped, lifting her head slowly with squinted tear filled eyes and said, "My son is dead! I just heard it!"

"Let's go back so you can lie down," Para tried to comfort her.

Emera and Officer Wodderspoon walked with them. Clemedeth went back into the room to get the crystal ball, remembering that Emera told her never to leave it alone.

Outside, Avanna heard crying from inside the cottage. She tilted her head to listen. "Is that my mother?" She hurried to the door and the others followed. As soon as she entered inside, she saw her mother awake and crying. She sat quickly beside her and put her arm around her shoulders. "Mom, what happened?"

She quietly sobbed, slowly lifting her head, wiping her overflowing of tears. "Avanna… Jack… he's… gone."

"I know, but we'll find him, right?" she smiled nervously, nodding to the others standing around them."

"No, Avanna," she explained softly as she held her close to her side, looking directly into her big blue eyes, "He's gone… forever."

Avanna looked up at Rena, who then placed her hand on her shoulder. "I'm sorry."

Avanna raised her voice, "No, I don't believe it!"

"It's true, Avanna," Emera confirmed regretfully.

Micah was speechless and heartbroken. He desperately wanted to save Jack from Devilea and bring him back to his mother and sister.

"We'll go back to Wishing Willow and we'll find Devilea! We'll make her tell us where he is," Avanna insisted.

"No, we can't. There's something I haven't told you," she paused, "I… I can't go through another tunnel."

She paused and then asked, "Why?"

"I'm dying, Avanna. My heart is weak. When I went through the tunnel, it became worse," she shook her head mournfully. "I knew my end was coming near after I felt a strong gust of wind go through me as I was running out of Wishing Willow, and into Wanderamid. It was at that time, I thought it had taken my last breath."

All kept quiet; they knew she had more to say. Silently and curiously, they waited.

"You should let me pass away… here… in Wanderamid. Please, don't bury me, Avanna. Bring me to the water and let my body drift away… peacefully."

"You can't die. I need you!" Her eyes filled with tears that slowly fell down her face. She rested her head next to her mother's and wept as they held each other's hand.

Para walked to the nearest room; the others followed solemnly, their eyes filled with sadness.

"Rena," Ms. Marsail called out to her in a weak voice.

Rena heard her clearly in the quiet cottage and walked up to her slowly.

"Yes, Ms. Marsail," she whispered delicately and then knelt down beside her.

"Could Avanna live with you? I mean… if it's all right with you and your family."

"Yes, we'd love to have her with us."

Avanna listened to her mother's request. She grew stronger knowing she had to show her, in such little time, that she would be all right, and not to worry during her last moments, however long that would be. She moved her head away from her mothers and looked into her eyes.

"No."

"What?" her mother asked, seemingly confused.

"I said… no." She then looked at Rena. "Thank you, but I'll be staying here, in Wanderamid."

"Please…." Ms. Marsail pleaded, slowly tightening her grip on her daughter's hand.

"I want to be close to you and Jack. Right now, that's here. I'll be all right."

"But, this world is much different than ours."

Clemedeth walked up to Ms. Marsail gradually and knelt down in front of her beside Rena.

"Lystra, if it's all right with you, she can stay with me at my cottage."

"Thank you, Clemedeth," Avanna responded gratefully.

Ms. Marsail's eyes had become darker and weaker, unable to respond to Clemedeth's kind offer. Avanna's thoughts slipped away from the surreal moment into thoughts of revenge. She blamed Devilea for everything that had happened, from her missing brother, to worsening her mother's health.

"Avanna," Rena gently patted her shoulder to get her attention.

She turned her head and slowly gazed at her while her thoughts remained elsewhere, "Yes?"

"It's your mother," she said sadly.

She tilted her head slightly to the side, not understanding what she meant. "What?"

Lystra watched, as everyone gathered around the couch.

"Thank… you for welcoming me, and my children, into your home."

Tears fell from their eyes as they listened to what seemed to be, her final words. She turned to Avanna, as she felt her time would end at any moment.

I love you and Jack so much. I wish that I could have saved… him and he would be with you now. I….” Her eyes closed and she looked as though she had fallen asleep.

“Mom?” Avanna rested her head lightly on her mother's lifeless body and cried.

All gathered around her for support. It was time to pay their last respects to Ms. Lystra Marsail.

Para and Oula both helped Avanna to stand, gently pulling her away.

“Officer, could you please carry Ms. Marsail into my bedroom?”

“Yes, Para," he walked sadly to her and then carefully carried her away.

“You boys stay here; the officer will be right back."

She turned to Avanna, who stood still, watching him carry her mother into the other room.

"I have a pretty gown in my closet never worn. I would like to give it to your mother, to wear in her passing,” she offered respectfully.

Avanna looked at her with no expression on her face and nodded gently before she sat on the couch where her mother closed her eyes, forever. Rena sat beside her.

“We'll need your help, too,” Para looked at Emera and Clemedeth.

“Rena, will you stay with Avanna?” Emera asked with a soft grin.

"Yes, I'll stay with her."

"We'll be outside if you need us," Micah said, before he walked out the door.

"If you need anything," added Jodon.

Rena gave them a soft grin while Avanna sat quietly, staring down at the floor. As they shut the door behind them, Avanna began to think about how her mother described her entry into Wanderamid. 'A gust of wind went through me as I ran out of the tunnel'.

"Rena? Did you feel a gust of wind go through you when we walked out of the tunnels?"

Rena had no idea what she was talking about; although it made no sense to her, she respectfully responded, "No... I didn't. I would have remembered that. Why?"

"No reason," she gave a heavy sigh. However, there had been a reason, a reason she would keep only to herself.

Para and the others came out from the room Lystra lay in the gown given to her from Para.

"Avanna," Emera stood tall and then knelt down as she spoke to her, almost in a whisper, "We must go towards the water, as your mother requested. My grandmother and my mother will not be able to accompany us. We must leave now."

"I'll help you up, Avanna." Rena gradually pulled her up and walked with her to the door.

Emera stood back up, walked behind them, and then stopped. They both turned and saw everyone standing, quietly still.

"With my powers, I will glide your mother beside us as we travel towards the nearest waters to release her body, towards the destination she so chose to be her last," Emera said, respectfully.

"I will be contacting your mother, Rena." Para placed her hand on her shoulder. "I will let her know all that has happened."

"Will you tell her that I love her?" she asked politely.

"Yes, my dear, I will," she assured her.

Officer Wodderspoon walked up to Para. "Will you tell Officer Morley something for me?"

"Yes. What is it you would like me to say?"

"Tell him he was the best partner—and that I'll be staying." He looked at Emera and then asked, "If that's all right with you."

Emera smiled and nodded, "Yes... that's fine with me."

Her heart softened with his words once again, although not all of her heart. She still held resentment towards others, she felt she could never forgive.

Micah heard his mother's answer as he and Jodon walked back inside, but his thoughts on Avanna took the place of their differences, for the time being. He wished he could have done more for Avanna and his feelings begun to lean towards her.

"The sun will be rising soon. We must go now before it does," Emera urged them to begin their short journey.

Emera, Clemedeth, and Officer Wodderspoon, walked ahead while Ms. Marsail's body glided above ground behind them, as she lay on a long, soft, white satin cushion. Her white gown hung over the sides, with her long hair parted over her shoulders. The girls walked on either side of her and the boys walked behind. All were quiet as they traveled to the place, where she would be making her final way, into another world that not even the crystal ball could bring her.

They headed north through uncharted woods, a different direction other than where they had arrived. The trees were spread apart more than what they were used to, making it easier and faster to get to where they were going. Nevertheless, they were still inside ghostly territories, walking through the home of unknown spirits from the past. The last thing the ghosts wanted to remember was life, something they could never have back.

"What's that?" Jordon whispered strongly. He thought he saw a white figure.

"What's what?" Micah seemed unconcerned, but looked around anyway.

"I saw something… up there, in front of Emera," he pointed.

Emera and the others heard what he said and they all looked up slowly. They saw a ghostly figure floating up high before them, the one Emera, Clemedeth, and Lystra had encountered earlier.

"Just ignore him," she ordered strongly. "Walk faster and show no fear."

As they walked faster, Avanna remained close beside her mother, floating in an increased speed, Rena on her other side.

"What does it want?" Avanna asked in a nervous tone of voice.

"Whatever he wants, he will have to fight me for it!" she shouted loud enough for the ghost to hear.

"I'll walk behind Ms. Marsail," Officer Wodderspoon told Emera. "Micah and Jodon, walk behind the girls."

Clemedeth yelled, "Watch!" She tightened the cloak around her to keep the crystal ball safe in her pocket.

"STOP!" the ghostly figure bellowed.

Emera and Clemedeth stopped and so did the others behind them. Officer Wodderspoon immediately took out his gun! Micah turned when he heard a clicking sound and caught sight of him aiming towards the spirit.

"You're kidding, right?" he chuckled. "Mom, is he serious?"

Emera turned slightly and saw Officer Wodderspoon from the corner of her eye, holding a gun in his hand.

"That won't work," she whispered firmly. "Put—it—away. I have this one."

Officer Wodderspoon hid his embarrassment and looked at the others whose eyes glued to the gun aimed in their direction.

"Impulse," he shrugged his shoulders and placed it back in his holster.

Micah shook his head and gave a huge sigh.

"I know who you want, and you can't have her!" Emera yelled.

"ANYONE WHO TRAVELS THROUGH IS MINE– IF I CHOOSE!" his mean spirited voice roared.

"Emera, I've dealt with his type many times."

"Flynn!" she yelled and then quickly after, calmed. "He's not a person. He's a ghost."

He looked up at the ghostly figure ten times his size, floating many feet above ground and came to realize, she was right, as he tried not to show the fear that instantly filled his body.

"Yeah… uh, right… I'm… here if you need me."

Micah once again shook his head in disappointment. Emera noticed her son's unneeded expression, but ignored it as she continued to take charge of a much more serious situation.

"LET US THROUGH!" she held her hand high, "OR YOU WILL BE BANISHED!"

Everyone gasped with eyes wide open and their mouths drooped down to their chests. Clemedeth remained beside her, ready to help in any way she could, with what powers she had.

"Emera, how will you do that?" she whispered loud enough to reach up to her ears.

"With everything I have," she responded with confidence.

"Ha, Ha, Ha, Ha, Ha-Ha, Ha, Ha, Ha, Ha!" he laughed in a deep, horrifying voice, "BE GONE!"

His figure expanded wide, pushing them all down on the ground; all except Emera and Avanna's mother, who still floated peacefully, untouched by their fight. The others moaned from the unexpected thrust and then helped each other get back on their feet.

"Mom, are you all right!" Micah yelled.

"Yes, I'm fine," she stood unmoved. "All of you... hide behind the trees!"

Officer Wodderspoon helped gather everyone behind the trees, as they all waited to see her reaction.

"ARE YOU READY TO HAND OVER THE SOUL WHO LEFT YOUR WORLD AND WHO'S MORE ACCEPTABLE TO MINE?" he spoke undefeated.

"You ask me that, even when you think I'm defeated? Ha, Ha, Ha," she responded scornfully. "You're a sorry soul who roams in the night. Deep down inside you know I have only begun to fight!"

She lifted her arms and then waved all she had within her, at him. A magnetic force lit the tips of the branches like enormous candles and then, pushed the ghostly sight of him away; he was gone in an instant! She turned all around and saw him nowhere.

Clemedeth immediately called out to the others hiding, "Hurry, come out!"

Avanna ran to her mother's side, and so did the others, protecting her in case he returned unexpectedly.

Emera saw glimmering from the light of the sun about to rise in the distance. "We must all run, quickly!" She continued to lead the way.

"Don't look back!" Officer Wodderspoon warned.

"We won't," they all replied and only looked straight ahead.

CHAPTER THIRTY-ONE

THE FINAL CALLING

Ms. Winterton and Officer Morley were preparing black tea, while the officers sat in the living room, watching over Ms. Kennings, who lay resting on the couch. She catered into the next room and placed the tray down in the middle of the table.

"I found some tea," she smiled and passed one to each of them.

"Thank you," they responded at the same time, grateful for her hospitality.

"My pleasure," she nodded. "Did either of you notice her move at all?"

"She did a little," answered Officer Oxnard, before taking a sip from his hot black tea.

"Well, I think we should go back down to the cellar, just in case Para tries to contact us."

"What about Ms. Kennings?" Officer Wysor asked.

"She'll be fine up here." She watched the felines roaming the floor and pointed at them, "They will watch over her I'm sure. They're quite intelligent little animals."

"Shall we?" Officer Morley stood up with his tea in hand, leading them all back down to the cellar.

"Um, Trent, wouldn't it be best you kept your tea up here?" Rylia suggested. "It does get sort of windy down there."

"I suppose you're right, Rylia." He set his cup back down on the tray.

Meanwhile, Ms. Kennings awakened from her sleep. She sat up moaning, rubbing her forehead. Ms. Winterton and the others heard her.

"Ms. Kennings," Ms. Winterton walked over and sat beside her. "Are you all right?"

"Hmm, I guess," she groaned, still rubbing her forehead.

Ms. Winterton held a cup of black tea up to Ms. Kenning's mouth. "Here, have some."

She slowly grabbed onto the cups handle and brought it to her lips. She was aware it was hot when she felt the heat touching her face and then carefully took a sip. Then, she noticed the officers standing. "Are you going somewhere?"

"We were going down to the cellar. We thought it would be best if you rested. This has all been so–how can I say it–so…." Officer Wysor had a loss for words.

"Out of this world," Officer Oxnard finished.

"So—nicely put," Ms. Winterton looked to Officer Morley and rolled her eyes. "Well, I was not going to relate the situation as such, but..." She also had a loss for words. "Are you well enough to come with us Ms. Kennings?"

"Yes, I'm well enough. Thank you for your concern. In the future, before all this ends, I would appreciate being included in everything."

"Of course," she nodded.

Ms. Winterton, and the officers, respected her wishes.

They all walked to the cellar door and then proceeded down the stairs, while the felines remained sitting on the end of the couch, staring with their glowing eyes.

"Let's all take the same positions we took before," Officer Morley advised.

Everyone agreed.

"Before I begin to open the peephole," Ms. Winterton said, "I want to let you know that the only way the children can find the entrance to Whilom, is by someone calling for them, from the tunnel at Fountain Lake Park, to let them know it's the right one. Keep that in mind, for whatever happens."

She sensed Officer Morley's stare from the corner of her eye. He knew why she made such a speech and was ready for any sudden decisions she already had planned. She looked down in front of her and opened the grimoire. They were amazed once again, how it grew to an enormous size. With her arms stretched out she immediately recited briefly, *We must see the loss of two; eliminate our worries with a mind easing view!"*

The wind blew against their faces as an inch size peephole appeared, growing larger by the second. Ms.

Kennings and the officers stood stronger and braver than the last time, only with the same chills running up and down their arms.

"Para," she called out as the peephole opened even wider, filling the space between the ceiling and cellar floor.

"Ms. Winterton, something terrible has happened," she said, sadly.

Ms. Winterton's heart suddenly stopped along with the others when they heard those alarming words. She stood horrified and suddenly speechless, not knowing what she had meant. Ms. Kennings grabbed hold of her arm to keep from falling. Finally, she had control of her emotions and ask, "What has happened, Para?"

"Ms. Marsail–Avanna's mother—she passed away."

Ms. Winterton was instantly saddened for Avanna, yet relieved the children were still safe. Ms. Kenning's tight grip quickly loosened, and her hand fell to her side. Although she never met Avanna, it saddened her to hear a young girl just lost her mother. The officers stood silent and listened.

"Please send our condolences and let her know she is welcome to stay with us."

"I will let her know, but she has already decided to stay here in Wanderamid."

"Oh—well—then if she changes her mind. Where are Rena and Jodon?"

"They left with the others to pay their last respects to Ms. Marsail. They've gone to bring her to the water. It was one of her wishes. Rena and Jodon will be searching for the tunnel leading them to you. Soon you will have to help them find their way."

Ms. Winterton turned to Ms. Kennings and smiled softly.

Ms. Kennings nodded and then a tear fell from her eye.

"How did Ms. Marsail end up in Wanderamid, Para?"

"She came across Devilea in Wishing Willow, where Avanna is from. Somehow, she took the crystal ball from her and came here, to search for her children.

Para thought it best not to mention Jacks death, as it would only cause them to worry more.

"Devilea sounds like a handful."

"That she is, Ms. Winterton, however, she too is a young girl lost and can't seem to find her way back to her heart. I don't think she even cares to try at this point. Oh, Officer Morley," she almost forgot to mention, "Officer Wodderspoon wanted me to tell you that you were the best partner he ever had. He will be staying here in Wanderamid with Emera."

"What?" he asked with a surprised look.

"He is determined to help make things right around here. He is a very brave man."

Officer Morley was worried about him, just as Ms. Winterton was worried for her daughter and Ms. Kennings for her son. He began to have the same thoughts Rylia had about going through the peephole. He turned to the officers and then to Ms. Kennings, slowly walking towards Rylia.

Para saw the look on their faces and quickly responded, "Don't even think about it! There's already been one parent taken away. You need to stay there and wait for them. They both love you very much!"

Ms. Winterton looked at Officer Morley. "She's right. We might cause more confusion. They have everything under control. We should all just stay together and help them find their way home from here."

Officer Morley hesitantly agreed and then looked back into the peephole. "Para, we'll be calling them from the tunnel. We'll give them one day to begin searching for the right one."

"They will probably begin after they place Ms. Marsail on her final journey. Good luck to you all." Para and Oula waved them goodbye.

"Thanks, for everything," Ms. Winterton smiled gratefully and they smiled back. The peephole closed thereafter. She turned and advised the others, "We must find a way to make the park scarce. No one can be around when they walk out of the tunnel."

Officer Morley looked at the officers, who were seemingly confused. "We'll need you to make up an excuse, calling off the investigation, at least away from the park."

"How can we do that?" Officer Oxnard asked with a doubtful expression.

"I don't know. Tell them anything. Tell them you found other evidence elsewhere; anything that will get them away from that tunnel."

"OK," he agreed to what was seemingly impossible. "We'll try our best."

"Ms. Winterton and I will stay here with Ms. Kennings, until you let us know it is safe to go down there. Remember, it has to be cleared by tomorrow night."

"Got it, let's go, Wysor."

Officer Wysor looked at Officer Morley, shaking his head. "You know what you're asking us to do is a little far-fetched."

"I know, but it's the only suggestion I've got."

They all walked up the stairs to see them off.

"I'm shaking, I'm so nervous," Ms. Kennings stood trembling. "I can't wait to see Jodon. I wish I could just go down to the lake right now."

"I know, I feel the same way," Ms. Winterton giggled nervously and then noticed Trent quiet, seemingly worried about his partner.

While she and Ms. Kennings were excited about seeing their children again, they had forgotten Officer Wodderspoon would not be coming back.

"Trent," she placed her hand on his slumped shoulder, "I'm sorry about your partner. You never know; he might change his mind and come back."

"No, I don't think so," he sighed with a smile. "I could see how he was with her. I could tell he liked her a lot. He's like the brother I never had. I wish him all the best." He gave another big sigh and added, "Well, time is ticking away and before you know it, we'll be walking down to the tunnel, where it all began. I went to your home earlier to get you a change of clothes. They're down the hall, in my duffle bag. I'll wait here."

"Thank you, Trent," she replied appreciatively.

She and Ms. Kennings walked away to prepare for their children's arrival, the felines followed.

"No, no, you stay here with Trent." She shooed them towards him.

Officer Morley lay back on the couch and rested, thinking about how his job would be without his friend and partner.

*   *   *

In Wanderamid, they all ran through the woods as they surrounded Lystra's lifeless body, each holding on to a part of the white satin cushion. Pure white clouds lowered, touching the tips of the trees and the thick mist swirled, covering any sight of the ground.

Emera turned around, "Stop! We're here."

Everyone stopped and Avanna gripped the cushion tighter, her heart began beating rapidly. She looked all around confused. There was no water in sight.

"Where's the water? There's no water!" Micah looked all around.

"Micah, everyone, listen carefully," she urged in a hushed voice.

Everyone listened first to the sound of sudden silence and then the sound of calm waters entering gently into their ears, magically releasing any fears once imprisoned within their bodies. Avanna's grip loosened and then she took hold of her mother's hand, unwilling to let her go.

Emera slowly turned and faced the pure white, heavenly view in front of her. They all watched as her head unexpectedly leaned back and her arms swiftly lifted towards Wanderamid's sky. The thick mist before them separated, revealing the waters they once only heard and the entrance to Lystra's new path. She spoke out strongly and the wind began to blow.

"I call onto my powers to create a divine ride in bringing our dear friend and mother safely to the other side. Heavenly sky above, watch as she sails; omit any disturbances for her destination to prevail!"

A beautiful white raft appeared with a silk cushion, glossy white and glittering. Emera turned around and noticed everyone's eyes sparkled from the reflection of the lovely raft she had created for Lystra.

"Avanna, we must prepare for your mother's departure."

"I can't just let her float away all alone. I'm going with her," she insisted as tears flowed uncontrollably down her face.

"Avanna, her body is here, but her spirit has already left."

"What if there's a storm and her body goes into the water? I need to be with her, so that doesn't happen."

Micah walked up to her slowly and then gently took hold of her hand.

"Let's give your mother her wish. We'll place her on the raft together," he said.

"We'll all help you," Rena added, with a mild grin.

"Mom, could you put a protective shield all around the sides so she doesn't go into the water?" Micah suggested to help ease Avanna's worried mind.

He surprised Emera, yet again, with his caring words, and she answered, "Yes, I can." She smiled and gave him a soft wink.

Avanna was pleased with his thoughtful request and gradually walked beside her mother, along with the others, as Emera slowly descended her body gracefully onto the beautiful glittering raft.

The time had arrived to set Lystra on her final journey to no return.

"Is there anything you want to say, Avanna?" Clemedeth asked in a gentle voice.

Avanna lifted her head and saw those who were there with her in the most solemn time of her life. They were all she had, friends from two other worlds. She gazed at them with her glassy, blue eyes and gave a soft smile. It was then she felt sudden strength to say her last words to her mother. To her, it seemed as though she was sleeping peacefully, ready to wake at any moment in time.

"I–can't believe you're really gone," she spoke while caressing her mother's hand and then leaned down to whisper in her ear. "Will you wake up?" She remembered Rena's inspiring words, that 'anything's possible'.

Nevertheless, Lystra lay still and breathless.

"I love you, Mom, and Jack does, too."

She looked up at Emera with tearful eyes and gave her a simple smile, stepping back and away from her mother. The others did the same and then gathered around her as Emera placed the surrounding protective shield, blind to any eye, setting her into the divine waters of Apatura Sea.

A rabble of butterflies with wings as big as the palm of a hand flew past them.

"Look, Avanna, butterflies. They're following her." Rena pointed out in amazement. She knew they were a sign of renewal of life and thought, 'Could it happen here, in Wanderamid?'

Avanna watched as they flew delicately, and she believed they would guide her mother.

The raft soon after disappeared into the thick mist, drifting away and carrying her away.

"Look at the sky," Rena pointed up as silent lightning flickered above them.

"That's a sign of rain!" Clemedeth announced loudly.

"They say when it rains at a funeral, it means good luck," said Jodon.

"How can rain at a funeral mean good luck?" Micah asked with a scrunched expression.

"I guess you could call it... luck," said Officer Wodderspoon. "It means the departed soul is at peace and on the way to heaven."

Avanna was heartbroken and could not accept her mother's death. She fought with her whole being to keep what hope she had left inside her alive, as she thought, 'anything's possible'.

They heard thunder and lightning become one of many and began running back through the ghostly, and misty woods when suddenly, it began pouring rain. Emera quickly placed an invisible shield to keep them from getting soaked. Then, Rena saw what appeared to be a shelter, made of concrete blocks, just like the one in Whilom.

"Look!" she pointed towards it, "Let's go in there!"

They ran inside what appeared to be another tunnel, a tunnel, she thought could be their way home.

"Clemedeth, I have to see if this is our way home. I'll need the crystal ball. If it's ours, I'll roll it back to you. If not, we'll return along it."

Clemedeth looked at Emera for approval. She gave a nod and Clemedeth reached inside her cloak pocket, and handed it over to her.

"Before you go, Rena, I want to apologize for the sorrow I've caused you and your mother."

"Apology accepted, Ms. Biddock," she smiled and then looked at Avanna. "Are you sure you won't come with us?"

"My place is here now. Thanks for being a good friend. I couldn't have made it without your help."

Rena nodded with a soft grin and then looked at Micah. "Thanks for helping us. I'll miss you."

"I'll miss you, too." He walked up to her, gave her a hug, and then nodded to Jodon, before standing back with the others.

"Thanks for all your help, Officer Wodderspoon."

He gave her a mild grin. "It was my pleasure. Tell my partner and your mother that I wish them the best."

"Clemedeth, I want to thank you, too. Please take care of Avanna."

"I will." She turned away to hide a tear that dripped down her cheek.

Jodon gave his gratitude briefly, but in a sincere manner.

"Sorry if I caused any trouble, and thanks for everything."

"Are you kidding?" Officer Wodderspoon responded. "We couldn't have had a better addition to this crowd. You're welcome anytime, uh, I mean that figuratively."

"Rena, it might not be your tunnel," said Avanna.

"If you ever need us," Jodon offered, "I know you'll find a way to reach us."

Rena ran up to Avanna and gave her a hug.

"I'm sorry about your brother, and your mother. If you ever need me, you know where I am." She held back her tears and then walked away with Jodon. A bright light filled the tunnel and they all partly covered their eyes, keeping them in view. Rena turned around slowly and shouted, "Please tell Oula and Para we said thanks… for everything!"

Jodon shouted, "So long, bro!"

They were gone, only the bright light still shined. A faded rumble had become louder. They all looked down to see the crystal ball had stopped in front of them. Avanna sadly picked it up. Although she was happy for them, she felt somewhat… alone. In one day, she lost her mother, Jack, and her best friend. There was no proof her brother was dead, only that he was certainly gone.

"Let's go back to the cottage," Clemedeth suggested. She turned to Avanna and saw her saddened by yet another loss. She placed her arm over her shoulder as they all walked out.

Emera used her powers to shield them again from the pouring rain. The light in the tunnel was no more.

*　　*　　*

They managed to travel back without any obstacles in the way. The mean-spirited ghost seemed to be gone.

Was he gone for good?

As they reached Para's cottage, Avanna thought again, about what her mother said before she died. 'A gust of wind went right through me."

Meanwhile, Emera and the others entered, as Para and Oula greeted their safe return.

Officer Wodderspoon turned, looked up at Emera, and asked, "How are you? Do you feel you've made everything right, like you hoped?"

Emera thought about what she had done years ago and answered in a calm voice, "Yes," and then gave a soft smile.

Micah heard his mother's answer; she was still hurting from what the trypalls had done to her, many years ago. Whatever he knew, at least for that moment, would remain unsaid.

"Jodon and Rena found the tunnel that led them home," Officer Wodderspoon told them. "Oh, and they said thank you for everything."

"Their mothers aren't expecting to go to the tunnel until tomorrow! We'll go right away and let them know to go now," Para replied excitedly.

"I'll go with you," Oula responded nervously and then turned full circle, "Where's Avanna?"

"I don't know," replied Clemedeth. "I'll look in the kitchen."

"We'll go with you. I'll fix us something to eat," said Emera.

"I'll take a look outside," Micah added calmly. "Let me know if you find her first."

Everyone left the room and when Micah opened the door, he found Avanna standing under the awning, staring out at the pouring rain.

Avanna whispered strongly, "Devilea's back!"

She slowly turned and then gasped when she saw Micah behind her, and wondered if he heard her.

Did he hear her?

"Come inside, Avanna," he said in a relaxed manner.

She looked at him with her sad eyes before walking inside. When he was about to close the door behind her, a heavy lightning bolt struck in the direction from which they had returned.

"Mom!" she cried out and quickly pulled the door wide open.

"She's gone, Avanna! We'll take care of you." He gently placed his arm around her and then slowly closed the door.

Meanwhile, the lightning bolt they heard, struck through atop the raft's protective shield, striking Lystra's heart. She rose up and gasped for air, then, she lay back down to the sound of gentle flowing waves passing beneath her pure white raft.

Emera shouted, "My felines!"

THE END

When The Taste Of Revenge

Seeps Into Your Soul

It Creates A Beginning

That Is About To Unfold!

CPSIA information can be obtained at www.ICGtesting.com
Printed in the USA
BVOW06s0124150416

444329BV00008B/51/P